My Not So Wicked Stepbrother

Copyright © 2019 by Jennifer Peel

All rights reserved.

This book is a work of fiction. The names, characters, places, and incidents are the product of the author's imagination or are used fictitiously. Any resemblance to actual events, business establishments, locales, or persons living or dead, is entirely coincidental.

All rights reserved. Without limiting the rights under copyright reserved above, no part of this publication may be reproduced, stored in, or introduced into a retrieval system, or transmitted in any form or by any means (electronic, mechanical, photocopying, recording, or otherwise) without prior written permission of the copyright owner. The only exception is brief quotations in printed reviews. The scanning, uploading, and distribution of this book via the internet or via any other means without the permission of the copyright owner is illegal and punishable by law.

Dedication

To Rebecca, one of the most intelligent and kind people I know. Thank you for being a rock star friend and for not being afraid to get your hands a little (or a lot) dirty.

Prologue

"Emma! Emma! Emma!"

"Mom! Mom! Mom!" I put my overenthusiastic mom on speaker, so I could continue to write my report for work.

"Funny, sweetie."

"I thought so."

"I have some news. *Big* news," she squealed as if she was much younger than her fifty-four-year-old self.

"I already know it's six months until Christmas today. I'm sorry, I don't have my wish list ready for you. Things have been crazy at the plant."

My mom's blood ran red and green. She lived for Christmas, or pretty much any holiday, but Christmas was her favorite. If she didn't have at least half her shopping done by July, she thought something awful would happen, like the couple from *The Notebook* would break up. I never had told her that Ryan Gosling and Rachel McAdams went splitsville a long time ago. She would have blamed it on the fact that she only made seven side dishes instead of ten for Christmas dinner that year, or maybe because she forgot to buy the postman a gift.

"Then it's a good thing that I already know what I'm getting you for Christmas this year," she sang to the tune of "Santa Claus is Comin' to Town."

Perfect. It was so hard to think of at least twenty things I wanted. Sometimes I thought Mom forgot I was thirty—not thirteen—and that I owned a house, a Jeep, and even had a big girl job as a metallurgist for the steel plant. "I can't wait to see what you picked out."

"Oh, honey, he is a cool drink of water—make that a hot toddy on a cold winter's night. Actually, he's more like a present you are going to want to unwrap all year long."

I minimized the melting efficiency report on my screen and gave Mom my full attention. I sadly knew where this was going but decided to try and divert her. "Are you finally getting me the Golden Retriever I've been begging for since I was nine?"

"Emma Elaine Loveless, you know I wanted to, but your sisters were allergic and now you work all day, and who would you raise it with?"

"Mom, single people have dogs all the time."

"But it would be so nice to share a puppy with someone. Or you know, maybe a baby?"

I pinched the bridge of my nose. "I have to get this report done by the end of today. Do you think we could talk about this for the 76,985th time again tonight?"

She giggled. "It's only been 56,321 times. Besides, I've found the perfect man for you and he's going to look fantastic in our Christmas photos. Seriously, you will be the cutest couple. Even cuter than that *Notebook* couple. They're still together, right?"

"Um . . . well . . . What about my Christmas gift?" I hated lending fuel to her unquenchable fire, but I couldn't bring myself to torture her.

"Oh, honey, really, he's the one. I have this feeling. I got tingles all over."

I hoped she didn't have nerve damage; that was the only reason I could imagine she would be tingling. When it came to me, she had horrible taste. For herself, she had picked two winners.

"Tingles like when you set me up with Darryl who you met at the gas station and it turned out he had stolen the Mercedes he was driving that you admired so much?"

"That was just a silly misunderstanding."

"Mom, he was arrested before our dinner even arrived." Unfortunately, that wasn't my worst date.

"You don't even like Thai food, so you're welcome."

"Okay, what about the time you gave Adam my number and he turned out to be married to three women and was looking for a fourth?" That was my worst date. Creepy.

"You have to admit he was handsome."

I went from pinching the bridge of my nose to rubbing my temples. "Mom, report, remember?"

"You're the one who keeps interrupting me."

"My apologies, please tell me who I will need to be blocking from my phone in the near future?"

"Believe me, you are going to want to put Sawyer, I mean *Dr. Sawyer King* on speed dial."

"What's he a doctor of? Let me guess. He has a PhD in folklore," I said dryly.

"My sides are hurting; you are so funny. No. He's my new optometrist."

"What happened to Dr. Alvarez?"

"She retired, and *Sawyer* has replaced her."

I squirmed at the way she emphasized his name. "You're on a first name basis?"

"He's going to be my son-in-law."

I rolled my eyes. "Does he know that? Please say no."

"Sweetie, I know how to be subtle."

"Like a sledgehammer," I said under my breath.

"Do you need some cookies? You sound a little snarky."

Cookies did sound good, especially Mom's cookies. Maybe some of her peanut butter ones. "Just tell me what you told him."

In her pause I could hear her trying to spin the tale she had told him. It probably went something like this: Emma Loveless is my oldest daughter. You may wonder why we don't have the same last name. Well, don't you worry, she's never been married, it's just that her dad died when she was a baby and I remarried. And just because her last name is Loveless doesn't mean she's cursed never to have love. The fact that she believes it doesn't make it true. Honestly, she is the sweetest girl. Smart, clever, athletic, she coaches soccer, and she can bake about anything your heart desires. And did I mention she's cute?

She would forget to tell him I was ten to fifteen pounds overweight depending on the season, though I worked out more than any of my friends, even my model twin sisters. I may or may not have a love affair with cookies, cake, brownies, and basically anything with refined sugar. I mean, sugar is always there for you, and it comes in so many forms, showing up exactly as you needed it, when you needed it. Like now—I needed it in liquid form to get me through the rest of this conversation, and there it was, waiting for me on my desk in all its dark and handsome glory. I took a long swig of my Dr. Pepper and let the fizz settle my soul.

Mom finally got her story straight in her head. It must have been bad. I finished off the entire bottle of Dr. Pepper while bracing myself. The good news was there was more in the breakroom. See? Sugar is always available.

"I told him you are the smartest girl ever and a metall . . . meta something . . ."

For some reason she could never say metallurgist. Technically, I was a melt cast metallurgist, but that was really a mouthful for her to say.

"I told him you were an engineer who worked with steel," she said, frustrated with herself. "And I told him that you were no prissy thing. I said, my Emma works hard and plays harder. Told him you even played football."

"Mom, I was the kicker." Seriously, it was no big deal, I walked on the field, kicked, and walked right back off. Too many of the boys were afraid to touch me, which our team used to its advantage.

"I know," she squealed. "That's the best part I wanted to tell you. You two know each other. He was the quarterback for Edenvale High the year you played."

I leaned back in my chair and thought for a moment. Sawyer King? In a rush, a memory hit me. It was our homecoming game and Edenvale High was the *it* team—they still were. They were the largest high school in the neighboring three counties at the time. The small town I grew up in, Carrington Cove, didn't have a high school back then so we went to the county school in Pine Falls. I remembered him because he was one of the best football players in the state during my senior year, not to mention extremely good looking. I've always had a bad habit of forgetting things, like everywhere. The night we played them my senior year I left my shoe behind. Just one. You would have thought I would have noticed the cold grass beneath my foot or my uneven steps, but I guess I was so used to walking out and kicking barefoot that it didn't faze me, or maybe it was because I was so bummed we'd lost. But regardless, Sawyer King, for some weird reason I'll never know, found my cleat.

I remember being embarrassed when he came running after me and called, "Hey Cinderella, you forgot your shoe." Embarrassment had been a new feeling for me. I was the girl who pretty much did anything, whether I was dared to or not. I belched louder than the guys, jumped off cliffs, got dirty, and obviously I felt comfortable enough to "play" football. But then Sawyer King, the epitome of every girl's high school fantasy, acknowledged my existence. He had the prettiest amber eyes and the all-American good boy looks. The kind of looks that rendered my seventeen-year-old self speechless. He must have been used to it because he flashed me his pearly whites and tossed me the shoe. "Good game, Loveless." I stared after him, watching him run to catch up with his teammates. He did football pants justice, that much I remembered. And when he looked back and caught me staring. Good times. Hopefully he didn't remember any of that.

"I think I remember him." I felt bad lying to my mom. She was the best. She drove me crazy with her relentless matchmaking attempts, but there was no better mother alive than Shannon Carrington. I was only tired of trying to pretend that I had any hope of finding *the one*. Truly, I believed my name was a curse. I was the friend, never the girlfriend, certainly never the wife.

"He remembers you."

Great. "Well, it's not every day you see a girl play football."

"Or kick fifty-five-yard field goals." She and dad were still proud of that.

That too. "I hope he's a good eye doctor for you." That translated into *please can this conversation be over with?*

"He's amazing. Best prescription I've had in ages. I'm seeing better than ever."

My plan worked? Fantastic. "I'm happy for you. I should get back to my report."

"Wait. Wait. I didn't tell you what he said when I showed him a picture of you."

"Mom," I whined, "which picture did you show him?" Not like there were a lot of good ones floating around out there. Normally I wouldn't care if someone saw me eating ice cream with my fingers or covered in mud from running an obstacle course, but for some reason I didn't want this virtual stranger to see those things. Maybe because I thought he might be normal, not a felon or a polygamist.

"Honey, you're so beautiful. I wish you would see that."

How could I when all my life I always heard, *your sisters are so gorgeous.* Nearly every guy I ever knew asked me how old they were, and could he get their numbers. Even today I had guys befriend me to get to the M and M twins—Macey and Marlowe Carrington, genetic perfection. They got the best of Mom and Dad. Mom's stunning ice blue eyes, Dad's height and raven hair. I got Mom's squishy middle and my biological dad's hairy legs. I should buy stock in razors and Nair.

I sighed. "Which picture?"

"You know, our family picture we had taken in the spring."

"Mom, that's an unfair representation of me. I Spanxed every inch of my body and Marlowe did my hair and makeup." She might have mentioned a few times I would be so pretty if I tried. I worked in a steel factory with crude, beer-guzzling men who I mostly loved, in 140-degree conditions at times. Even if there was anyone to try for, makeup would melt off my face.

"Oh, honey, you're being silly; they don't make Spanx for everything. I've looked."

We both loved our cookies. But unlike me, my mom truly was beautiful, and she'd married the most handsome man in the county. He owned most of it, too.

It didn't matter, I'm sure Dr. King only had eyes for my sisters. I wasn't jealous. I loved Marlowe and Macey despite how opposite we were. "Did he get the girls' numbers from you?"

"Why would he? They're a little young for him."

"Mom, they're twenty-four and he has to be my age or close to it."

"Six years is a lot of years."

I didn't argue with her.

"But I did give him your number after he said you looked exactly like he remembered you."

Now I know he's a liar. Not only was I not carrying around an extra ten pounds, okay fifteen, back then, but I had massive football helmet head the last time he saw me. It didn't matter, because if he looked anything like he did back in high school, he probably had a girlfriend, or plenty waiting to occupy that title. Not that any of that would deter my mom. Even if he had one, she would push me on him like a used car salesman. Either way, rest assured, Sawyer King was not calling me.

"Love you, Mom."

"I only want you to be happy."

"I'm happy." Truly, I was. I had a great life. Loving family—okay, Marlowe and Macey were a bit self-absorbed and acerbic at times, but I knew they would eventually grow out of that phase. I hoped. I had a terrific job and a dozen girls who adored me. I got to be a soccer mom without having to drive a minivan; that was a major win. And I had friends. Lots and lots of friends. Who needed a boyfriend?

"I love you, Emma. You made me believe in love at first sight. Someday, I hope you get the chance to know what that feels like."

Me too.

~

Text from Unknown Number: Is this Emma?

Me: It depends on who's asking. If this is the IRS, no, but I paid my taxes even though you could really give a single girl a break. I mean, sheesh, I'm sorry I don't have any dependents to deduct. Now if this is

Baskin Robbins, yes, I'm Emma and I love you. I'll take a double scoop of chocolate ice cream with peanut butter sauce.

Unknown Number: I don't want your money and I don't have any ice cream, but now that you mention it, I could go for some.

Me: This is very disappointing, stranger. At least tell me you're not a serial killer.

Unknown Number: I'm a doctor.

Me: All that means is you're smart enough to get away with it.

Unknown Number: I am pretty smart.

Me: Now you're starting to creep me out. I hope you have the wrong number or are texting from a penitentiary. Do they let prisoners have cell phones?

Unknown Number: I don't think so.

Me: Do you know this from personal experience or because you know someone on the inside?

Unknown Number: Neither. Do you normally have conversations with strangers like this?

Me: Not typically, but I'm bored.

My team's soccer game had been rained out and all the shows I liked were in summer reruns.

Unknown Number: So, you're using me for entertainment?

Me: I'm not sure how entertaining you are. Do you know any good jokes?

Unknown Number: This is Sawyer King.

I sat up from my prostrate position on the couch.

Me: Haha, Jenna. Whose phone are you using? This isn't funny.

I knew I shouldn't have told my best friend about Sawyer, but she'd had a crush on him like every girl this side of the mountains. That was, until she finally figured out that Brad, my other best friend since preschool, was in love with her since he was an embryo. Jenna and Brad fancied themselves jokers. I guess since they owned a comedy club they were, but this wasn't funny at all.

Not So Funny Best Friend: Who's Jenna?

Me: Seriously, Jenna, the joke's over. Sawyer King, god among men. Mr. I Hold the State High School Record for Touchdowns in One

Season isn't going to text me. An angel doesn't text. He appears in your living room, hopefully wearing something akin to his cousin Cupid.

Jenna and I had stalked Sawyer on Facebook after I talked to my mom. Dr. King had grown up just fine. As in, he was ridiculously gorgeous and I'm so embarrassed my mom tried to set me up with him. How could she possibly think he was meant to father my children? Not that my ovaries didn't scream that they deserved to breed with someone as beautiful as him, but even they knew it was a pipe dream. To punish me for not being able to snag such a catch, my period started early—while I was at work and without a tampon in my purse. Did I mention I worked with all men?

Really Not Funny Best Friend: You think I'm an angel? And I didn't know Cupid was related to heavenly beings. I guess it's the wings.

Me: Jen, joke's over. Don't you have work to do? I thought tonight was comedy sports night and you and Brad were facing Heidi and Oscar. I'm going now. I need to pluck that one stupid hair on my chin that acts like its high on miracle grow.

I threw my phone on the couch cushion next to me, wondering if maybe I should let the hair chin grow out and tie a bead to it. That could be fun. I could ask my friends, "What's hanging?"

My phone rang before I could fully explore the possibilities of the fun conversations I could have about my chin hair. I picked up my phone to find it was Jenna calling from her mystery number. I bet she asked to use some random person's phone at their comedy club, High on Laughs. It was a tribute to Colorado's new marijuana law and all the potheads who now called our state home.

"Okay, Jen. I forgive you."

"I'm so glad to hear that," a gravelly masculine voice replied.

"Uh . . . Brad?" Please let it be Brad. He was good at imitating voices.

"It's me, Sawyer. Mr. Ninety Touchdowns in a Season."

No. No. No. I mean anyone could know that stat. Right?

"I'm sorry I'm not related to Cupid. No wings, and I haven't worn diapers in years."

I was losing feeling everywhere except in my brain, which remembered all the embarrassing things I just said, including plucking my chin hair.

"Are you there?" he asked.

"Um . . . yes. Why are you calling me?"

"I promised your mom I would."

Grr. Mom. "Whatever she bribed you with, I'm willing to pay double if you forget our little texting conversation and my number."

He laughed the most fantastically beautiful laugh I'd ever had the pleasure of hearing. "Are you sure? The price was pretty steep."

Oh my gosh, she had resorted to paying people? I had been joking, as in figurative speech. "How much?" I internally cringed.

"Cinnamon rolls every week for a year."

"Oh."

"I refused the offer," he said hastily.

"I thought you said you were smart. My mom's cinnamon rolls are to die for. So, why are you contacting me then?"

He thought for a second. "I wanted to see for myself if it was true."

"What?"

"Well, your mom made it sound as if you could walk on water."

Of course she did. "You know you can too?"

"What? How?"

"If I tell you, do you promise to never ever reveal our little discussion even under threat of torture?"

"What if someone is pulling out my fingernails?"

"They grow back."

"You're harsh."

Extreme measures for extreme possible embarrassment. "Walking on water is pretty amazing knowledge."

"True. But what if I don't want to forget your number?"

Uh, why wouldn't he? "You don't even know me."

"That's why I'm calling." He thought for a moment. "How about this, in exchange for learning how to walk on water, I will forget everything except your number and that you think I'm god-like. And perhaps I can negotiate how you came to that conclusion and how you know about my football record."

I fell to the side of my couch. I think I was literally dying from embarrassment. My heart was beating erratically enough for me to consider dialing 911. On the bright side, it would give me a good excuse to end this call, and he may even take mercy on me if I ended up in the ER or died. Either option sounded fantastic right about now.

"What kind of negotiations are we talking about?" I managed to squeak out through heart palpitations.

"Nothing too painful. You only have to admit to stalking me on, let me guess, Facebook, and tell me your secret to walking on water. In return, I promise I won't ever stare at your chin hair and I might confess that I also looked you up on Facebook."

I sat up. That did not make me feel better. Oh no, if anything, this was worse. Cardiac arrest, here I come. I had the most embarrassing pictures and videos on Facebook. Everything from bad Spice Girls karaoke and burping out the alphabet song, to Halloween pictures where I'd dressed up like a bowl of Froot Loops, or when Jenna and I were a bra. I was the left saggy boob. And I wondered why nobody found me to be a catch. I didn't mind everyone else in the world looking at my life in pictures, but not him. Not after looking at Sawyer's profile filled with professional pictures of him doing things like skiing or graduating from the University of Houston College of Optometry. Not to mention all the gorgeous women he'd dated over the years. They had names like Candy and Sasha. He even looked fabulous blowing out his birthday candles. No one should look good doing that. Needless to say, it all made me feel self-conscious. Maybe I should feel like that more often. I might get more dates.

"You're stalking me on Facebook?" I homed in on that factoid.

"I think the deal was for you to admit that first."

I melted into my comfy leather couch to help me get through the trauma I was experiencing. "See . . . the thing is, my mom, as wonderful as she is, has this awful habit of setting me up with less-than-scrupulous men, so I was preparing myself in case I had to get a restraining order."

"Understandable. But why is she setting you up when according to your Facebook profile, you are in quite a few relationships already.

It's stiff competition. The Pillsbury Doughboy, Duncan Hines, Dr. Pepper, Mr. Pibb—"

"I only see Mr. Pibb if the Dr. isn't available. And the Doughboy's real name is Poppin' Fresh. No one really knows that." It was sad that I did, but bread would always be my first love.

"Consider me informed. Thank you. But what about Tony the Tiger and Captain Crunch? Do you see them at the same time?"

"All the time."

He laughed. "Should I ask about Betty Crocker? I'm not judging."

I sighed with content. She was my favorite. "Betty and I have a special relationship. I go to her when all the guys have let me down."

"Is that often?"

I paused, not sure how to respond. "Are you asking how often Betty and I hook up?" Based on the pictures I saw of his girlfriends he probably thought I should dump Betty altogether.

He cleared his throat. "No. No," he scrambled to say. "I meant, do men disappoint you often?"

"Are we talking about *my guys* or *guy-guys*?"

"Guy-guys."

"Well . . . how do I put this?" I didn't want to sound bitter, because I honestly wasn't. There were perks to being the friend, never the girlfriend. I never had to worry about silly things like three-month anniversaries or if I had garlic on my pizza, because there was no one to kiss. I'd be willing to stock up on mint gum, because I really did like garlic. But no matter how fresh my breath was or non-felonious my dates were, I always managed to end up in the friend zone. "I tend to keep my expectations low unless it's Colonel Sanders or my dad, so the answer is no."

He thought about that for a second. "So you like chicken, your dad, and cereal. Anything else?"

The fact that I hadn't scared him away yet surprised me. "That's only the tip of the iceberg, but I'm sure you have better things to do than listen to me ramble about why I love spreadsheets and soccer."

His masculine laugh filled my ears. "You say the most unexpected things. I can't think of anything I'd like to do better right now than to hear more about you."

This couldn't be real. "Did my mom already bring you cinnamon rolls?"

"Not one."

I sank back against my couch, more confused. But what the heck, my shows were all in reruns. "Okay, spreadsheets or soccer first?"

"You choose."

I started with spreadsheets since that tied into my job and all the data I constantly analyzed that for some reason brought me ridiculous amounts of joy. From there we moved on to soccer, which turned into a full-blown sports conversation. He was more of a football and hockey guy. We ended up talking about lots of different subjects, including our families. He had an older brother and his parents were divorced. Like me, he was also a lover of the great outdoors and his favorite food was pancakes. I could get on board with that. He sounded intelligent, unmarried, and supposedly had never been arrested, which made me wonder what was wrong with him. But the more I talked to him the more I liked him, even at two in the morning when I could barely keep my eyes open, but neither one of us was in any hurry to end the call. For me it was like talking to your best friend who you never knew existed, and all you wanted to do was catch up with him.

However, I did have to be at the plant at six. I hated to end our marathon call that was only paused when I had to pee—twice. Eight hours is a long time. "I suppose I should tell you the secret to walking on water and let you get some sleep." I yawned, already curled up in my bed. I had even brushed my teeth while he seduced me with tales of disgusting eye appointments, like removing parasites from patients' eyes.

"Wait," he sounded panicked.

"You don't want to know?"

"I do . . . but I want you to tell me in person." He paused. "Would you like to go on a date?"

Chapter One

One Year Later

SAWYER RESTED HIS hand on my thigh under the crowded table while I thanked my lucky stars that he picked a firm spot. A few inches up and it would have been more like Jell-O with a massive dollop of whipped cream. While his touch made my heart skip an entire song's worth of beats, I stared up into his amber eyes that always managed to play between mischievous and charming schoolboy. I resisted reaching up and running my hands through the curls in his dark hair that danced above his ears. As if he knew I wanted to, he flashed me his pearly whites that *tinged* in the low lighting of Sage Café, one of our favorite hangouts. For a few blissful seconds, only he and I existed. What I wouldn't have done to stay in our own little world. We could have called it Sawma, Emyer, or Semma. Any combination of our names would do, as long as it was only a population of two.

Sawyer gave my thigh a little squeeze. "How was your day, Em?"

Instead of my fingers frolicking through his beautiful locks, I ran my hand through my sweaty, matted down hair that was once referred to as the color of dirt by a date. The hard hat required at work and then soccer practice in the summer sun hadn't done much for my medium length mop. "It was—"

"Y'all are so cute," an alluring Southern accent interrupted. The new office manager at the eye center where Sawyer worked, with her perfect figure and gorgeous blonde hair, sat across from us. Sawyer had invited her to our monthly dinner with friends, to my dismay. "How long have you two been together?" Shelby, I believed was her name, asked with a hint of disappointment.

Sawyer removed his hand from my thigh in a hot second and without even thinking we both scooted our chairs away from each other.

Kellan, Sawyer's best friend since high school, grabbed his midsection and laughed. "They aren't a couple." He pointed between Sawyer and me. "But for siblings they're pretty cute." Kellan smirked.

Jenna gave me a sympathetic grin from across the table while I tried to hide my cringe.

"Brother and sister?" Shelby, who now was getting excited, asked.

"Stepbrother and stepsister." Kellan was happy to clarify for her through his fits of laughter.

Sawyer cleared his throat before reaching for his ice water. "Em and I are *friends*."

Ugh. The dreaded F-word. The past year's events had landed me smack dab in the middle of not only the friend zone, but also the twilight zone. All I could say was my last name had struck again. This time with a freaking vengeance.

I flagged down our server. "More Dr. Pepper, please. And keep them coming." I needed a sugar coma, stat. Might as well waste all the calories I'd burned during my five-mile run earlier this morning and the running I'd done with my girls during soccer practice.

Shelby leaned forward and put her hand on the table in front of Sawyer. I took notice of her long, tan, delicate, and manicured fingers. One finger stuck out. The wedding one had a stark white tan line around it. Huh? Was she recently off the market? She wasn't exactly acting like it.

"So, Sawyer." She flashed him some seriously white teeth. I almost reached for my sunglasses, except I had forgotten them at home.

Sawyer gave the epitome of Southern charm his attention. With her free hand, Shelby tossed her golden tresses and batted her baby blues. Oh, she was good. I had to wonder, though, if her eyelashes were fake. Those lush babies made it look as if two beautiful black butterflies landed on her eyes and were flapping furiously.

"You know, I just moved to town." She bit her lip in that sexy don't-you-want-a-taste way. "And I was wondering if you would be willing to show me around?"

I grabbed my tall, cool glass of Dr. Pepper and began to down it while watching the man I loved get stalked by a jungle cat in heat. Okay, she was lovely. But that made it worse.

Sawyer cleared his throat and stretched his neck from side to side like he did when he was thinking. What was he waiting for? She was absolute perfection, and as much as I didn't want to admit it, I could tell she was nice. Like, I would have tried to get to know her if she wasn't eyeing my man like he was a sundae drenched in the deepest, darkest fudge and she wanted to swim in it before tasting every drop. Get in line, sister. I'd been standing on the diving board for almost a year waiting to take the plunge. Me and every single woman in Edenvale. I wasn't sure what he was waiting for. He obviously had unrealistic expectations. I'd seen him turn down every beautiful woman this side of the mountains in the last year. Maybe this Southern Belle would catch his fancy.

I began gulping the Dr. Pepper to help me cope. Too bad my chug fest didn't account for the carbonation. My favorite beverage went down the wrong way. It was all I could do not to spray the table with my backwashed drink. I began to splutter and cough violently, all while praying it didn't come out my nose. It had happened. Jenna had it on video.

Sawyer turned his attention from Shelby and jumped into action by patting my back. "Em, are you okay? Lift your arms," he said through his smile. This, unfortunately, was a pretty regular occurrence around him.

When I didn't raise my arms, Sawyer took the liberty and lifted them for me while shaking his head. "Maybe you should start seeing Mr. Pibb again; he doesn't have as much kick."

It took me a moment to catch my breath before I could respond. "You know how I feel about the doctor."

Sawyer placed my arms gently by my sides; his eyes were smiling.

As I did all too often, I found myself gazing into those pretty amber orbs wishing he knew how I really felt about the doctor and that he could find it in himself to reciprocate. By doctor, I meant the optometrist staring at me, not the tasty beverage. But Sawyer had never made a move after our first *meeting*.

Sawyer tapped my nose in a brotherly fashion. "I know you're hopelessly devoted to him." Truer and more disturbing words had never been spoken.

I swallowed and smiled. "Maybe we should order."

"Good idea." Sawyer picked up his menu. "Do you want to order the cilantro lime quesadillas and I'll get the caprese grilled cheese sandwich so we can share?" He knew me so well.

"Perfect." I turned from him to meet several sets of eyes staring at us with interest, especially the beautiful blonde who was eyeing us carefully.

"Did you two grow up together?" Shelby asked.

Sawyer and I both vehemently shook our heads while I silently begged her not to ask any more questions.

Jenna saved the day. "Hey, Em, are you still up for doing our gender reveal party next week at the club?"

"Yes!" I flashed a grateful grin at my best friend. "Wait until you see what I've come up with. Wear something you don't mind getting dirty."

Brad and Jenna scrunched their faces at me.

"Believe me, it will be mild compared to what you're going to see come flying out of your baby."

Brad turned green. Poor guy had the worst gag reflex. It only took someone pretending to vomit for him to toss his cookies. Jenna rubbed her husband's back. "Breathe."

I couldn't believe my best friends were procreating. Jenna had had a tough time convincing Brad that they should. Brad had some serious reservations, as he himself was a big kid, and that gag reflex thing. But he loved Jenna and they babysat Jenna's sister's baby last year for the weekend and survived. Brad only threw up twice. So Brad agreed they could try. Honestly, I think the blizzard we had back at the beginning of February when we were snowed in for a few days had something to do with it. I expected a huge baby boom in Edenvale come November.

"Y'all are having a baby?" Shelby beamed at the pair. "I love babies." She turned her sights back on Sawyer with her unnatural lashes flapping again as if she were asking him to father a few for her.

Sawyer gave her an uneasy smile and clapped his hands together. "Is everyone ready to order? I'm starved."

Goddess Divine's smile faded with confusion as if this sort of thing had never happened to her before. I was confused on her behalf. She was like cotton candy perfection in her baby blue off-the-shoulder sundress. Why Sawyer didn't want to devour her and let her melt in his mouth I had no idea.

I felt so bad for her, I swallowed my pride—not that I had much left after my soda incident—and decided I should help her to feel included. I didn't want her to think us Westerners lacked hospitality.

"Where are you from, Shelby?"

She sat up straighter, which I didn't think was possible. I had already noted her impeccable posture. My guess was she had been to finishing school and was probably a debutante. Which made me wonder why she was an office manager for an eye clinic. Whatever she was, she made me feel like a slouch. I tried pulling my shoulders back like hers, but that expended way too much energy.

Some of Shelby's enthusiasm returned. "I'm from Roswell, Georgia," she said in her refined Southern drawl.

"What brings you to Colorado?"

She swallowed hard and smoothed her dress out while avoiding any eye contact. "I . . . needed . . . I wanted a change of scenery."

Right. I tilted my head and studied the Georgia Peach who was now sipping her strawberry lemonade as if she was filming a commercial. How did she do that so daintily? The better question was what was she hiding, and did it have anything to do with my man, I meant my friend? You know, the one I was sort of related to. I downed some more Dr. Pepper. This time I remembered to breathe between swallows.

Miss Perfection set down her drink and found her dazzling smile again. "So, Sawyer, about that tour?"

Dang Dr. Pepper went down the wrong way again.

"Arms up, Em."

Chapter Two

"Em, wait up."

I had almost made it to my Jeep parked down the street from the café when my favorite voice called my name. I turned around to find Sawyer jogging toward me with a takeout bag in his hand. My grin came out.

Sawyer landed in front of me and held out the bag. "You forgot your leftovers . . . again."

I swiped the bag from him. "Thank you."

"What would you do without me?"

He probably didn't realize it, but that was a deeply complex question. Ever since he entered my life, much of it had changed—and not all for the better, except he had become the best of my best friends. Of course, I would never tell that to Jenna, Brad or even Aspen, who was one of my closest friends from junior high and the mom of one of the girls on my soccer team. But Sawyer got me like no one else ever had. Did you see anyone else running after me bringing my take-out box? He knew I would be severely disappointed tomorrow morning when I left for work and had to pack a lunch instead of being able to grab the scrumptious leftovers from the meal we'd shared. And no one had ever shared their meals with me before. They never quite got how I loved options with each meal. Why settle for one dish when you could have a taste of two? Sawyer totally understood that. But as wonderful of a friend as he was, his presence had not only introduced the crap fest that was unrequited love, but he brought along a person who had fundamentally changed my life and still had me reeling. I couldn't tell him that, though.

"I would eat PB and J tomorrow. Who knows, I may forget this," I held up the bag, "in my fridge tomorrow."

"I'll text you in the morning to remind you to take it."

See? Best friend ever. I would have preferred best boyfriend of all time, but that dang last name of mine was a killjoy.

"I have to be at the plant at six, so I'll be leaving my house before you're even up."

He pressed his lips together and thought for a second. "Hand me your phone."

"Why?"

"I'm going to set a reminder for you."

"I can do that."

He held out his hand. "But you might forget, so hand it over."

I reached into my pocket to comply. While I wasn't making direct eye contact I decided to rub some salt in my wounds. "Did you ask Shelby out?"

"No, no," he spluttered.

I dared a peek into his eyes when I handed him my phone to see what those gorgeous amber jewels had to tell me. They were darting all over the place, so I couldn't read them. "Why not? She seems . . . nice." And determined. She'd made sure to get him alone after we paid and had said our goodbyes.

His hand started doing what I'd been wanting to do for almost a year now. It ran through his dark locks. "I suppose, but . . . I don't want to get involved with someone I work with." He hastily took my phone and went to work setting a reminder.

"That makes sense."

"I'll probably show her around this weekend, though, since I'm a gentleman." His lip twitched.

That was true. Dang him for it.

"I recommend skipping the Sawyer King glory days portion of the tour."

"Hey, you enjoyed it. If I remember correctly, you got to relive a bit of yours on my alma mater's field."

"I don't think Shelby is interested in kicking field goals."

Sawyer smirked. "Probably not, but Southerners do love football."

"True."

"You know," he fiddled with my phone, "you could come with us."

That's just what I needed. A front row seat to my own personal horror show starring the man of my dreams and the nightmarishly perfect woman poised to capture his heart.

"I'm busy this weekend. We have a game on Saturday and Sunday is . . . um . . . you know."

Sawyer gave me a strained smile. I'd never come right out and said that I hated how we'd come to be stepsiblings, but he wasn't stupid.

"A barbecue at the Ranch. Should be fun." He sounded unnaturally cheery.

Fun wasn't the word I would use.

His smile went from strained to sincere. "I'm still planning on being at the game."

"My girls will love that." Sawyer stole the hearts of women of all ages, including eleven and twelve-year-olds who were about to hit puberty. For the girls on my team, he was right up there with their celebrity crushes.

He held out my phone. "All set."

When I took the phone, our fingers did a little dance together. A rainforest of butterflies took flight in the pit of my stomach, so much so that a high-pitched squeak leaked out of me. I was an idiot.

Sawyer tipped his head to the side. "You okay there?"

"Fine." My voice was keeping to the high notes. "I better go." Before I did something really embarrassing like lick his face.

"All right." Sawyer shoved his hands into the pockets of his these-make-my-butt-look-amazing jeans. "Are you sure? We could go get some ice cream."

Ice cream did sound good, but I stared at the man who would never be mine and an outstanding sense of loss filled my entire being. "Can I get a rain check?"

He studied me for a moment, I'm sure in shock that I had passed up ice cream. "You can cash it in anytime."

I gave him a subdued smile. "Okay. Good night."

Sawyer reached out as if he was going to touch my face, but his hand awkwardly landed on my arm where he patted me a few times. "Good night. Drive safe."

I nodded. "You too." I walked toward my Jeep a little dazed and confused. Sawyer waited on the sidewalk until I was in and pulling out. He waved and watched me drive off.

I didn't feel like going home to be alone. My house was feeling more and more lonely. As if my Jeep knew exactly where I would end up, it sped past the exit to my house in Edenvale and kept straight on to Carrington Cove. On the forty-five-minute drive, I blared mom's favorite band, REO Speedwagon. "Can't Fight This Feeling" was my parents' unofficial song. Mom loved to tell us the story of how she couldn't fight her feelings for Dad. Sometimes she went a little too far when she mentioned things like Dad's rippling chest. Not sure how many ripples he had anymore, but I didn't need a visual or a verbal description.

It wasn't only Mom who had to fight her feelings. Dad had to as well, because my biological dad had been his best friend. But when the man who gave me life died, Dad stepped in to make sure Mom and I were taken care of. Their friendship blossomed into a whole lot more. Mom always said she was twice blessed to know true love. She always told me I was the luckiest girl in the world to have the two best men God ever created as my fathers. For a long time I believed her, but I didn't feel so lucky anymore. Now I felt betrayed. I'm sure Mom did too.

I turned my radio down as I wound my way around town. The sun was about to set, but the last rays of light illuminated my hometown. No longer was it the sleepy town I'd grown up in. Now it was a bustling village full of shops and restaurants. A tourist trap, really. I rolled my eyes thinking how my sisters' new overpriced boutique, M&M on Main, played a part in it all. And how they were selling out $200 shirts. On a positive note it was good they had something better to do than flirt with the Ranch guests and wranglers all summer.

I took the hidden back road to the Ranch to see Mom. I needed her to tell me what to do. My Jeep easily traversed the bumpy dirt road almost obscured by overgrown pine trees. I loved the cool summer nights and the smell of distant campfires with the crickets providing background music. The clearing up ahead told me I was close. I slowed down even more until I reached Mom's meadow. Shannon's Meadow, as we called it. It was as lovely as she was, with wildflowers and tall grass as far as the eye could see. It was punctuated with a crystal blue pond in the middle and the small cabin where my life began. My dads served in the military together in the same Army Ranger Regiment. After seeing their fair share of conflict, they both decided to settle here. It was home for my dad Dane, and a new beginning for my biological father Anders, who was already married to the lovely Shannon at the time.

I parked on the dirt drive that looped around the old place. So many memories, both happy and sad, filled me. Mom loved this little one-story log cabin with the pink door. I think Dad shook his head every time he saw it, but I always saw the smile in his eyes as if he was thinking, *that's my girl.* Now I didn't know what the man was thinking. How could he have gone from Mom to *her*?

I ran my hands across the tall grass as I walked toward the back of the cabin. It didn't seem right that Mom was here when . . . Josephine—I could hardly think her name—was living with Dad in the main house not that far up the road. In the distance I could hear the night's festivities. Old Grady's band was playing country tunes for the Ranch guests. The smoke of the nightly bonfire could be seen in the dusk filled sky. Last year I would have been tempted to drive over and join in on the fun, but the Ranch no longer held the magic for me it once had.

Tonight, I made my way through the white picket fence gate several feet behind the cabin. The creak I expected never came. It must have been oiled since I was out to visit last week. I tiptoed across the sacred ground until I saw her name engraved on her magenta granite headstone. The pink hue in the sky added to the granite's pinkness. I laughed and cried thinking about how delighted that would have made Mom. I knelt on the cool grass in front of the stone. July of last year, my life irrevocably changed. One slip on a ladder. The ugly words epidural hematoma still rang in my head. Why did she need to climb into the loft of the barn to see how many Christmas lights she had in July? Because that was her.

My eyes were drawn to one of her favorite quotes by Willa Cather inscribed on her headstone, *Where there is great love there are always miracles.*

I wiped my eyes. She embodied that quote. No mother loved greater than Shannon Carrington. She was my miracle. And honestly, I thought she had left me with one, but nothing was overcoming the curse of my last name. Not even the great love my mother had for me or the love I felt for Sawyer.

I picked the grass around me. "Mom, I know you would tell me you're not here and not to waste my time mourning you, but too bad. I will mourn you forever." I sank further into the ground. "I really need your advice. How do I get over Sawyer? Clearly, being in love with him is a lost cause. I have to say, I partially blame you." She'd made me promise to wear pink at her funeral even though it wasn't my color. I looked like a chewed-up wad of gum, especially next to the twins, who looked like sparkling pink champagne. I had no idea Sawyer would show up. For a minute there, I thought my mom had sent him. But she finally got her wish. I now believed in love at first sight.

I thought back to our first official meeting. It should have been our first date. Instead, he stood by one of the pine pews in the church after the service carrying a dozen pink roses as if he knew those were Mom's favorite. But they weren't for Mom, they were for me. Those dried roses hung in my walk-in closet now. The roses weren't half as attractive as him. I knew Mom wouldn't mind me ogling him at her funeral in his dark suit and tie. In fact, I smiled thinking how pleased she must have been by my reaction to him, especially when I clung to him for the world's longest hug.

My Not So Wicked Stepbrother

"Yep, Mom, I was certain you pulled some weight with the man upstairs and had him hand delivered." I sighed. What a foolish thought that was. Sure, Sawyer was extremely kind when he had found out about Mom. When I called him to break our date due to the most unfortunate circumstance of my life, he let me cry to him for hours. What did he say? "It would be an honor to listen to you all night. You don't have to say a word." Between my fits of crying, I entertained him with silly Mom stories, like how one year for Christmas she made about a hundred nativity sets out of toilet paper rolls all for the sake of recycling. I loved and missed her so much I physically ached.

I smoothed her headstone. "Mom, please tell me what to do. He's never asked me out again, yet I spend more time with him than anyone, which has only made me fall deeper in love with him. And then there's *her*. Who comes to the funeral of a person you don't know with their son? A money-grubbing tramp, that's who."

Oh, yes, I saw right through her though she was playing it cool and acting as if she was only there to pay her respects and offer comfort to our family. A family she didn't know except that everyone this side of the mountains knows the Carrington name.

I sniffled. "I bet you saw her conniving ways too. Are you dying over her? No pun intended. You really need to shake your husband, or zap him. People survive lightning strikes all the time; I'm just saying, think about it. If Josephine was standing near him when it happened, that wouldn't hurt." I would love to see her perfectly coiffed dyed auburn hair frizz and fry.

"I know. I know. I'm being terrible, and you taught me better, but she's awful. You have to admit that. Look at what she's done to our house. Have you seen that black mohair furniture that no one is allowed to sit on? Not that I would want to; it's uncomfortable. Don't even get me started on her 'art.' I've seen better paintings from kindergartners. And I had to beg Frankie to stay on as cook at least through the end of the summer. Josephine has done nothing but complain about her food since January when she married Dad. Frankie may hate Josephine more than I do, which is saying something. I can hear you say 'hate is for the weak and simpleminded', so maybe I'm both."

Tears poured down my cheeks.

"I thought he was the one. I had those stupid tingles you talked about. I still get them even though he's offered me nothing but friendship and his mother is the worst of the worst. Why is Dad so blind to her? Everything about her is fake, from her cheekbones and liposuctioned thighs, to the way she pretends to adore Dad. It's his money and status in the community she loves. Did you see the fancy sports car she bought herself and told everyone it was a gift from Dad? Dad would never spend that much on a car, and I have it on good authority from Rick at the car dealership that Dad had words with the sales manager when he got the invoice."

I had to take a minute to catch my breath before I could continue. "Why can I hear you tell me to calm down? You are supposed to be on my side and telling me what to do about Sawyer."

And why was I arguing with a headstone? I laughed despite how distraught I felt. I lay back on the grass and looked up to the heavens. I could only see Venus in the distance. The hellish environment on the planet second closest to our sun had nothing on my situation. To love someone and know you could never have him was torture. It was like the lady at Baskin Robbins asking you what kind of ice cream you want, only for you to choose your favorite and have her laugh in your face and tell you you'd never in a million years get a taste of it. And it would be dangled in front of you for eternity. And just for the fun of it, let's make him your stepbrother and best friend so you get an up close and personal view of each woman who wants to land him. And wow, there had been several. Our Southern Belle tonight was only the tip of the iceberg. They all had been as beautiful as Miss Shelby Duchane. Maybe not as sweet, but surely Sawyer would have been interested in at least one of them.

I should probably be a better friend and tell him to lower his standards, or at least get some attainable ones, but the thought of helping him find love made even me lose my appetite.

"Mom," I whispered into the night air, "should I walk away?" I knew I would have to see him at what were now excruciatingly painful family events. We could become like distant cousins who only caught up when forced to. It would mean me separating our friends and having to make up several atrocious lies about why I was too busy to associate with him. I held my stomach. The thought of severing our connection was like me dumping Betty or cheating on the Doughboy with some no carb diet. What a preposterous thought. But so was pining for my best friend and stepbrother when he obviously wasn't romantically interested in me. Maybe I should have worn Spanx to the funeral or used waterproof mascara. My hazel raccoon eyes weren't pretty.

My mind turned to more morbid thoughts as I lay on my mother's grave. Not sure it got more morbid than that, but I began to imagine my own headstone's epitaph. *Here lies Emma Loveless. Her name says it all. She was a loving daughter and devoted to Poppin' Fresh, the Doughboy's proper name. She never met a cookie she didn't like. Her most notable accomplishment was breaking the world record set for longest living member of the friend zone.* I might also add in, *Where there is love there is a good chance somewhere else there is a rejected woman eating her feelings.*

I needed to write this down and put it in my will.

"Please, Mom, send me a sign. Anything." I closed my eyes and waited. My phone buzzed in my shorts pocket. Um . . . I sat up a tad unsettled. A text message from heaven? That would be a new one. I carefully took my phone out of my pocket and slowly pulled it up to take a peek. I one-eyed it just in case it was a heavenly message. I let out a deep breath when I realized it wasn't Mom texting from beyond. No, it was the man I was in turmoil over. With both eyes wide open I read what he had to say.

Sawyer: Hey Em, I know that look you get when you are thinking about your mom. I can guess where you are. Tell her hi for me. I'm here if you need to talk. By the way, I left some ice cream in your freezer. I'll talk to you tomorrow.

I lay back down on the grass with my phone weighing heavily on my chest. Was that a sign or an unfortunate coincidence?

Chapter Three

"Good morning." Sawyer's groggy voice on speaker phone filled my bathroom.

"What are you doing up so early?" I managed to get out between brushing my teeth. "The reminder you set for me hasn't even gone off."

"I was worried you would forget your lunch reminder went off and . . . I was worried about you."

I dropped my toothbrush in the sink and stared into the bathroom mirror. It wasn't exactly a pretty sight in the morning, unless I had the help of my sisters. Even then, it was subjective. I think I was blushing. I wasn't sure I ever had.

"Um . . . you're worried about me?" I tugged on my ponytail. It was about as fancy as I got with my hair.

"Of course, Em, that's what friends do."

My reflection snarled back at me. The dreaded F-word had struck again.

"I know how hard this past year has been on you," he continued, "and we are coming up on the anniversary of your mom's death. I just want you to know I'm here for you and I've been thinking that . . ." He paused for an uncomfortable amount of time.

"Thinking what?"

"I . . . was thinking if you wanted to, we could do something to celebrate your mom. Maybe . . . do . . . a camping trip next weekend since you said she loved it so much."

Mom did love to camp. She taught us silly songs about yodelers and fried ham to sing around the campfire. And she could make some amazing food over a fire. I would only eat pineapple upside down cake now if it was made in cast iron. But back to camping with Sawyer and blushing.

"Mom would love that. Were you thinking of getting a group together?"

He didn't answer right away. "We could . . . I mean . . . yes. That's a *great* idea."

"Are you sure?" He wouldn't want it to be only the two of us, right? Seriously, that would have been like a dream.

"Yeah. Usual suspects?"

That's what I thought. No dream camping trip. "Okay. I'll ask Jenna and Brad. I'll even see if Aspen can come."

"I'll talk to my brother and Kellan to see if they're in."

"Thanks, Sawyer."

"Anything for you."

If that were true, he'd be in my bathroom right now kissing my neck and making me late for work.

"Oh, and thanks for the ice cream last night. You didn't need to buy three pints of it."

"I didn't know what you would be in the mood for."

"I'll admit I tried all three." Chocolate chip, chocolate, and rocky road.

He laughed. "I would have expected nothing less. I hope you didn't mind me using the housekey you gave me. I figured it was an emergency."

"Feel free to put ice cream in my freezer anytime."

"You got it."

"I better go before I'm late."

"Don't forget your lunch."

"I won't."

"I'll call you after work."

"Talk to you then. Bye." I hung up, feeling all sorts of conflicted. On one hand I felt loved—you know, the platonic kind, which was not bad at all. On the other hand, it kind of sucked when you considered that he had the makings of the world's best boyfriend. Not to mention my love for him went well beyond platonic. Maybe I could help him change his mind during this camping trip. I could accidentally fall into the river next weekend and fake hypothermia. He'd then feel obligated to strip down to his undies and cozy up with me in a sleeping bag. That would be great until he felt how squishable I really was under my clothing, which wouldn't help catapult me out of the friend zone. And knowing my luck, Jenna would jump to the rescue first and we would end up in a very awkward situation like we did my senior year of college. A situation we shall not visit again either in my mind or in real life.

Fine. No faking illness or injury. Not sure what I had left up my sleeve. He already knew I could make any kind of pancake, his favorite food. Maybe I should get cozy in the friend zone.

I walked out the door when Sawyer's reminder went off. I looked at my phone.

Go back in the house and get your lunch. Have a good day.

Oh crap. I marched back into my house to get my lunch. Sometimes I amazed myself. How could I be so forgetful, yet I had the capability to graduate from the Colorado School of Mines, one of the toughest engineering schools in the nation, with a B+ average? I probably could have had an A average except Jenna came to visit me one too many times and maybe I forgot a homework assignment or two. I'd needed Sawyer in my life then. Well, maybe. Not sure I could have handled over a decade of this kind of torture. In ten years, if I was still pining for him, I might move away and join a support group or something. Heck, make that a year. A year from now, if I couldn't get over Sawyer, I was moving.

I had to stop and think about that. I never thought of moving out of Colorado. There was so much to love about every season here, from camping in the summer to skiing in the winter. Not to mention most of my family and friends lived here. What would I do without Jenna,

Brad, and their little bambino who I was going to be godmother to? I could still be a rocking godmother from out of state and I would visit, of course, though it wouldn't be exactly the same. However, if I moved, perhaps I could find someone. Perhaps my name only cursed me here. I doubted that, but it was worth a shot looking elsewhere. What if Mr. Right-After-The-Real-Mr.-Right had gotten the wrong GPS coordinates and he was waiting for me to find him? And it wouldn't be all that bad living away from my wicked stepmother.

I grabbed my lunch and continued to give this some serious thought.

In the summers, I went to work earlier for two reasons. First, the steel plant became Satan's spa in the middle of the day. The temperatures could get above 140 degrees near the furnaces in the melt shop. Also, summertime meant internship time, and for some reason I was in charge of babysitting them. That was, I was tasked with molding and shaping them. Basically, weeding out those who could hack it and those who, let's say, needed a softer environment they could pin all their hopes and dreams on. Babysitting them meant I had to come in early, so I could get some actual uninterrupted work done. You don't know how many times a day I was asked, "Can I take a break now?" or "What does KPI stand for again?" Was it really that hard to remember key performance indicator? My favorite was the guy last year who kept asking me how to do basic formulas like addition and subtraction in Excel. He went in the *maybe you should think about a new career choice* pile. I really wanted to tell him he should probably pick a new major altogether.

I settled in my tiny office that was dingy like most offices in the mill. I'd tried making it cheerier by putting up pictures of family, friends, and the Colorado landscape, but nothing helped. If Sawyer's face didn't make a place look better, you knew it was a lost cause.

I was ready to face my day armed with Dr. Pepper and a protein bar, the breakfast of champions. On my screen was the data for a recent corrosion test I had been conducting. I had barely started my analysis when I had a welcome interruption.

Wallace Hodge walked in wearing an old, worn-out smile on his weathered face. He was not only my boss, but one of the reasons I decided to be a metallurgist in the first place. Wallace had been around long enough that he was once my biological father's boss. He thought the world of Anders Loveless and had made sure to keep in touch with Mom over the years. I remembered Wallace taking me on tours of the plant when I was a girl. Something here called to me. I thought maybe it was Anders. Like he wanted me to get to know him and working here would help me. I had to say it had. Wallace wasn't the only guy from back in the day still around. The old timers all loved to tell me stories about how Anders worked harder than anyone they knew but played just as hard. Kind of like his daughter. He was the resident prankster on top of being the melt shop electrician. He was infamously remembered for setting up mannequins in each stall in the men's bathroom. It took them hours to figure out why the stalls were never unoccupied. They'd also been wary of any food he brought to share. Caramel apples could have been caramel onions. He sounded like my kind of guy.

I learned more about my funny first father working here than I had my entire life. It wasn't that Mom had been keeping him from me. We talked about him, but I don't think she ever wanted to make Dad feel as if he had someone to live up to, so I never knew a lot. And I don't think she ever wanted me to feel as if I was loved any less by either her or Dad because Dad's blood didn't run in my veins. Dad never treated me any different than my sisters. Well . . . until Josephine entered the picture. Marlowe and Macey had a lot in common with Josephine, like running up Dad's credit cards and preening for hours, so my sisters embraced the new marriage.

I didn't have a good poker face or mouth. Dad knew I was unhappy about the union. I felt a distance between us that had never existed before. I knew I bore some of the blame. I resented Dad for not only marrying Josephine, but Sawyer's mother. I knew that sounded silly as they were one and the same, but in my mind the only marriage that should have happened between our families was the Sawyer and Emma one. Which was absolutely ridiculous when you considered we had never been on a date and he thought of me as a friend.

I smiled at Wallace instead of continuing to contemplate my bizarre family relationships.

"Morning, Emma," Wallace's rumbly voice filled my small corner of the plant. If you didn't know him, you would have thought he'd smoked all his life, but his voice was naturally rough.

"Good morning. To what do I owe the pleasure?"

He scrubbed his face filled with salt and pepper scruff. "I wanted to see how it was going with the interns. I heard some crying in the men's bathroom yesterday."

I tried not to smile. "That was probably Carson; he gets a little emotional when he doesn't get over a hundred likes in the first hour of his Instagram post. Yesterday it was only thirty. An all-time low for him."

Wallace shook his head. "What's Instagram?"

"It's a social media site where you can post pictures of your life and people can like it."

"How do they like it?"

"By clicking on a little heart."

Wallace's eyes narrowed. "Guys do this too?"

"Yep. It's a whole new world."

"What was the picture of?"

"His lunch." I grinned.

"Are you yanking my chain?"

I laughed. "I'm afraid not. Carson fancies himself an amateur chef and photographer. He spent hours making a dish made with SpaghettiOs, not to mention all the time staging it in the break room. The low stats were a real blow to his fragile ego."

Wallace crinkled his brow, not sure what to say. "Well . . . huh. Maybe . . . I got nothing."

"I think I might need a raise after this year's batch of interns."

Wallace leaned against the door frame and gave me a contemplative smile. "If you can keep the tears out of the men's bathroom, I'll think about it."

"No problem, I'll tell Carson to use the women's next time."

Wallace chuckled. "Deal."

"Wow. You should visit my office more often."

He stepped inside. "I probably should come by more often, but you're always on top of things."

"I do try."

"You do a good job. I'm proud of you."

"Thank you." I thought that was it. Wallace was a man who usually cut to the chase and skedaddled. This time, though, he shifted his feet and gave me a good look over.

"How are you doing, kiddo?" He hadn't called me that in ages. Never at work. I believe the last time was at Mom's funeral.

I didn't answer right away as I was confused by his tone and his thoughtful stare. "I'm doing good. Are you okay?"

"Right as rain. Speaking of which, we could probably use some."

Now he wanted to talk about the weather? This was not like him at all. Now I was concerned. "How's Bev doing?"

Wallace cracked a smile for his wife. "She keeps me on my toes and out of most trouble."

I knew he was a little bit of a troublemaker like my father, Anders, from the stories Wallace would tell of their hunting and camping trips. Lots of drinking and late nights from the sounds of it. Even Dad had joined in with them. It was hard for me to imagine Dad being anything but serious. He was probably the one to go to bed early. I always thought he and Mom balanced each other out.

"Tell her hello for me."

"I will." He shuffled his feet but stayed in my doorway.

"Is there anything else you wanted to discuss?"

Wallace sauntered into my office. His salt and peppered scruffy face was pinking up a bit. If he hadn't just agreed to give me a raise, I almost would have thought he was going to fire me. But he did something else most unexpected when he picked up the picture of Sawyer and me riding in a hot air balloon together. We were smiling at each other as if to say *what are we getting ourselves into?* That was a fun day last month during Edenvale's annual hot air balloon festival. We couldn't get anyone else to go up with us, which was fine by me.

The exhilarating views of the mountains and nearby peach orchards weren't half as mesmerizing as when Sawyer had held my hand. I admit I'd had a moment where I panicked when an unexpected gust of wind jostled us. Heights normally didn't bother me, but when there was nothing between you and the earth, it gave a whole new meaning to free falling. Sawyer held my hand for the entire excursion while we talked about his plans for opening his own practice one day instead of working for Hobbs Eye Center. He had a five-year plan, which included living in his crappy apartment and driving his old truck until it died so he could save as much money as possible. I liked a man with a plan who wasn't afraid to work hard. I also loved the feel of his strong hand. It was the perfect amount of smoothness and our hands fit comfortably together. It didn't hurt that it gave me those tingles Mom had talked about. Or maybe it hurt more than I wanted to admit.

Wallace cleared his throat, making me jump and get out of my head.

"You know, kiddo, you are more than an employee to me."

I smiled up at him. "I know."

"If there is anything you want to talk about you could come to me. Or if you needed me to talk to someone for you, I would be happy to."

I tilted my head. "Okay . . . I'll keep that in mind."

Wallace smiled down at the photo. "You two are an attractive couple. It's about time some guy finally wised up and—"

I pushed myself back in my rolling chair. "Whoa, there. I think you're mistaken about the kind of relationship Sawyer and I have."

He turned the picture around so I could see it. "I know it's a little strange that you're otherwise related, but it's not by blood, so no harm done."

I shook my head. "Wallace, we're only *friends.*" Every time I said it, I got this sucker-punched feeling in the pit of my soul.

Wallace's brown eyes squinted into slits. "Bev and I've seen you together, and this picture," he pointed to the two of us, "says it all."

"Says all what?"

"It says Anders would have wanted me to have a chat with him about how he expects his daughter to be treated."

My body deflated in my chair. "I promise you that won't be necessary."

Wallace gently placed the picture back on my desk. "Funny thing about promises. You should never make them until you know all the facts."

Unfortunately, I knew all the facts. And the biggest fact was Sawyer would never be mine.

Chapter Four

SUMMER WEEKENDS WERE my favorite, especially when it involved soccer. I was thrilled when Edenvale's Recreation League added a shortened summer season this year. It was basically conditioning for the fall, which was fantastic. My girls were excited because they were determined to win the fall championship. It meant new strategies and trying new field positions. They had been practicing hard and I was proud to call them my Pink Ladies. I smiled every time I thought of the name they had chosen this season. As weird as it sounded, I could always hear Mom giggle when I said it or when I put on my pink jersey. Pink was not my color, yet it followed me everywhere.

Our game was at eleven, but we met at the soccer fields at ten to warm up and make sure everyone had the proper gear. Inevitably, shin guards or cleats were forgotten every game. Parents would have to hustle home to retrieve forgotten items. I couldn't ever get upset at the girls, being chronically forgetful myself. To try and be a good example, I kept a crate in my Jeep filled with all my coaching gear, including things like my clipboard and our practice and gameday plans. So I may have already forgotten the crate this morning. The jog back to my Jeep was good for me.

My only complaint this season was with my assistant coach, Gwendolyn, or as I thought of her, the annoying warm body. To follow the rules, each team had to have two coaches always present. She was the only person who volunteered. All I could say for her was that she was present, at least physically. Most of the time, Gwendolyn, who gave me a lecture the first time we met that at no point was I ever to call her Gwen, was on her phone or filing her nails, even painting them on occasion. She brought a lounge chair and umbrella to each practice and game. It mortified Poppy, her daughter, who played on the team. Beggars couldn't be choosers, but I would have paid some parents under the table to take Gwendolyn's place.

Speaking of my partner in crime, she showed up in the tiniest white shorts and a halter top, wearing sunglasses bigger than her face. Her newest husband trailed behind her carrying all her gear. Poppy was running ahead of them, hoping not to be associated with them. I could feel her pain.

Gwendolyn was upon us, in heels I might add. "I brought everyone a treat today," she sing-songed unnaturally high. "Set down the cooler, Mario," she ordered her new, younger Latin lover husband. He did so with a loud thunk before stretching his back.

Was that glass I heard jangling in the rather large cooler?

"Ladies, gather round. Gwendolyn," she loved to refer to herself in third person, "brought you something extra special today if you win." She pointed at Mario with her ridiculously long, painted gold fingernail. "Open the cooler."

Her boy toy obeyed like he was a dog and she would pet him afterward. I hoped she didn't, especially not in front of me or the kids. I was pretty sure there were league rules against it. Poppy should probably plan on years of therapy. I knew I would have needed it if ol' Gwennie was my mom.

Mario obeyed and revealed Gwendolyn's surprise, which was more like a gotcha!

The smell hit us first. We all backed away, except Gwendolyn, who actually did some lifting and pulled out two crystal platters. Yes, I said crystal. She held them out as if she'd actually made them herself, which there was no chance of. A lot of what she did during practice was order takeout.

"Look, my little darlings, smoked trout crostinis and curried shrimp tarts, annnddd," she handed the trays to Mario before retrieving a nice, cold glass bottle of Perrier, "sparkling water. Isn't that exciting?"

All the girls looked at me to answer.

"You know, Gwendolyn, carbonated drinks aren't the best for kids to rehydrate." I know what a hypocrite I sounded like, because who was going to be downing a Dr. Pepper after the game? That's right, this girl. Win or lose I was stopping for one. "And a few of the girls have shellfish allergies." I so lied. It was worth it for the twelve beaming smiles I received and to see Gwendolyn's collagen filled lips pout.

"Why didn't anyone tell me this? I need an entire list of allergies. Do you know how much this food cost? What am I going to do with it? I can't eat it. Do you know how many calories are in these little delectables?" She gave me a scrutinizing once over. "You probably don't count calories."

She would be correct, but even if I did, I wouldn't admit to it, especially not in front of girls who needed positive body reinforcement. "You're right, I don't, and neither should the girls." I turned to twelve sets of wide eyes. "Let's warm up."

I grabbed my large bag of soccer balls and headed out to the field in a huff, running different backhanded comments through my mind that I could lob at Gwendolyn. Why was weight such a factor in a woman's life? She would have never said that to a man who was ten pounds overweight—okay, twelve now. Those additional two pounds were just the pre-pre-pre-period pounds I always carried, but who was counting? Apparently, everyone. I liked food. Sue me. I could run circles around the heeled princess.

Before I went unhinged and challenged her royal highness to a race, I was relieved of the bag of balls I'd been carrying. My head whipped to the side ready to be super annoyed, but instead I was pleasantly surprised to see my favorite. Not just person. He was simply my favorite everything. I almost smiled, but then I thought, would he love me if I weighed less? My almost smile then turned into a scowl.

Sawyer stopped and set down the bag of balls. "Are you okay?"

I had to shake myself out of my head. "I'm fine."

Sawyer stepped closer and brushed some of my flyaway hairs back, causing me to shiver in the warm summer air. Did he ever notice my reactions to him?

"Are you sure?" Sawyer asked.

I was about to tell him I was, but then I wasn't.

"Hey there, Miss Emma," Shelby's Southern drawl echoed across the field.

Sawyer stepped away from me, flustered. "I'm giving Shelby a tour of Edenvale today," he tripped over his words. "This is the first stop."

"How nice." I faked a smile.

Shelby was upon us and before I knew it, she was hugging me. Why did she have to be so dang nice? And skinny? Like, I could feel her bones. She smelled like heaven too. I had no other choice but to hug the man-stealing goddess back. "How are you?"

Shelby stepped back all smiles, wearing the cutest romper. Not many women pulled off the romper look, but she nailed it. Miss perfection leaned into Sawyer. "I'm doing just fine. This man here showed me the best place for breakfast. Have you ever been to the Brown Bear?"

I thought this was their first stop on the tour, and yes, I had been there. I was the one who introduced Sawyer to it because they made the best apple cinnamon pancakes with warm apple butter syrup. You know, I could go for some right about now. I nodded my response to the Southern Belle.

She rubbed her non-existent stomach. "I think I'll be full for a week."

My stomach was more lived in. I would have been full only until lunchtime. "Well, I need to go get my girls warmed up."

"GO PINK LADIES!" she shouted and jumped up in the air. I guess Sawyer had filled her in about the team name.

"Why don't you grab us a seat over there?" Sawyer pointed to the bleachers on the east side of the field. "I'm going to help Em for a minute."

Shelby patted Sawyer's arm. "You truly are the sweetest thing. You take your time." Shelby waved at me. "Good luck, Emma."

"Thank you," I mumbled while walking off.

Sawyer caught up to me.

"First stop on the tour, huh?" Came flying out of my jealous mouth before I could filter it.

Sawyer narrowed his eyes while smirking. "This is the first stop in Edenvale. The Brown Bear, as you know, is in Pine Falls."

"Clever."

Sawyer nudged me. "Em, what's wrong?"

"Not a thing." I picked up my pace.

Sawyer and his long legs easily kept up. "Are you trying to ditch me?"

"No. Why would I?"

"That's a good question."

"It's a silly question, because I'm not."

"If you say so," amusement played through his words.

"I do."

"Well good, because it would be futile. I run faster than you."

I smiled at the fool.

"There's my Emma smile."

I wasn't the only one smiling. As soon as the girls saw Sawyer, they all charged him. He was quick and started tossing the balls at them as if they were playing an impromptu game of dodgeball. The girls played right along. They started tossing balls back trying to hit him, but he was too quick.

It was such an attractive sight. Sawyer fit so well into my world. Even when he gave me a wicked grin and threw two successive balls at me. I dodged the first one, but the second one nicked me in the butt. Sawyer flashed me his brilliant smile, pleased with himself.

"Okay, ladies, let's warm up." I hated to end the fun, but it was important that we warm up.

They each tried getting Sawyer once more before lining up to stretch, but each attempt was unsuccessful, until I bent over pretending to stretch. I grabbed the ball nearest me and zinged it Sawyer's way, hitting him in his nice firm buttocks that I'd pretty much memorized the shape and contour of. He deserved an award for how good it looked in his khaki shorts.

"I'll give you that one." Sawyer tossed the ball back at me. "Good luck, ladies." He sauntered off without another word toward the woman who might finally capture his heart. I needed a Dr. Pepper right about then, you know, for the carbonation to make my ill stomach feel better. I really needed to get myself together and get over him. Maybe I should start looking for a new job now. Metallurgists were in high demand, especially female ones since there were so few of us. I could basically write my own ticket.

I would have to think about it later. I had to focus on my girls. We went through our series of stretches and then we ran several drills for dribbling, passing, and shooting agility. It didn't take long before it was time for us to take our side of the field where her highness Gwendolyn was already set up as if she was laying on the beach in Monte Carlo. I was waiting for Mario to start fanning her. Thankfully, some sanity awaited me in the form of Aspen, my friend and mother of Chloe, our fabulous goalie. Aspen would have been the perfect assistant coach as we were former teammates back in the day, but as a single mom of a preteen, she was busy trying to make a living working at the bank and going to school so she could get a promotion. Aspen's road hadn't been an easy one, but she was a fighter and an amazing mom and friend.

The always well put together Aspen, with tresses of golden brown, hugged me tight. "Hey, girl. You ready for today?"

"Always. Our girls are looking fierce today."

Aspen pulled me a little closer and whispered in my ear, "Who's the blonde with Sawyer?"

It took everything I had not to look their way. I'd already noticed them front and center, chatting cozily. Miss Shelby was a leaner and was practically in his lap. I guess she was getting the deluxe tour. I took a deep breath and let it out. "Her name is Shelby and she's the new office manager at the eye center."

"Looks like she's managing something this morning," Aspen remarked.

Unfortunately for me, my friends knew how I felt about Sawyer. I may have been a little exuberant when he first asked me out. It wasn't often I was asked out, especially by sane individuals, so I'd celebrated prematurely. There had been several conversations since on why he never asked me out again. My friends kindly thought it was because my mother had passed away and then his evil mother put the moves on my dad, but I think deep down we all knew why. It was me, plain and simple, because I was plain.

"They make a pretty couple," I responded.

Aspen leaned away from me with her narrowed emerald eyes. "Are they seeing each other?"

"Not yet, but from the looks of it, it won't be long."

Our eyes both darted to the two of them laughing in the bleachers.

Aspen rested her hand on my arm. "I'm sorry, Em."

I shrugged and plastered on a fake smile. "What for? I'm happy for him. He deserves someone like Shelby. As far as I can tell, she's sweet as can be."

She pressed her lips together and thought for a moment. "I'm here for you if you want to talk."

I gave her one more quick hug. "Thanks, girl, but I'm good." What other choice did I have?

Back to my girls. Twelve reasons to make me smile. It was time for my motivational speech and the chant we had made up and shouted before each game. We gathered around in a circle, arms wrapped around each other, heads leaned in.

"All right, my little warriors. You need to accomplish three things today. The first and foremost is to have fun. The second is to be your best. Remember, your best isn't the same as anyone else's. And third, learn something new on that field today. Study your teammates and opponents, learn from their successes and their failures. But remember, you only truly fail when you give up. And I know my girls aren't quitters. Are you ready to go out there and take command of that field?" I shouted.

"YES!"

"Who are we?"

"THE PINK LADIES!"
"What does P stand for?"
"POWERFUL!"
"What does I stand for?"
"INTELLIGENT!"
"What does N stand for?"
"NIMBLE AND NICE!"
"What does K stand for?"
"KICK BUTT!"

Yep. Kick butt. That's what I was going to do. I had a feeling it was going to be painful because it was my own that needed the kicking.

Chapter Five

I WAS STILL living off the glow of yesterday's soccer match, but the closer I got to Carrington Cove, the more I felt the light being sucked out of me. It didn't help that I kept getting flashes of Shelby touching Sawyer any way she could yesterday. You know, those little flirtations and touches that say all you have to do is say the word and I'm yours? Shelby was skilled at them. Her delicate hand resting on his chest or playful pats on the arm. And man, could that woman lean. Sawyer invited me to have lunch with them and continue the tour, but I passed on account of I liked to enjoy my food and seeing them would only upset my stomach. And you know Dr. Pepper would have been involved. Knowing my luck, it would have gone down the wrong way again and there was a good chance it would have come out my nose.

I hoped he wasn't bringing her to the barbecue. I was almost certain he wasn't, as he'd asked me if I wanted to drive out to the Ranch together, but who knew. Maybe he liked having me around as the third wheel to provide entertainment. I was good at it. I'd been Jenna's and Brad's third wheel for years. I even ended up with them on their wedding night—in the emergency room. Poor Brad ate some strawberries by accident and had a major allergic reaction. It was so romantic, the three of us all night. Jenna and I cuddled up on the couch to watch late-night TV talk shows and discuss if this was a bad omen for them while we watched her new husband go from looking like a puffer fish to the adorable goofball he normally was. Fortunately, it hadn't been. Unlike me, they weren't cursed.

I ended up declining Sawyer's offer for a ride because being the third wheel was getting old, and I was doing that butt kicking thing by doing my best to distance myself from him. I almost wished I hadn't agreed to go camping with him the coming weekend, but all our friends were on board and I knew Mom would love that we were all getting together to remember her. She would love that I was there with Sawyer, though I had to believe she could see by now it was a lost cause. I'd finally come to that conclusion myself.

I cranked up my radio and tried to get in a good frame of mind. After all, there was a wedding to witness before our "family" barbecue. Carrington Ranch was a popular place to elope or have a planned wedding. We had a wedding officiator on staff all summer for any lovebirds ready to take the plunge at a moment's notice. Our new officiator happened to be Sawyer's older brother, Ashton, who was also a wrangler for the Ranch. Ashton had moved back to Colorado a few months ago from Las Vegas, a little down on his luck. He was recently divorced and had lost his job at the construction company he'd been working for. Like Sawyer, Ashton was a fun-loving guy and seemed like a hard worker so far. Not sure how Josephine had managed to raise such nice men. Maybe their dad was nice, but according to Sawyer, he wasn't. He blamed his dad for his parents' divorce. I knew infidelity was involved but that was about it. Sawyer had such bad feelings for his dad he rarely spoke of him, even though he apparently lived in Edenvale. Come to think of it, I should despise his dad too. If they'd stayed married, I might have only known Josephine as Sawyer's mother and I would have avoided her like Diet Dr. Pepper. It was full-on sugar for me baby, or nothing.

I took the main entrance into the Ranch today. After this little soiree I would swing by and talk to Mom. No sense showing up in tears.

The Ranch was alive and full of people. Lovers and families could be seen walking in pairs or clusters along the well-worn dirt paths. Some looked as if they had just come back from the lake in bathing suits and wet hair. There were others on horseback and some playing volleyball. I loved this place. Honestly, growing up here had been like a storybook full of happy endings. I tried to remember that and hold on to those memories. Mom would always say that things were rarely as bad as they first may seem. I'd tried to believe that about Josephine, even though I felt Dad was moving on way too soon and that a decent person would have waited to put the moves on a man who had just lost his wife. But Josephine was happy to tell anyone who would listen, which was getting fewer and fewer, that she couldn't resist her handsome man and all she wanted to do was heal his broken heart. Then she would lean into Dad and practically knock him over. What was with these women leaning on the men in my life?

Was it awful for me to say that I'd hoped Dad's heart would never fully heal? I knew mine wouldn't. I didn't think it was supposed to when someone who was such a part of you died. Sure, you were supposed to learn to cope and move forward, but you didn't move on from them. You continued to carry them with you. Was Dad still carrying Mom with him? I couldn't say for sure, and that broke my heart even more.

I took a deep breath and chanted out loud, "Happy place, happy place, happy place." For Mom's sake I would be happy. It's what she always wanted for her children, so despite how life wasn't turning out like I'd hoped, I would find a way back to my happy, or find a new happy.

I took the turnoff toward the main house, passing by several of the cabins of varying size that dotted the property. It looked as if they were all occupied. That would have tickled Mom, as this had been her pet project. My parents didn't need the money the guest ranch brought in. The land and rights Dad's family had owned for generations made the Carringtons wealthy. Dad had only increased his wealth with the boom Carrington Cove was going through. Land was at a premium and Dad could name his price when selling off parcels or leasing.

While Dad wheeled and dealed, Mom had made her dreams come true and opened the Ranch. At first it was more like a bed and breakfast, but as its popularity increased, Mom and Dad started having cabins built that could be rented out. Stables and the barn were next. Dad eventually built Mom her dream home about ten years ago. Our old cabin was now used to house the ranch hands who lived full-time on the property during the summer. We had some local year-round employees who lived in town or in Pine Falls with their families, though we only had guests from Memorial Day to Labor Day. The Ranch and the animals needed year-round care and maintenance.

Frankie, our cook, was one of those year-round employees. Even though Mom had been a terrific cook, we'd hired Frankie because her family needed the money when her husband lost his job. That was a long time ago and her husband had been gainfully employed for years, but Frankie had become more like family and she'd stayed on. I was hoping to keep it that way since we especially needed her during the busy summer months. She took such great care of our guests and she was part of the reason so many of them came back. The woman had a gift with food.

I pulled around the semi-circle drive of the big, rustic house and admired the place I used to call home. The wraparound porch, complete with hearth, was my favorite. Mom's too. No detail had been spared when this gorgeous place was built, everything from the huge boulders in the landscape to the way the aspen and pine trees were planted around the home.

I pulled in behind Sawyer's old, beat-up blue truck. I couldn't help but smile. It reminded me of what a good and decent person he was. I know Dad had offered him a loan to start his own practice, but Sawyer wanted to do it on his own. I loved him even more for it. Unlike his mother, who was happy to take Dad's money, Sawyer never seemed interested in it.

I had to remind myself I was in Sawyer detox, so it was best not to dwell on his attributes. With my resolve kind of sort of in place, I hopped out of my Jeep.

I didn't even make it to the house before Marlowe and Macey ran out with more exuberance than they normally showed. They still called the Ranch home. Each of them was dressed up. Marlowe wore a stunning white maxi dress and Macey was in a navy halter dress that showed off her long, beautiful legs. The same legs Marlowe had. I looked down at my own legs; they were mostly shaved and tan, that was all I was going to say about them.

"Emma, you're late, everyone else is already at the chapel. We were waiting for you," Marlowe complained while shaking her ebony mane.

"I'm not late. The ceremony doesn't start for twenty minutes and it's not like we know the couple." I would have been earlier, but I had forgotten I wasn't wearing a bra. It wasn't like my girls were big enough to poke an eye out, but I was wearing a light blue T-shirt and it would have been awkward, to say the least, if I hadn't remembered halfway down my street that my tatas were flying free.

Macey, the sweeter of the two, looped her arm through mine. "But this is *Ashton's* first time officiating."

Did I detect some dreaminess when she said Ashton's name? Ashton was handsome. Not as handsome as Sawyer, but he had the athletic build and angular face most women found attractive. I probably didn't think he was gorgeous because he looked too much like his mother with his dark eyes and auburn hair. I could see why someone would find him so, but I didn't think it was a good idea for my baby sister to. He was eleven years older than the girls and recently divorced. Then there was the fact that he was our . . . dare I say it? Stepbrother. *Ugh.* If I couldn't be with a stepbrother, neither could they.

Marlowe practically jogged passed us in heels.

"Why are you two so dressed up? I thought this was casual."

Marlowe barely paused. "No reason." She picked up the pace again.

Macey broke loose from me and matched Marlowe's pace. They began to see who could walk faster, pushing each other on the gravel path. What was going on with them?

It didn't take us long to arrive at the "chapel." It wasn't a chapel at all, but an outdoor amphitheater with wood benches for seating. In the front stood a pergola covered in crawling roses, all pink, of course. Mom and Dad were married under that very pergola, except it wasn't here, it was at a country club in Edenvale. As a first-year wedding anniversary present, Dad had the pergola moved here. Mom planted the roses. There had yet to be a divorce for anyone who married under that symbol of love. Mom had made sure to keep tabs on each couple who had married here. That was my job now. I sent a gift basket filled with handmade truffles and other goodies to each couple on their anniversary, just like Mom had done. It was time consuming, but it helped me feel connected to Mom. And I knew she would fret if it wasn't done. I couldn't have her blaming herself for another celebrity breakup all because she died and didn't get the baskets out. I was sure she was already in a tizzy now that she knew Rachel McAdams and Ryan Gosling were no longer a couple. That information had to be readily available in heaven.

Marlowe and Macey raced to Ashton, who was looking nervous while he paced in a white shirt and jeans near the pergola. I guess it would be nerve-racking to join together two people in holy matrimony. There were several guests already seated in the audience. Typically, anyone who was currently vacationing at the Ranch was invited unless it was an invitation only ceremony. From what I knew, this couple was visiting from South Dakota and had decided on Friday to take the plunge and they welcomed any guests. The only reason they waited until today was because the bride wanted to find the perfect dress. My sisters had informed me they'd helped the bride out since they lived and breathed fashion. They were saints.

I admit I stalled on the precipice of the lowest level of the amphitheater. I pretended to look at how much the pine trees had grown since I'd last been there an entire month ago. I was sad to report I didn't see much change. Then I thought maybe I should wish Ashton luck. Anything to not face Sawyer or his mom, who I knew was sitting up several rows between my two favorite men. I had good peripheral vision. And her big hair was hard to miss. I headed toward Ashton, but it wasn't meant to be.

"Em, up here," Sawyer called.

Internally I sighed before plastering on a smile and looking up.

Sawyer was standing up waving at me. Josephine was tugging on his shorts telling him to sit down. I wasn't surprised. She didn't seem to care for Sawyer's and my friendship. She was always trying to keep us away from each other at family functions for some weird reason. Once, she went as far as suggesting I move seats at the dinner table. I declined.

I sucked it up and walked up the aisle to the fifth row where they all sat. Dad stood up as I approached, looking as handsome as ever in his signature plaid button-up. I noticed his raven hair had more gray in it and his brown eyes were tired. They looked like that a lot now. I gave up asking him if he was okay because he would only nod. He gave me a smile, but something was missing from it. It wasn't the warm, how-is-my-Emma-Bear smile. It was cordial. Nothing more. Nothing less.

"Hi, Dad." I hesitated to hug him, which made my stupid eyes tear up. When did I start questioning whether to show my own father affection? Josephine glared up at me from her sitting position, giving me all the answer I needed. I wasn't going to let her take that away from me. I wrapped my arms around Dad and took comfort in the fact that he reciprocated so strongly with no hesitation at all.

"Emma—"

"You were cutting it close," Josephine's acidic voice with a hint of fake sweetness interrupted Dad.

Our father-daughter moment was gone. I pulled away from Dad and faced the woman who was reaching up and digging her claws literally and metaphorically into Dad. If she gripped his arm any tighter it might require a crowbar to wrench it away.

I smiled at her. "As long as you show up before the bride walks down the aisle, I'd say you're in plenty of time."

Sawyer chuckled until his mom turned to him with her left brow raised so high I thought it might stick like that. With all the extra collagen she had pumped in there, it was possible. I had this urge to poke it and see if I could push it down.

Sawyer waved off his mom's attempt at intimidation. He patted the seat next to him. "I saved you a spot."

"Emma will probably want to sit up front so she can see better since she's, you know . . ."

"Short?" I laughed.

"I was going to say height challenged, but I didn't want to offend you."

I didn't believe that for one second but played along. "I appreciate your thoughtfulness, but I don't think that's going to be an issue." That was the beauty of amphitheater style seating. What was an issue was the man smiling sweetly at me waiting for me to sit by him. Perhaps Josephine was right, though I hated to say it. Maybe I should sit in the front row.

"You know, I think I will sit up front, so I can snap some pictures for the Ranch's social media pages." I turned to leave.

"I'll come with you." Sawyer stood up.

"Thank you, but—"

Sawyer tilted his head, his eyes begging to know why I was ditching him.

It panged my heart because, truly, he was the best friend I had ever had, and I hated that because I wanted more, we needed to be less. But I couldn't tell him that. Instead, I made up a pathetic excuse on the fly, which never turns out well. "What I meant to say was the seats up here are more comfortable and . . ." I had nothing. Absolutely nothing but three people staring at me as if I was crazy. Well you know what? I was. That's what being in love with your stepbrother does to you. There, I said the freaking S-word.

Dad reached out and touched my arm. "Are you feeling all right, Emma?"

I nodded, not trusting myself to say anything.

Josephine's eyes said she suspected all along I was crazy and now I was proving her right. I didn't dare look at Sawyer. Instead, I turned on a dime and hightailed it to the front.

Sawyer beat me there, jumping over benches and a small child all while his mom called after him to come back. Why was he acting like that? We were causing a scene.

I took a seat in the front row on the right side, trying to pretend I hadn't noticed Sawyer's crazy antics. Sawyer ended up on the left but made a quick course correction as soon as I sat down.

He cozied right up to me, making me feel as if heaven and hell had collided. "You're right, the wooden benches down here are much more uncomfortable than the ones up there." He nudged me and laughed before turning serious and hitting me full force with his amber eyes. "What's going on with you, Em? Did I do something?"

Yes, he had. He had given me false hope and the vision of what a life full of love and laughter could be like and it killed me that I could never have it, could never have him. Why couldn't he have been a polygamist or felon? Heck, I would have even taken halitosis, or that he chewed with his mouth open. But, no, his breath was amazing and his manners were impeccable. Darn him.

In response to his inquiry I shook my head and faced forward. What I saw in front of me was trouble brewing. My sisters were definitely flirting with Ashton, and worse, he was flirting back. There was copious amounts of touching going on and fits of giggles marked by leaning. Maybe that was my problem, I had never properly learned to lean. Instead of learning to burp the alphabet, I should have studied up on that.

Sawyer wasn't going to be ignored. "Em." He tugged on my ponytail.

I turned to face him. His concerned amber eyes glistened in the summer sun, making them even more attractive. It wasn't helping, so I did some butt kicking and yep, it was painful. "Did you have fun with Shelby yesterday?"

He squinted. "It was fine. But what does that have to do with anything?"

Basically everything. Couldn't say that either. "I was just wondering."

"It would have been more fun with you."

"I doubt that."

"Em, come on. Tell me what's wrong. Has something happened at work?"

"Work is great. I'm great. Like so, so, so great." I flashed him a sardonic smile.

He nudged me several times in a row. "You are so, so, so lying. Why?"

"What makes you think I'm lying?"

"It may have something to do with how you think the wood benches up there are more comfortable. And you've never turned down Las Delicias before yesterday."

I laughed and rolled my eyes. "Maybe I wasn't in the mood for Mexican food." That was a lie. I was always in the mood for smothered burritos. "And," I scooted my butt around the bench, "this bench definitely feels harder."

Sawyer let out a heavy breath. "Whatever you say, Em. I'm here if you want to talk."

"I know," I whispered. He didn't know how bad I wanted to blurt out that I loved him and ask if he could try to love me too. I already knew the answer.

Marlowe and Macey joined us on the *hard* bench, twittering with anticipation. Dad and Josephine ended up in the row behind us. Dad didn't look happy about having to move and Josephine gave me a look that said she had her eyes on me.

Why did she care if Sawyer and I were friends? It's not like I was saying bad things to him about her. I knew how much Sawyer loved his mother. And I had only said one bad thing about her to Dad. Before they were married, I begged him to reconsider or to give it some more time. I also may have mentioned that I thought she had the classic signs of a gold digger, and possibly her love for him had more to do with the size of his bank account. Dad hadn't taken kindly to my insinuations. He had muttered something about me not knowing what it was like to lose a spouse before he stomped away and slammed the door. He was right. I didn't. The fact that he had said it pierced my soul. Mom would have never said anything so cold. She knew how much I wanted to be married, to know that kind of love.

Maybe I didn't know what it was like to lose a spouse, but I knew what it was like to lose the person who had loved me more than anyone. I knew what it was like to lose love. I knew what love looked like because Dad and Mom had shown me, and it didn't look like the couple who sat behind me. Their affection always seemed forced, as in Josephine forcing it on Dad. I never saw him take her hand like he used to take Mom's. He never smiled at her like he did with Mom as he'd wondered how he'd gotten so lucky. Dad used to look alive with Mom. Now he was vacant and distant, even after I had apologized right before he got married.

The bride and groom came walking out of the forest clearing on the path that led to the honeymoon cabin. It was the most modern cabin on the property. The inside was stunning, done in all white. It was one big open room with the most incredible four poster bed covered in, you guessed it, pink linens and pillows. Mom loved that little cabin and was so delighted each time it was rented out. She made extra special care to stock it with her finest chocolates and wine from a nearby vineyard. She and Dad used to sneak away and spend the night there when they wanted alone time.

This couple looked about as in love as my parents had been. The tall, gangly groom only had eyes for his bride, who was dressed in a crepe ivory maxi dress. It was classic with a hint of casual.

"Love the dress," I whispered to my sisters.

"We just started carrying them in the store," Macey informed me.

"I told her it would look best if she wore her hair up," Marlowe complained.

I thought the bride's red hair was lovely draped to the side in waterfall curls.

"Keep your voice down." Macey elbowed Marlowe.

"Your elbows are looking ashy," Marlowe zinged Macey.

"Well, if someone would stop stealing my moisturizer—"

"Ladies," I whispered, "perhaps this could wait until after the ceremony."

"Okay, *Mom*," Marlowe snarled.

The girls had both complained over the years that I tried to act like their mother. Maybe there was some truth to it. When Mom brought home two baby girls, I thought one was for me. Mom may have reminded me a time or two growing up that they already had a mother. I was only trying to be helpful. That was my story and I was sticking to it.

We all went from focusing on the bride and groom to Ashton, who looked like he flipped a switch. Now he was all cool and confident.

Ashton smiled brightly at the couple in front of him. "Buddy, you lucked out." Ashton made everyone laugh.

I snapped a few pictures of the jovial scene.

Ashton held his hands out like a Southern Baptist ready to preach about hellfire. "We come together today to bring this lucky guy and this gorgeous woman together in holy matrimony." He began to sound like an Elvis impersonator. "Marriage brings two people together in a way nothing else can. It brings out the best and sometimes the worst in us."

Ashton was deeper than I gave him credit for.

Sawyer was nodding to my side, agreeing silently with his brother.

"The secret is," Ashton continued in his Elvis/preacher voice, "to never take each other for granted. To see each day together as a gift, for there is no better present than finding your soul mate."

Unless he was your stepbrother and about to be taken. Unfortunately, I sighed audibly while lamenting, wondering if I could get a refund or an exchange on the gift I'd been given.

Sawyer whispered in my ear, "You ever think about doing this?" He flicked his head toward the bride and groom.

I nodded. "How about you?" I tried to keep my voice down to peep level.

"Lately, all the time."

I object.

Chapter Six

THERE WAS NOTHING like cupcakes to soothe your soul, especially when they were pumped full of raspberry lemon filling and topped with the best buttercream known to man. Frankie was a culinary rock star. Cupcakes and punch in the barn were part of the complimentary package for anyone who eloped at the Ranch.

"Frankie, I could kiss you right now." I licked the buttercream on my second cupcake instead.

"What would you think if I added toasted coconut to the filling next time?" Frankie was adding more cupcakes to the cupcake stands. Word spread there was free food to be had and guests were filing into the informal reception.

"I think it's genius. Let's add them to the menu for the Farewell to Summer dance." I had taken that tradition over too since Mom's passing. At the end of the summer season before we closed the guest ranch, we always held a big dance here in the barn. All the guests that stayed with us that summer were invited to come, as well as the entire town of Carrington Cove. It was the hottest ticket in town, with a live band and the best food around. "I want to go all out this year to celebrate since it's the twenty-fifth anniversary. As a tribute to mom, I thought we could do a slideshow of years past and ask former guests to talk about their memories here and of mom."

Frankie looked up with a rare smile on her no-nonsense, smooth-but-aged face. "Your mom would love that. Let me know what else you want on the menu that night. Assuming I'm still here." She glared at Josephine, who had an iron grip on Dad while scanning the barn like a hawk.

"Don't say that," I whispered.

Frankie harrumphed, making her gray wispy bangs fly. "I promised you until the end of the summer, but past that I make no promises. And who knows, the wicked witch may decide to fire me before then."

I shook my head, startled. "Dad would never allow that."

Frankie's brows raised. "I'm not sure of that. Mr. Carrington isn't himself anymore."

I stared at Dad. Longing and loss filled me. I wanted him to make it all better like he used to when I was little and I'd had a bad dream. He would sit on the floor by my bed and hold my hand while telling me fairytales about the secret princesses who lived in our forest who were there to protect us until I fell back asleep. "I've noticed."

"Hey."

I turned to find a fierce looking Frankie.

"Don't you give up on him. That would devastate your mom, and if anyone can get through to him, it's you. He needs you now more than ever."

"He's not very happy with me."

"No, honey, he's not happy with himself. He's always been proud of his Emma. I still overhear him telling people you graduated from the Colorado School of Mines and how you can kick a ball farther than most men."

I gave Frankie a half smile.

"You go over there. You are the rightful lady of the Ranch now; don't let anyone tell you any different."

That sparked a tear in my eye and an idea. Every year we gave the dance a theme. This year's would be the Lady of Carrington Ranch. "I love you, Frankie."

She waved me away with a crooked smile. "Get out of here."

I took my half-eaten cupcake with me and headed toward Dad

and Josephine. They were standing just beneath the loft, right where my world had changed. Dad had since removed the ladder Mom fell from and replaced it with stairs. And no one was allowed to store anything up in the loft anymore. Frankie says she saw him burn the ladder once it was removed.

On my walk over, I noticed Ashton doing card tricks in front of a good-sized crowd. My sisters were front and center as he dazzled people with his sleight of hand. Sawyer was part of the crowd too, until he saw me and headed my way.

He sidled up next to me. "I see you're still trying to avoid me."

"You could have joined me at the cupcake table." Though I was relieved he hadn't. Ripping off this Band-Aid was killing me. But I had to, especially now since Southern Perfection had entered the picture and was making him think of getting married.

"You know, Frankie scares me," he half teased. She could be intimidating if you didn't know her well, or if you were related to Josephine.

"Too bad, you're missing out on the best cupcakes." I waved mine in front of him.

"Why don't you offer me a bite of yours?"

"Uh, no way. Did I mention this is the best cupcake ever? Get your own."

He chuckled before dipping his finger right in my frosting.

My eyes widened. "Excuse me."

He stuck his finger in his mouth with a wicked grin. Dang that was a tantalizing scene. Visions of me licking frosting off him filled my mind. Holy crap, I needed a pause button, more like a delete button and some ice, stat.

He leaned in only a few inches from my face. "What do you think about that?"

I couldn't think, but I might tinkle my pants or do something really embarrassing and kiss the frosting lingering on his sensuous lips. I was a nanosecond away from doing it. My body was overriding my mind. I was leaning in.

"What are you two doing?"

It was the only time I had ever been grateful for Josephine's irritating voice. Sawyer and I jumped apart as if we'd been caught being naughty. If only.

Sawyer grinned at me before addressing his formidable mother who was dressed in black. Her facial features were sharpened by that big hair of hers. "Emma was just sharing her cupcake with me."

Her dark eyes bore into me, more like my figure. "You might want to go easy on the desserts to save room for dinner." Her fake concern was transparent through her falsetto voice.

"Don't worry, I'll be ready."

Her thin neck stretched upward, almost as if it was a hydraulic lift. Her tongue clicked as if she was holding back an insult, but she didn't dare go too far in front of Sawyer. I was sure the first moment she could catch me alone she would mention I should try the Keto diet or something like it, because she only had my wellbeing in mind, of course.

Before the wicked stepmother clicked and clucked her tongue some more, Dad meandered over with a cupcake in his hand.

Like a magnet, Stepmommy Dearest suctioned up to him. "Dane," she whined, "I thought we were avoiding sugar."

On purpose? Who would do such a thing? I think a sugar plum fairy just died somewhere.

Dad cleared his throat, not sure how to respond.

I decided to help the guy out. "Dad, I was just talking to Frankie about the food for the Farewell to Summer dance and I got to thinking. Since this is the twenty-fifth anniversary of it and Mom founded it, I thought the theme could be the Lady of Carrington Ranch. What do you—"

Josephine leaned into Dad more, which was hard to do. She was already stuck to him like cling wrap. Her meticulously manicured hand landed on Dad's chest in a loud slap. "Honey, didn't you tell Emma that I was in charge of the Farewell to Summer dance this year?"

There suddenly seemed to be no air to breathe. I stared at Dad in disbelief, suffocating and begging him with my eyes to tell me it wasn't true.

Dad wouldn't look at me, but his wife was happy to. She hit me with a snake-like smile filled with killer venom. "I know you were in charge of it last year, but there is a new Lady of Carrington Ranch now. I do like that name. Thank you. I think I will use it for the theme. It's fitting, don't you think?"

I was only able to catch enough of a breath to say, "Dad?"

His brown eyes pleaded with me before he handed Josephine his cupcake and walked out.

My cupcake fell to the ground before I followed after him. Before I was out of earshot, I heard Sawyer say, "Mom, you know how much that dance means to Emma."

She knew exactly how much it did, which I had a feeling made this an even sweeter victory for her.

Dad was almost to the stables by the time I caught up to him. "Dad."

He paused but didn't turn around.

I stopped and waited for him to face me. The scent of horse manure lingered in the summer air. It was fitting, since that's how I felt about this new twist in my plot.

I could see his shoulders rise and fall with each deep breath he took. It took him several seconds before he turned around with steel conviction in his eyes.

"Why?" was all I could ask.

"Emma, she's my wife now."

"But I'm your daughter."

"And you always will be."

"What about Mom? She would want me to do it."

He shook his head. "She would understand. She knew the roles husbands and wives played in each other's lives."

A sheen mist coated my eyes. "Something I don't understand, right?"

He ran a hand through his thick hair, sighing. "No, Emma, you don't." He walked off without another word. That hurt more than anything.

I did the only thing I could think of. I ran straight to Shannon's Meadow. I didn't bother to return any of the greetings from several ranch hands who offered me a hello, even Ray who'd been with us since the beginning and was like an uncle to me. Once I was past the Ranch, the tears began pouring down my cheeks. I ran as fast as my Tevas would take me down the gravel road that led to the meadow and the cabin where my life began, literally. Not only was I conceived there, but I was born there as well. There was a blizzard that closed all the roads on the night I decided to make my entrance into the world. Both my fathers helped bring me into the world that night, safe and sound. I always thought that was lovely, almost poetic. Now I felt neither safe nor sound.

Out of breath from the half mile full-on sprint, I fumbled up the porch steps of the cabin. I bent over trying to catch my breath while racking sobs came falling out of me. It felt as if everything or everyone I loved was being stripped away from me. I thought my last name precluded me from romantic love, but now I realized it was on a mission from hell to take everything I loved. I should probably do some family research on the Loveless side to see what horrible misdeed had been done in the past for me to deserve such a fate. Maybe I wasn't the only one, but as far as I knew no else on my biological father's side was as unlucky in love as me. I got wedding invitations all the time from cousins I hardly knew.

Once I caught my breath, I fumbled with the thermometer near the pink door where we hid the spare key to the cabin. Stepping into the cabin was like entering a museum dedicated to the eighties and my parents. The floral-patterned baby blue furniture got me every time. How did Mom think that looked good? Anders must have really loved her. There was not a hint of masculinity in the small, two-bedroom cabin with pink ruffled curtains and fake flowers in several vases. I swore it still smelled like Mom, a hint of cinnamon and gardenia lingered in the air. I'm not sure how much she used to visit this little place, but I had followed her out here once when I was sixteen. I watched her through the window crying over the wedding photo of her and Anders that rested on the mantle now. She was lovely in a simple white cotton gown. My biological father wore slacks, a white shirt, and a hideous wide paisley tie. But the way they stared at each other with wonder in their eyes said it all.

My Not So Wicked Stepbrother

I waited for her that day on the porch and asked her why she came out here and why she was crying. She took my hand and said, "Baby girl, the kind of love that made you is the kind that never dies. There is room in my heart for both of the men that love us."

With tears streaming down my cheeks, I walked over to the mantle and picked up the old photo encased in an etched glass frame. Next to it was a baby photo of me. I had to say I was a beautiful baby, with lots of dark hair and big eyes. I peaked early, even though I had chubby thighs then too. If only everyone thought they were still cute. The last photo on the mantle was of both of my dads dressed in their combat gear. Two handsome, smiling men stared back at me. Brothers in arms and in spirit. I ran my fingers across the glass, wishing I knew what to do to bring Dad's smile back. I felt as if I had lost both men.

I took the wedding photo and curled up on the couch with it. I hoped it would make me feel less lonely. Perhaps my parents would know I needed them, and I could feel them somehow and the love that used to fill this place. While I waited for them to get the memo, I looked around, thankful I at least had this place. Dad had promised it would always be mine. I always thought it was sweet that Dad maintained it, even making sure the cleaning crew came in once a month to dust the place.

I also began to wonder how Anders felt about my mom moving on so quickly with Dad. And how maybe Dad was right, there were things I just didn't understand. Obviously Mom loved both men with all her heart. And I was thankful Mom had married Dad. He was the best Dad growing up. Not only did he quiet fears in the middle of the night, but he was present. He never missed a soccer or football game. He was a shoulder to cry on, like when I was voted homecoming queen, but no one asked me to go to the dance. I had to ask my friend Micah to be my escort. I only won because I was fun and everyone's best friend. Dad told me that day that the right boy would come around, but he still wouldn't be good enough for me. I wanted to believe him.

I hugged the picture tighter. Perhaps I had been too judgmental. Maybe Dad had room in his heart for two women and it didn't mean he loved Mom any less. But why Josephine? Sure, she was beautiful, but did she make him happy? I didn't see that she did unless it was in private. And maybe that was it. Perhaps that's what Dad was talking about when he said I didn't understand. I wanted to. I really did, because it wasn't only me who thought Josephine was a questionable choice.

I waited forever for my parents to make themselves manifest. They could have knocked a book over or something, but not even a rustle happened. I had almost given up hope until there was a knock on the door. I didn't think ghosts knocked.

"Em, are you in there?" Sawyer's voice surprised me.

I sat up straight, still clutching the wedding photo. He wasn't being very helpful with the Band-Aid ripping process. "I'm okay," I yelled out, half-hoping he would leave it at that, but the other part of me yearned for him to do exactly what he did.

Sawyer walked right in, carrying a plate covered in foil.

I let the picture fall to my lap while I wiped my tearstained cheeks. "How did you find me?" I'd never let him in here before. He'd visited Mom's grave with me behind the cabin, but for some reason I was saving this place to share with the person who I not only wanted to share forever with, but they had to be a willing victim. Sawyer only filled half of the requirements.

He gave me a sad smile. "You left your Jeep at the house and I could see you weren't at your mom's grave, so I figured you came in here. Em," he walked closer, "I'm sorry."

"What do you have to be sorry for?" Other than making me fall in love with him.

He set the plate that smelled of Frankie's baby back ribs on the coffee table in front of me before taking a seat right next to me, like our legs were touching we were so close. His long, muscular legs made my heart pitter-patter. The rest of him had my stomach doing an entire gymnastics routine. When he took my hand and squeezed it, it made my stomach feel as if it had just flung itself off the uneven bars and crash landed. I knew for him it was all in the name of friendship, but for me it made my heart take hope, and I couldn't afford that. Yet when I peered into his eyes, they begged me not to pull away from him, so I let myself be tortured by his touch.

"Frankie wanted me to bring you dinner. She told me if I ate anything off the plate, she would stab me."

I laughed. "I hope for your sake it's all there."

"I may have eaten half your roll."

"You're a brave man."

"It was a long walk."

"Since I like you so much, I'll keep your secret."

He tilted his head to the side thoughtfully. "I like you too, very much."

Could I get a side of *and by the way I love you and can't live without you*? No? I didn't think so.

The picture on my lap captured Sawyer's attention. "You look like your mom."

"I wish." She was so slender and beautiful in the photo, with long, cascading blonde hair. I looked more like my dad with brown hair and a solid build, though his was pure muscle.

"Wish granted," he was kind enough to say. I didn't argue, even though there was no way I looked like the stunning woman in the photo.

"Em," Sawyer squeezed my hand, "I'm sorry about the dance. I know how much your family traditions mean to you. My mom does too."

I refrained from rolling my eyes. I had no doubt she knew; she just didn't care.

"She's not trying to hurt you."

I had to keep my head down so he didn't see the incredulous look on my face.

"Living in your mom's shadow makes her feel insecure. She's not trying to take anyone's place; she's trying to make her own place. Does that make sense?"

His comments slapped me right in the face. I'd never looked at it from Josephine's point of view. If I was being honest, I saw her as someone who didn't have feelings. I turned and looked at him.

A sweet smile filled his face. "I hate to see you so sad. Can you try and see this as a good thing?" He pointed at the picture I held. "I didn't know your mom all that well, but judging by how happy she was in this picture and the ones I've seen of her and your dad, I would say she, better than anyone, would understand. I think she would even celebrate that your dad has found happiness again."

That was the problem—I didn't know if he was happy.

"I know for me, I'm glad my mom has finally found someone who treats her the way she deserves." Could he shove the knife in any further?

I let out a deep breath that sounded more like shudders after a good cry. "Sawyer, so much has changed in the last year. I'm not trying to be selfish."

"No one would accuse you of that. You are the least selfish person I know, unless cupcakes are involved." He gave me a heart stopping smile, making me smile too.

"You could have had your own."

"I like sharing with you." He pulled my hand closer to him. If I hadn't known better, I would have said it felt intimate, especially the way his thumb glided back and forth against my skin. My entire body was aflutter. I should have pulled away, but I couldn't, and heaven help me, I didn't want to.

I could hardly breathe, but I managed to respond, "Thank you, Sawyer, for always being so generous with me."

"You make it easy." He paused for a moment. "Do you think you could help my mom with the dance?"

My eyes bugged out before I could stop them.

"It would mean a lot to me if you two got to know each other better."

I wanted to ask him why, but I was too stunned, and then I remembered a conversation we'd once had about how family unity was important to him. I didn't think he had a lot of that growing up. I had until recently, and I missed it.

"I know this has been a hard year for you and your family, but maybe this can be a way to heal some wounds. Maybe help you move on."

"I can't move on from my mom," I choked out.

"Em, that's not what I meant. I just . . . thought if your heart could mend a bit, it might be open to other possibilities."

"Like what?"

He paused and squeezed my hand. "Something that requires your whole heart."

I tilted my head. "I'm confused."

"I know."

Chapter Seven

"You're helping enemy number one with the dance?"

I looked around the comedy club to make sure Sawyer hadn't sneaked in before I responded to Jenna. We were hiding out in the sound booth, which wasn't exactly private as it was near the stage on the floor. It's where Brad typically emceed depending on what acts they had on tap for the night. Brad's commentary alone was worth the price of admission. The man in question was nowhere to be seen. That same man was making it hard to distance myself from him. If he didn't see me, he called me every day and he was coming tonight for the big gender reveal I had planned. I couldn't wait for Jenna and Brad to know what I already knew.

I lowered my voice before saying, "We probably shouldn't call her that anymore. I promised Sawyer I would help her and try to get to know her better. She's as thrilled about it as me." I thought back to Sunday night when Sawyer and I finally made it back to the main house. There Josephine waited. She was annoyed Sawyer was gone for so long and when she asked me to help her, she choked on her words. She had to hold onto Sawyer for support, as if it was the hardest thing she had ever done. I wanted to say, believe me, lady, this is no cake walk for me and the only reason I'm doing it is because your son is the best person I know and his happiness means the world to me. Instead,

I graciously accepted her offer, well, as gracious as it was to say yes through gritted teeth.

Jenna narrowed her pretty blue eyes at me. "Don't you think it's weird that Sawyer wants you to get to know his mom better?"

"Not really. When you think about it, it makes sense since we're *related*. Though I use the term lightly."

Jenna started twirling her bobbed curly hair that had turned a darker shade of blonde throughout her pregnancy. "So, you don't think there is any other reason?" She flashed me a devious smile.

"What other reason would there be?"

She rolled her eyes. "Come on. Do I have to spell it out for you?"

"What am I missing?"

"Emma," she smooshed my cheeks, "have you ever stopped to consider that Sawyer is into you?"

I snorted so loud it hurt my nose. "I think you have pregnancy brain," I said through smooshed cheeks, which made us laugh because I sounded ridiculous.

Jenna dropped her hands. "That may be, but I'm pretty sure I'm right about this."

I waved her silly declaration away. "Do you know how many times he's called me his friend in the last year? And let's not forget, after he met me in person, he never asked me out again."

"He doesn't need to, he sees you more than I see you."

"It's not my fault you got married," I teased her.

"Actually, I do blame you for it." She smiled.

"I'm so sorry you've been tortured by a man who worships the ground you walk on and spoils you rotten. Please sign me up. I mean, not with Brad, but, you know."

"There are some days I would let you have him, but I'm pretty sure Sawyer would like the job."

"Like I said, pregnancy brain."

"Why don't you just ask him?"

I spat out a laugh. "Are you crazy? He's my freaking stepbrother. It's not like I could avoid him after he lets me down gently." As kind as Sawyer was, I knew he would be gentle about it after he tried to hide his disgust.

"You don't know that would happen."

"I'm 99.9999 percent sure. I'm not risking my heart on the one ten thousandth of a percent chance."

She pressed her lips together thinking of a good counter argument. "Maybe you should just kiss him."

"How would that be any less embarrassing?"

She grabbed onto my arm. "Listen to me. You two are always having cozy little chats, which by the way, proves my point that he's into you. But anyway, next time you find yourself alone with him chatting it up, lean into him and take him by surprise. If he kisses you back, great, keep on kissing him and seal the deal. If he pulls away, play it off like it was an accident."

"Oops, I'm so sorry my lips accidentally fell on yours. That sounds legit."

"If alcohol is involved, it's highly plausible."

"Speaking of poor decisions, I saw Macey and Ashton sneak off into the woods when I left Sunday night."

"Don't think we aren't coming back to you and Sawyer, but what the heck? How old is Ashton?"

"He's thirty-six, so eleven years older than her, which is fine. The problem is I think Marlowe likes him too, and you know the whole creepy stepbrother thing."

"Is that what's keeping you from pursuing Sawyer? It's not like you grew up together."

"What's keeping me from Sawyer is he doesn't want me, but regardless, the whole dating your stepbrother thing, it's weird, right?"

She tossed her head back and forth. "Kind of. Could you imagine explaining it to your kids?"

The honest answer was yes, because I had already named our offspring. We were going to have two girls and one boy. Eleanor Jane whom we would call Ellie Jane, Shannon Elaine after me and my mother, and our son, Dane Anders, after my fathers. I didn't mention this to Jenna, because, hello, it was crazy. "I don't need to worry about it, I think he has a mother in mind for his kiddos."

Jenna's face contorted in several expressions trying to land on one. "Who?"

"Shelby."

Jenna shook her head. "No way. He didn't act remotely interested in her at dinner last week."

"Oh, believe me, he's interested. He took Miss Sunshine on a tour of the town on Saturday."

Jenna pursed her lips together. "Huh. That doesn't necessarily mean anything."

I didn't get to respond because Brad entered the picture and wrapped his arms around Jenna from behind. "Hey baby, who's having my baby."

Jenna snuggled right into him. "I can't wait to find out what we're having."

"I already know it's a boy," Brad responded. "I was sure I saw his manhood on display today during the ultrasound." He sighed with content. "I'm so proud to have passed down the family jewels."

Jenna smacked his arm. "I think you were seeing things."

"Yeah, I was—my boy in all his glory. Am I right, Emma?"

"You'll have to play my game and find out." Ever since they handed me the envelope this afternoon, I was having a hard time not telling them what they were having.

"Speaking of games, Brad and I want to try out a new game on the crowd tonight and we need you to help." Jenna smiled coyly.

"We do?" Brad looked down at Jenna confused.

Jenna elbowed him in the ribs, making him groan. "Yes. Don't you remember?"

Brad nodded furiously. "Oh, yep, yep. New game. It's going to be awesome. Jenna just came up with it today."

I narrowed my eyes at my two best friends. "All right. As long as it doesn't involve slime, removing my clothes, or singing Spice Girls songs, I'm in."

"Come on, Em, no one sings 'Wannabe' better than you while in a vat of slime in your undies." Jenna laughed.

"As true as that may be, I'm not twenty-nine anymore." I smirked.

"You've really matured these past couple of years," Jenna smiled, "but don't worry, this will be even more fun."

"I'll be the judge of that."

About that time, patrons of the comedy club and our friends started filing in for the show and the gender reveal. Jenna and Brad had used their baby for marketing purposes, and judging by the crowd, it had worked. Tonight's theme was, Let's Talk About Sex, Baby. Sex apparently still sells. Not that they didn't normally do good business. Edenvale was home to Vale College. If there was one thing college students loved besides sex, it would be cheap entertainment. Come to think of it, sex could fall right into that category. Anyway, the comedy Jenna's and Brad's club provided was worth the ten-dollar cover charge. They also made a killing in concessions and merchandise.

One face stood out in the crowd. Unfortunately, the face right next to him stood out even more. It wasn't right for someone to be so beautiful, and I wasn't talking about Sawyer, though he was ridiculously handsome. But Shelby, Belle of the South, was stunning in her pencil skirt and silk camisole. Together they made a gorgeous couple.

Jenna looked wide-eyed at them. I gave her a look that said *I told you so*. She gave me one back that said she'd meet Shelby out back and teach her a lesson. For that she earned a smile.

"Hey, Em." Sawyer met us at the sound booth with his beautiful tagalong.

"Hello to you too, Sawyer," Jenna didn't take kindly to being excluded from his greeting or his guest.

Sawyer's eyes stayed on me while addressing Jenna. "How's the mother-to-be?"

Jenna scowled at him and Shelby before exiting the booth. "I'm fantastic. Excuse me, I need to go check on our glowstick supply for tonight." They threw glowsticks out into the crowd between sketches and performances. It was kind of their thing. She waddled off irritated.

"What's up with, Jenna?" Sawyer asked once she was out of earshot.

"She's just anxious to find out the gender."

"I'm so excited for them," Shelby jumped in.

I gave her a small smile, not exactly sure why she was so excited for someone she didn't really know, other than it fit her sweet demeanor. "How are you, Shelby?"

Shelby looked around the club walls filled with eighties and nineties movie memorabilia that Brad had been collecting forever. "I'm well. This place is just precious."

Precious? That wasn't a word I would use for it, but okay. "It's a lot of fun."

"I know I could go for some fun tonight." She leaned into Sawyer. She needed to quit doing that.

Sawyer gave her an uneasy smile. "Do you want to find us a couple of seats?" His voice seemed to be unusually high.

"Sure thing, darlin'."

I raised my eyebrows. She was using pet names now? I watched her walk off in her sky-high heels. Wow, could she swing those tiny hips of hers. A trail of hormone crazed college boys stared after her.

"Darlin', huh?" I asked Sawyer. "You two are becoming cozy little work buddies." After hours ones now too.

Sawyer undid the top button on his dress shirt while clearing his throat. "That's just how Southerners talk."

"Right."

"She calls everyone that at the clinic."

"You don't have to explain yourself to me. I think it's *precious*." I tried to keep the cattiness out of my voice. Honestly, I thought Shelby was a nice woman. I was only jealous.

He narrowed his gorgeous eyes at me. "We're friends."

"Friends are good." I stepped out of the booth. "I need to go set up and make sure Aspen is FaceTiming in Jenna's parents."

"Do you want some help?"

I looked up to find Shelby waving at him in the third row. "I think your *friend* is anxious for your company."

Sawyer cringed when he looked over to see Shelby beaming at him. "She can wait if you need my help."

"I'm good, thanks." Total lie. I wasn't good, but this was good. Reminders of my real relationship with him—friend and stepsister. I really needed to rip that Band-Aid off, but in so many ways he was a good healer of emotional scrapes and cuts. On the other hand, he created a big gaping wound of unrequited love.

"Are you sure?"

"Absolutely positive." I plastered on a fake smile before I grabbed my box of decorations with the reveal eggs and walked off. I met Jenna and Brad on the stage. Brad had set up a table for me. We weren't doing pink and blue—I used Jenna's and Brad's favorite colors of purple and black. It took me a few tries to get the right colors. I had to use purple cabbage and blueberries. Good thing I had a minor in chemistry. I'd even made a banner for the table that said, "Let's Talk About Sex, Baby." For some reason, when I made the banner I swore I could hear my mom giggling before she said, "Yes, let's talk about sex, and when are you going to have a baby?"

At this rate, the answer was never unless I decided to skip trying to do it the old-fashioned way. Or perhaps I would get that Golden Retriever I'd always wanted.

Aspen joined the three of us on stage. It was the four amigos again. It had been that way since junior high. During high school it might have been five or seven if the other three were dating someone. We were quick to weed out anyone we didn't like, no matter how good of a kisser they were, which was Jenna's only criteria for a long time, to Brad's dismay. He'd even asked me once to help him out, give him some pointers. Not sure why he'd asked me. I got the least amount of action in that department and kissing Brad would have been like kissing my brother. Not my stepbrother, because I was pretty sure that would be amazing, but a flesh and blood one. He should have asked Aspen; she was adored by many. Too bad she picked a loser in Leland, the father of Chloe. Since their divorce several years ago, she'd kept herself off the market.

The four of us gathered around the table where I was hanging the banner and doing my best not to spill the beans. I was so excited for Jenna and Brad to find out what they were having. Even more excited than Shelby, I might add.

Without saying a word, we all looked over at Sawyer and Shelby, who were chatting animatedly. Shelby talked with her hands in between her episodes of leaning and putting her hands on him whenever she could. Sawyer was smiling at her the entire time. Three sets of eyes landed on me to gauge my reaction.

"What?" I shrugged my shoulders before kneeling to more securely tack down my sign and my heart.

My friends congregated around me. Even Jenna—with her baby bump—knelt around me and began rubbing my back.

"I'm fine."

Aspen bit her lip. "I overheard Shelby," she whispered, which was unnecessary since the music was blaring in the background giving the place a beat of its own, "invite herself to the campout this weekend."

I dropped the tape I had been using. I must have blinked a thousand times before I said, "The more the merrier." It came out sounding like I'd sucked in some helium.

"Tell Sawyer to uninvite her." Jenna's face was turning bright red.

"I won't do that. Sawyer deserves someone like her."

"What is that supposed to mean?" Jenna asked.

"Look at them. They look like the perfect couple, and she seems really nice."

Jenna rolled her eyes. "Will you quit selling yourself short?"

"I don't want to talk about this right now. Tonight is all about you, Brad, and your little . . ."—oops, I almost blew it there—". . . your little banana." I had been tracking the pregnancy too and the site said a baby at twenty weeks was as long as a banana.

"Men are douche bags," Aspen growled.

"Hey, I take exception to that." Brad stood tall and proud.

Jenna stood up and patted his flat gut. "Even you, babe, can be a d-bag."

I stood up too. "Sawyer is a good guy. I've told you all along where we stand, so can we move on? We have a baby's gender to reveal and I bought the cutest freaking outfit for my godbaby that I'm dying to give you."

They made an Emma sandwich out of me in a group hug before dispersing. Aspen took her seat in the front row, ready to FaceTime Jenna's parents, and the parents-to-be took center stage while I arranged the colored eggs on the table. Eleven of the twelve eggs were hard-boiled, but the one that wasn't, revealed the gender. Jenna and Brad were going to take turns smashing the eggs on each other's heads until they got to the raw egg. If it was purple it was a girl, black was for a boy.

"All right, all right," Brad yelled into his mic. The music ceased to thump. "Let's talk about sex, baby!"

The crowd went nuts.

Brad looked his pregnant bride up and down. "Maybe we should have done a little more talking and a lot less action," he teased her.

"Oh, honey, if I remember correctly, there wasn't a whole lot of action," she zinged him back, making the crowd cheer loudly.

Brad rubbed Jenna's stomach. "Now, baby, it's not nice to lie. You know it took a whole two minutes."

"I'll give you a solid ninety seconds."

Several guys in the audience yelled, "Burn!"

Jenna and Brad were good with roasting each other on stage. Off stage they were at times nauseatingly wonderful to each other.

I snatched the mic from Brad. "Save your pillow talk for bed. We're all here to see what you two lovebirds created." I got a lot of applause. I went over the rules while Jenna and Brad put on ponchos to protect their clothes from egg yolk just in case they were the recipient of the raw egg. I laid out a plastic tarp for them to stand on and stood back to let them do their thing. They weren't timid about it. Jenna was smashing the black eggs on Brad, and Brad the purple on Jenna. The first few smashes they really pushed the hard-boiled eggs into their hair, but they were getting anxious and started going quicker, hardly cracking the egg before tossing it to the side. That was, until Jenna grabbed the winner and cracked that raw black egg on her hubby's hair. Yellow goo slid down his hair into his face. Brad was so ecstatic it was a boy he didn't care that he could have had a raging case of salmonella on his head. He picked Jenna up and swung her around.

There I watched from the outside, so happy, yet wondering if it would ever be me. I looked out into the crowd where Sawyer and I happened to lock eyes. His eyes screamed he longed for a day like this too. My eyes drifted toward Shelby, who beamed up at him. I had a feeling one of our wishes was about to come true, and it wouldn't be mine.

Chapter Eight

THERE WAS SOMETHING extremely satisfying about bowling. Balls colliding with pins and the sound it made. And there was something about sliding in bowling shoes on the wood floors. It was like ice skating, but not as cold. Or maybe it was the view. Holy crap, Sawyer's butt. Or maybe Sawyer was a butt. He wouldn't take no for an answer when he'd asked me to go bowling with him tonight. He'd gone as far as holding my phone, which I'd left at the comedy club last night, hostage until I'd agreed. This all went down on my office phone at the plant. The Band-Aid was never coming off at this rate. I had pretty much resigned myself to getting a fungal infection from not letting my skin breathe. Make that my heart. Yep, fungus of the heart. That's what I had.

I was surprised Shelby hadn't come. Maybe she was packing for our camping trip tomorrow. I was miffed she was coming. I was certain Mom wouldn't want her there. Sawyer apologized but felt like he couldn't tell her no when she asked what he was doing this weekend and she asked if she could come. Apparently, she loved to camp and that's one thing she'd been dying to do since she'd moved to Colorado. More like she'd been dying to share a tent with Sawyer. If that happened, I wasn't sure what I would do. For now, I was praying Miss Sunshine had her own tent. What she and Sawyer did was none of my business, but I didn't need to be a witness to it, especially since this weekend highlighted so much of what I had already lost. Although, if they shared a tent, it would rip that Band-Aid off in the most painful fashion ever. It would be a quick cure for fungal heart.

Sawyer missed a spare by one point. I stood to take my turn, trying not to smirk. "Bummer. Looks like I'm still winning," I taunted him from near the ball return.

"We're only in frame five. I've got this."

"That's what you said last time."

He met me by the ball return and flipped my hair that I had partially styled, which meant I'd run a flat iron through it a few times. "I'm feeling lucky tonight," he whispered.

My cheeks blew up like a chipmunk gathering nuts while I held my breath and seriously contemplated that stupid suggestion Jenna gave me. Too bad I'd only been drinking Dr. Pepper. I wasn't sure I could say, *sorry my elevated blood sugar made my lips fall on yours.* Maybe I could use the excuse that last night's kiss from that stupid game Jenna and Brad made me play was so awful that I needed something to make up for it. My cheeks deflated, and I blew so much air out Sawyer backed up. "Sorry, I was just thinking about that kiss last night."

Sawyer's brow furrowed. "So, you liked it?"

"No. It's not exactly how I like to meet guys, and that idiot tried to stick his tongue in my mouth."

"Is that why you punched him? I thought it was part of the game. Pucker or Sucker." He grimaced.

Dumbest game ever, and completely made up by Jenna so she could see how Sawyer would react to me kissing someone. Her report was that while the crowd was supposed to be clapping and cheering as loud as they could—because the louder they were, the closer Jenna and Brad pushed me and that idiot together—Sawyer was doing neither. And when that guy kissed me, Sawyer stood up, concerned, as Jenna put it. Brotherly concern, I was sure.

"It was a good sucker punch, if I do say so myself."

Sawyer grinned.

I turned to get my bowling ball from the ball return.

"So . . ." Sawyer let out a heavy breath, "tongue is out for a first kiss?"

I snorted and turned toward him, almost dropping the bowling ball. "What kind of question is that?"

He ran his hand through his wavy hair. "A guy can't be too careful nowadays. These are good things to know. I'm just trying to get a pulse on how women feel on these issues."

"Taking a poll, are you?"

"Maybe." He flashed me his sparkling smile.

I thought for a moment. "Hmm. Well, I would say if you are strangers, definitely no tongue, but it would probably be best not to go around kissing strangers; that would certainly land you in hot water."

"What if you know the guy?"

"How well?"

"Very."

"If we knew each other that well, he would know exactly how to proceed if he kissed me."

"What does that mean?"

"I'm saying he would instinctively know by how I respond to his kiss whether he should risk slipping me his tongue."

"You wouldn't want him to ask?"

I laughed. "Uh. No. That would totally kill the mood. 'Hey baby, would you like to feel some of my papillae?'"

Sawyer chuckled. "Sounds romantic to me."

"Try that on your next date and let me know how it goes." On second thought, please don't. I didn't need to hear any tonsil hockey stories between him and Miss Sunshine.

"So, let me clarify, if you know the guy well and you're attracted to him, tongue is totally appropriate for a first kiss?"

"That sounds about right, unless he's Jude Law. He can French kiss me any day without introduction or delay."

Sawyer narrowed his eyes. "He's getting so old."

"He's refining with age. Speaking of Jude Law, do you want to watch *The Holiday* later?" *Crap!* That invitation slipped out before I remembered I should be trying to be prevent fungal heart. It was just so easy to want to be around Sawyer. Plus, he always brought my favorite caramel popcorn with him. And he always had a tissue ready to go for when I cried during the scene where Jude Law tells Cameron Diaz he loves her. Maybe that's what I should do. Swap houses with someone in England for a week and pray they had an amazing brother I wasn't related to who comes to visit and wants to make out with me passionately, sight unseen. I would definitely be amenable to tongue in that scenario.

Sawyer shook his head at me, amused. "Sure."

"First, I need to finish kicking your butt."

He waved his arm out for me to proceed. I was about to until an unfamiliar voice said, "Sawyer."

Both Sawyer and I turned to see a man and a woman standing pensively by the chairs in our lane. The handsome gray-haired man looked so familiar to me, but I couldn't place him. The younger woman next to him, gripping his hand was probably in her mid-forties with long, blonde hair. They were an attractive couple, whoever they were.

"Dad." Sawyer's hand clenched until his knuckles were white.

What? I dropped the dumb ball, barely missing my toe. Sawyer jumped into action and swooped up the ball before placing it back in the ball return for me. I could feel Sawyer's body shake next to me. Without thinking, I took his hand. Never once had I initiated such contact, but it seemed so natural. For me, our hands were meant for each other. He accepted my hand without a second thought, squeezing it.

"Are you okay," I whispered.

He said nothing, but continued to stare at his father. The familiarity I had recognized in him became obvious. Sawyer looked so much like his father, from the curl in his hair to his build. They even shared the unusual amber eyes. Sawyer was going to be a babe in his late fifties.

Mr. King braved moving toward us. The woman he was with continued to cling to him and followed alongside him. I recognized pleading in the unknown woman's eyes, like she was asking Sawyer to please not turn them away. The closer they got, the tighter Sawyer's grip on my hand became.

"Son, it's good to see you," a nervous Mr. King stuttered. "Who's this lovely young lady with you?"

Sawyer continued to stare hard at his father while pins and balls collided around us. I had a feeling Sawyer's insides were doing the same thing.

I wasn't sure what to do, but I hated the awkward silence. "I'm Emma Loveless." I held out my free hand. "It's nice to meet you."

Sawyer whipped his head toward me with eyes agape as if he couldn't believe I was fraternizing with the enemy. His dad looked so kind and his physical appearance reminded me so much of Sawyer's it was hard not to be polite.

Mr. King gratefully took my hand and shook it. "The pleasure is all mine. I'm Warren, by the way." His wide smile looked exactly like Sawyer's toothy grin. It made me smile. Warren looked at the woman near his side. "This is Bridget."

Sawyer's grip reached vice-like levels. Was this *the* woman? Sawyer had never mentioned a name or whether his dad was still with her. She looked so nice. So opposite Stepmommy Dearest. She was pretty, but she wasn't stunning like Josephine. Bridget was more naturally beautiful. No collagen or fillers. She even had a muffin top. This was my kind of woman.

Bridget held out her small, semi-rough hand. I noticed some dirt under her fingernails. I was liking her more and more. That was, unless she was the man stealer and the reason why my dad was now married to Sawyer's mom.

I took her hand, giving her the benefit of the doubt.

"It's nice to meet you, Emma." She dared to catch Sawyer's gaze. "It's nice to see you again, Sawyer. It's been too long."

Sawyer scoffed.

"I've missed you, son." Warren held his breath, waiting to be lambasted for his remark.

Sawyer said nothing, but stared coldly at them.

"What brings you here tonight?" I couldn't help but try and make the situation more comfortable. But seriously, what a dumb question. Why else do you go to a bowling alley? Believe me, the snack bar wasn't worth the trip.

Warren's smile thanked me. "It's date night for us. Looks like for you too."

I cleared my throat and regrettably dropped Sawyer's hand. "Oh, um . . . we're just . . ."

"This is Dane's daughter," Sawyer jumped in unwillingly.

Warren and Bridget both tipped their heads.

"When Emma was a baby, her mother married Dane after her first husband died."

They nodded like that cleared up the last name discrepancy.

"We are sorry about the loss of your mother," Bridget offered.

"Thank you," I replied.

Warren looked between Sawyer and me with interest. A hint of a smile could be seen in his eyes. I had seen those glints in Sawyer's many times. "It's nice you two are . . . *friends.*"

It was freaking dandy.

Warren scrubbed a hand over his face while taking a deep breath. "Would you mind if we used the lane next to yours? I would love to catch up with you." His eyes begged Sawyer's before he focused on me. "And I'd like to get to know you better."

"That would be great," I responded without thinking. Warren had this effect on me, like Sawyer. He was so easy to like, just like his son.

Sawyer didn't appreciate my willingness one bit. He grabbed my hand. "Can I speak to you?" He didn't wait for my response before he began pulling me away toward the shoe rental counter. By the time we got there, Sawyer's face was a dark shade of red. I'd never seen him angry before and I hated that it was directed toward me. He let go of my hand. "Em, what are you doing?"

I glanced over at a forlorn Warren before focusing back on a seething Sawyer. "He's your dad and he obviously cares about you."

"He left my mom for Bridget."

Oh. So she was *the* woman. She looked so nice. I was having a hard time hating her. "I didn't know that, but Sawyer, he's your father."

"You don't know what it's like to have your dad betray his family."

I raised my eyebrows. "Not in the way you experienced it, but . . ." I hesitated, "when my dad struck up a relationship with your mom so soon after my mother's death, that felt like a betrayal to me."

Sawyer opened his mouth to respond, but nothing came out. He took a deep breath and let it out. The red began to dissipate from his face.

"I don't know everything that went on in your family, but if you want to talk about it, I'm here to listen. But I do know what it's like to lose a parent and how much I would give to talk to my mom again if for only one second, or to even have my dad reach out to me now." My eyes teared up.

"Em." Sawyer rested his hand on my arm. "Your dad loves you."

I wiped my eyes. "From the looks of it, your dad loves you too. And aren't you the one who told me that I needed to move forward and mend my heart? Maybe it's time for you to do the same."

Sawyer's head dropped while he mulled over what I had to say. "Maybe you're right," he spoke low.

"If you want to leave, we can; if you want to stay, I'll help you through it."

He tipped up his head and gave me a crooked grin. "What would I do without you?"

"You might actually win a game of bowling." I smiled.

He pulled me to him for a hug. I settled into his chest and soaked in his clean scent. For a moment I closed my eyes and only concentrated on the strong, steady beat of his heart. What I wouldn't have given to stay there forever. I knew I couldn't, so I pulled away. "We better join your dad and Bridget."

Sawyer's brow furrowed. "Okay, Em." But he wasn't done torturing me; he put his arm around me on the walk over and gave me a squeeze. "Was this our first fight?"

I laughed at him. He said the strangest things sometimes. It was one of his endearing qualities. "I think I've had more heated discussions with the soda dispenser at the convenience store than I just had with you."

"Well, that's good; it means we're good communicators."

"If you say so."

It didn't take long for us to reach the lane where his dad and Bridget waited for us. This time, though, I think Bridget was keeping her distance from Warren on purpose, as if she thought it might help. Infidelity was awful, and I didn't condone it, but I could tell Bridget loved Warren. I wanted to know their story. Whether they realized it or not, it intertwined into my own.

Warren stepped forward. "We can go."

"Don't," Sawyer offered.

Warren smiled at me as if it was my doing. I suppose I had something to do with it. Both he and Bridget looked relieved.

Warren clapped his hands together. "Great. Let's play."

Yes, let's play. I took my turn while Bridget and Warren set up the screen on their side. Not to brag, but I rolled a strike. Okay, I was totally bragging. I turned around and gloated. "Yes!" I high-fived Sawyer on my victory march back.

"Don't count me out yet."

"I've already counted twice, and you're totally coming out on the losing end. You might as well get ready to pay for the ice cream tonight." That was our friendly wager for the evening.

He reached for his ball with a serious demeanor. "This is about more than my ice cream. This is about my dignity."

"You must have checked that at the door." I loved talking smack with him.

"Those are fighting words." He pulled his ball up to his chest, determined to finally best me.

"Good luck." I threw myself into one of the chairs at the electronic scoreboard. Warren was occupying the other chair. I admit I was a tad nervous to sit next to him, but his disarming smile put me at ease. And now that I was closer to him, I noticed his arms were buff and his polo shirt said King Steam and Sauna. Huh. Sawyer never mentioned his dad owning a business. It wasn't surprising, considering he tried to never speak of him.

"Emma Loveless, you wouldn't be the same girl who used to be the kicker for the Pine Fall Eagles now would you?"

"That would be me."

"You were impressive. Best high school kicker I've ever seen."

"I'm not sure about that, but I had fun doing it."

"I could tell. And if memory serves me correctly, I think the night we watched you play you were made homecoming queen."

That memory held dueling emotions for me. It was a happy memory. I was honored to have been chosen, but it was accentuated by the fact that no one had asked me to the dance. "You have a good memory." I smiled. Though it probably wasn't every day you saw a girl get crowned homecoming queen wearing a football uniform and pads.

"It's not as good as it used to be, but I do remember telling Sawyer that night if he wanted to be happy, to choose a girl like you—a girl who wasn't afraid to get dirty but knew how to stand tall and keep her crown on straight."

Wow. I didn't know what to say. It was a profound and flattering statement, but so depressing knowing that was never happening. I wanted to ask how Sawyer responded back then, but present him caught my attention with his victory dance by the ball return.

"Strike, baby." He pointed at me.

"I'm still ahead by twenty points," I taunted him while standing up. "Why don't you take a seat while I go get a refill on my Dr. Pepper?"

Sawyer knew what I was doing. He looked between me and his dad, uncertainty flooding his eyes. I could understand the hurt and hesitation. With my eyes, I tried to convey that I was here for him and I believed in him. I knew he had it in him to forgive his dad.

Sawyer approached slowly, but he came, and that was the most important part.

"Do you want a bottle of water?" I asked him. He didn't really believe in drinking his calories. No one was perfect.

"I'm good."

"Yeah, you are." I gave him a wink and left him to spend a few minutes with his dad.

"I'll come with you." Bridget finished tying her bowling shoes and stood.

This was going to be awkward hanging out with the mistress, but it was good of her to give father and son a few minutes alone.

Bridget and I walked to the snack bar with our hands in our pockets. I almost started whistling because I thought it would be funny, but instead my mouth took over and went with an embarrassing question. "So how long have you and Warren been together?" Smooth move, Emma. Way to serve up the elephant in the room on a crap platter.

Bridget's kind brown eyes, while shocked, looked understanding. "I suppose Sawyer hasn't said anything about me."

"Not once."

She nodded. "That makes sense."

We each took a stool at the snack bar. "Dr. Pepper, please," I ordered before turning my attention to a nervous Bridget. "I'm sorry I tossed that question out there. Sometimes my mouth and brain have a serious disconnect."

She was nice enough to laugh. "I've been there, and I don't blame you for being interested. You and Sawyer are obviously close, so it's only natural."

"He's one of my best friends."

"Friends, huh?"

"Yes, friends."

She gave me a coy smile. "If you say so."

I knew so.

She turned in her stool and looked at father and son trying to have a conversation. I did the same. Even from a distance you could tell it was uncomfortable. Sawyer was hardly looking at Warren and all Warren could do was look at his son in adoration.

"I've known Sawyer since he was in high school. I moved next door to his family to help take care of my ailing father."

Yikes. Were they having an affair all those years? I did know Sawyer's parents had only been divorced for three years.

She turned my way. "I know what you're thinking, and the answer is no." Her head lowered. "For many years we were only friendly neighbors. Sawyer used to mow my dad's yard when he was in high school and when he came home for the summers during college. He was a sweet kid. He would never let me pay him. I didn't know Josephine well; she spent a lot of time away from home. And Warren and I... well... he was helpful with doing minor repairs around the house. He knew Dad didn't have a lot of money and what I earned mostly went toward my dad's medical bills. We never meant for any of this to happen, though we know we are to blame." She rubbed her lips together. "We were both lonely and dealing with loss. My father was dying, and his marriage was. We let our emotional connection go too far. For that, I'm ashamed. As far as how long we've been together, that's a hard question."

I tilted my head. How hard could it be? The math had to be simple.

She looked up and tucked some hair behind her ear. "We only had one, uh... physical encounter while he was married."

That was a nice way of putting it.

"The guilt was too much for us to take," she continued. "He confessed to Josephine right away. As you can imagine, it spelled the end for them. This sounds awful, but it was a relief for Warren to be out of his marriage. But it devastated him to lose his relationship with Sawyer. Those two were very close. Ashton has been more forgiving, but Sawyer wanted nothing to do with his father. That ate at both of us, so we decided it was best not to see each other. We both hated that our relationship caused so much damage and I think we both wondered with his marriage gone and my father passed away if what we had was even real."

"Did Sawyer know you broke things off?"

"Warren told him he would do whatever it took to make things right between them, even if that meant not seeing me, but the damage had been done. That was a few years ago." She gave me a small smile. "You must wonder why we are together now."

I nodded. Did it make me bad that I was so curious?

"I moved out of my dad's house after he passed away, but last year, Warren and I literally ran into each other on the ski slopes. I lost my footing and ran smack into him on a black diamond run."

They must be good skiers to navigate black diamond slopes. I preferred the intermediate blue slopes. "Sounds like something that would happen to me."

She grinned and nodded. "If you're not willing to be embarrassed, you're not really living, right?"

I tilted my head. "That sounds like something my mom would have said."

Bridget patted my knee. "It's funny how we still hear them after they're gone, isn't it?"

"I hear my mom talking to me so much, sometimes I think I'm crazy," I admitted.

"I don't think so. I think the connection between a parent and child is strong, it supersedes death and it feels like death when it's severed in life."

Bridget spoke to my heart. I felt that way about both my mother and my father respectively. I glanced at Sawyer and his dad. They must be feeling that same pain. "It must be hard for you and Warren to be together."

"More than you know. We discovered that day on the slopes and the days after that what we had was real. The best relationship either one of us has ever had, but there were consequences for our wrong choices early on in our relationship. Our happiness will never be complete until we have Sawyer's blessing."

My brows raised. "I think that's a tall order."

"Maybe impossible."

"I don't know. Give it some time. Sawyer has a good heart."

She squinted, studying me. Then her eyes lit up in an ah-ha moment. "Warren and I would love it if you two would come have dinner with us."

"Do you live together?" My hand flew to my mouth. "I'm sorry, that's none of my business."

She wasn't upset at all, in fact, she smiled. "Don't apologize. You're protective of Sawyer. I respect that." She leaned toward me. "But the answer is no, we don't." She blew out a deep breath. "We have no intention of marrying until we can make things right with Sawyer."

"What if that never happens?"

Her entire body deflated at the thought. "If I have to, I'll leave Warren for the sake of Sawyer." Tears welled up in her eyes.

I took her hand, though I barely knew her. "I'll see what I can do."

She patted my hand. "This may sound weird, but I feel like we're supposed to know each other."

You know what was weirder? I felt the same way. Not sure how I was going to explain that to Sawyer.

Chapter Nine

"You're doing what?" Jenna yelled into the phone.

"I'm not happy about it, but there's no way Sawyer's old truck is making it over Freedom Pass." And Sawyer and I had already been planning on driving up together.

"Tell him if he can't drive Shelby, she can't come. Doesn't she have a car?"

"I assume she does, but even Colorado natives have a tough time going over that Pass. I can't have her blood on my hands." None of us had wanted to attempt it last night in the dark after we got off work, which was why we were leaving this morning.

"I don't mind getting bloody. I'll take the blame without an ounce of guilt."

"Aww. Now I know who to call when I need to bury a body."

She laughed. "I'll be the first one there with a shovel. It wouldn't take long to dig a hole for miss little thing."

"You know, sometimes you scare me, and to think you're going to be a mommy soon."

"No one better ever mess with my boy."

I had no doubt Jenna would be a scary mama bear. "For the safety of those around you, I hope that's true. And by the way, try and be nice to Shelby this weekend."

"Ugh," she spat. "I make no promises. I don't understand why you're being so nice to her. She's putting the moves on your man."

"He's not my man."

"Oh, really? Who were you out with last night?"

"Friends go bowling together. Besides, we weren't alone. His dad and his dad's girlfriend crashed the party."

"Oh, yeah. You're going to need to fill me in on that."

"I will. I need to go or I'm going to be late picking up Sawyer and his *friend*. I'll see you in a few hours."

I could hear Jenna sigh in disgust before she hung up. I wasn't thrilled about the arrangement either, especially given that Sawyer and I parted last night in disagreement. I guessed you could call it our second fight. Two fights in one night. When he dropped me off, he barely muttered a goodbye.

He didn't think we should accept Bridget's dinner invitation and I think he felt betrayed that I didn't loathe her. It's not like I didn't try for a few seconds. I had fully intended on hating the woman who'd stolen Warren away from Josephine, but she seemed really nice and it was apparent she loved Warren. And I wasn't so sure she had stolen Warren away. I had a feeling the divorce had been inevitable. The question was, why? Like, why was Josephine never at home? Why was Warren relieved to finally be divorced? I mean, what kind of woman was my father married to?

I felt like there were two sides to the story, and Sawyer needed to learn the other half. Maybe if Sawyer could see the whole picture, it might help him forgive his dad. Again, I wasn't condoning infidelity. It was obvious Bridget and Warren weren't making excuses and that they felt remorse over it. Sawyer needed to see that too.

I looked up into the clear blue Colorado sky. It was the perfect July morning. Not a cloud could be seen. The birds were digging it too, by how loud they were chirping. It was going to be hot in the valley today, but where we were going, it would be warm in the day and cold at night. I threw the last of my gear into the trailer I'd hitched to my Jeep. I was excited to try out my new tent—it came with a porch.

Aspen was going to be my roommate for the night once she

joined us after work. The bank was open for half the day. My stomach wriggled thinking about who Shelby was probably going to stay with. I had a feeling that Band-Aid was going to come flying off this weekend and my fungal heart infection would clear right up when it broke in two. If they were getting that cozy, going to dinner at his dad's with me would be a moot point. He'd want to take his girlfriend, or not go at all and hang out with Shelby instead. I should be happy for the distance it would create between us, but even though I knew it was probably the best thing for me, it filled me with profound sadness and loss.

I checked that I had everything. I even looked down my T-shirt to make sure I had a bra on. The girls were secure. My shorts were zipped. I had on both hiking boots. I reached up and felt my sunglasses on the top of my head. My cell phone was in my pocket. Not that there was service where we were going. The primitive camp site was at the base of Freedom Pass near the river. It was pristine and untouched. It was Mom's favorite camping site because it was so remote. She loved taking us there growing up because she felt like she had us all to herself. Dad couldn't do any business and we weren't calling our friends or watching TV. It was a place free of distractions, until now. I was going to try not to be distracted by Shelby and Sawyer, but I wasn't sure that would be possible.

All the way over to Sawyer's I worried about what I would say to him. I'd never really felt that way around him. Maybe we weren't the great communicators he thought we were. By the time I arrived, I'd decided not to mention last night unless he did. I still felt like he should go, but it wasn't my place to push him.

Every time I pulled into Sawyer's apartment complex with the peeling green painted buildings, I couldn't believe he lived in such a dive. But not as much as his mother, who was constantly telling him he needed to live in a place worthy of his profession, so she could come visit him. I wondered if his neighbors knew he was a doctor.

I had to drive extra slow through the parking lot, as it dealt with more crack than a drug lord. At least his beat-up truck fit in. There he was, looking fantastic and ready for an adventure in his khaki shorts, tight T-shirt that showed how toned he was, and of course he had sunglasses on. He was always reminding me how important it was to protect my eyes from the sun's rays.

Sawyer was surrounded by coolers, his tent, and a large duffle bag. He had said he wanted to handle all the food for the trip. When I parked behind his truck, he looked up from his phone and flashed me a tentative smile. Was he still upset with me?

I put my Jeep in park and hopped out to see what the verdict was. I met him around the trailer. He was already hefting his duffle bag into it.

"I would have met you at your place to help you hitch the trailer."

"I know, but . . ."

I wanted to say I did it by myself because I was too afraid to become dependent on anyone of the male variety. They never stuck around all that long unless they married one of my friends. I wasn't even sure Brad could hitch a trailer, come to think of it.

Sawyer turned and met my gaze. "But what?"

I shook my head, clearing out my thoughts. "Nothing. It was easy enough for me to do." So I had sworn a few times and bruised my thumb.

Sawyer met me by the coolers with a look of contrition. He rubbed his neck. "I feel bad about how we left things last night." So we were going to talk about it.

I leaned against his truck, knowing I was current on my tetanus shot. "I get it."

He gave me a half smile. "I know you were only trying to help."

I stared down at my hiking boots. "Not sure how helpful I was."

"Em," he took his shades off, and rested them on his head, "I acted like a jerk last night."

My head popped up and met his sincere eyes.

"My dad and Bridget," he could hardly get out her name, "showing up came out of left field for me."

"I wouldn't say jerk. Maybe whiny and immature."

He raised his brows. "Whiny and immature? For that, this cooler," he nudged one with his foot, "isn't coming."

I knelt down. "What's in the cooler?" I tried to lift the lid, but Sawyer bent over and slapped his hand on it. "I think you owe me an apology first." A playful smile danced on his face, which was now inches from my own.

"I stand by my assessment." I dared him, with my own smile, to contradict me.

He took a deep breath and let it out. "Perhaps I was a tad irritable."

"Okay, I'll let you have that."

"For your concession, I will let you have this." He threw open the cooler lid.

I could have kissed him. Like really, really kissed him. Lots of tongue. Instead, I did something more embarrassing in the glow of an entire cooler full of Dr. Pepper made with real sugar. The kind you have to special order in the green cans. The king of all drinks.

"I love you!" Yes, that's what I said. Biggest freaking Freudian slip of all time. We are talking I fell on my butt I was so taken aback by what I'd said. With my butt on the pavement, I began to stutter, "I mean, you know what I mean, like a friend, a sis . . ." No, not like a sister. There were laws against the way I felt for him if we were truly related.

Sawyer reached over the cooler and took my hands, trying to hoist me up. "Are you okay?"

Uh, that was a negative. I just told the man I love that I loved him. My stepbrother.

In one big pull, Sawyer had me on my feet, all while laughing at me. "Wow. I should have bought you 'real' Dr. Pepper a long time ago." He gave my hands a good squeeze before letting them go.

I couldn't make eye contact. "It was very sweet of you."

"Anything for you. Should we load this up and go pick up Shelby?"

Oh, Shelby, you lovely, awful reminder of what would never be. P.S. I think I might hate you.

∽

I know I told Jenna to be nice to her, but on the drive up all I could think about was ways to torture Shelby. Maybe a push in the rushing river, a snipe hunt, a burned marshmallow rubbed in her perfect blonde hair. Where were these violent thoughts coming from, you may ask? It wasn't just that she was there, but when we picked her up, I didn't see a tent. Not only that, but she brought designer luggage. We are talking Louis Vuitton monogrammed luggage. She better have a dang tent stuffed in there. Oh, and she was wearing wedges with tiny denim shorts that proved she was a freak of nature—she had not one ounce, not even a ripple of cellulite. I was born with more fat than she had on her entire body.

If that wasn't enough, I began to question her story of only being an office manager for an eye clinic. Really? What was that salary? Around forty thousand, maybe fifty if she was lucky. I was thinking she was very lucky, or a liar. She lived in an upscale townhome at the new Bridge Park development that was like a mini town in and of itself. The community boasted a country club, expensive restaurants, boutiques, and its own fitness center. The starting price was half a million. The mortgage payment alone would take her entire salary before taxes.

The worst of it, though, was Miss Sunshine was about ready to wet her pants when we drove over Freedom Pass. She was sitting in the backseat of my Jeep. Sawyer was riding shotgun. I would give her credit that it was a tad frightening. Guardrails were few and far between, the windy roads were narrow, and you could see a car or two that had gone off the road and landed in the pine trees below. The views were breathtaking, though. The only sights for miles were mountain vistas, pine and aspen trees, and a bald eagle or two. With the top down on my Jeep, we were able to soak in the clean mountain air that settled in your soul and made you feel more alive than you imagined possible. The abundant sunshine added to the energy of it all.

All Shelby could focus on was the sheer height we were at . . . and Sawyer. She had him in a stranglehold for miles while squealing. If she was that worried, she should have stayed in her seatbelt instead of reaching up and hugging Sawyer from behind. Sawyer kept patting her toned arms, telling her it would be okay and that with me at the wheel, she was in good hands. He shouldn't have been too sure. I wanted to rip those perfectly tanned arms off her and start whacking her with them. And with her out of her seatbelt, devious thoughts had run through my mind. No need to say them in case of self-incrimination.

By the time we arrived at the campsite, I needed a vacation from my mini vacation. I had a feeling that cooler of Dr. Pepper wasn't going to last long. And if that chick thought I was sharing my Dr. Pepper with her, she had another thing coming. Sawyer I had no say over, but that real Dr. Pepper was all mine.

I pulled over on the tiny rutted dirt road near a clearing where my family had camped before, about fifty yards from the river. The pine trees made an almost perfect circle around the clearing, as if they had been planted with campers in mind.

I couldn't get out of my Jeep fast enough. I wished some of our other friends were already there. Without a word, I hopped out and headed straight for the river. The sound of water calmed my soul. At least it used to. Before I could get too far, I heard Shelby ask, "Where's the cabin?"

What?

"Cabin?" Sawyer laughed.

I turned around to see her bite her lip all sexy and cute. "Well, yes, when my family goes camping, we rent this really beautiful cabin in Blue Ridge. It has any amenity you'd ever want."

"That's not camping." Sawyer grinned.

"Oh," her lip started to quiver, "I didn't realize that this is what you meant when you said camping. I didn't even bring any bedding."

Was she serious?

Sawyer hugged her and began patting her back; she settled right into him. That's when I headed back for the cooler. It was going to be a six-pack day.

"Don't worry. I'm sure between all of us we can take care of you." Sawyer gave me a pointed look. "I know Em has plenty of room in her tent."

Make that a twelve-pack kind of day.

Chapter Ten

ONE THING SHELBY didn't forget was her white bikini. We all stood at the bank of the river mesmerized by the blonde goddess ready for some tubing, minus mommy-to-be Jenna, who would be reading a book about natural childbirth. I kept tilting my head wondering how her boobs stayed in that tiny top and what kind of torture you had to endure to get those perfect lines and curves. I guaranteed it meant not drinking Dr. Pepper. Totally not worth it, I kept telling myself as I yanked down my swim shorts to cover my cellulite thighs and sucked in my gut under my slimming-paneled black tankini top. Newsflash, it wasn't all that slimming.

I was acutely aware of how Sawyer's eyes lingered on her as he explained tubing to her. Seriously, what world did this chick come from? Who had never heard of tubing? While Sawyer was explaining how to stay in the current and avoid giant boulders, I was more concerned with how the cold water was going to really perk her girls up, perhaps enough to bust through her life jacket, and what kind of a show we were all in for. By the way Kellan and Ashton were ogling her, it looked as if they were praying for the cold water to do its thing.

Jenna was tsking and snarling under her breath, debating with her eyes whether she should shove the Southern Belle into the river, while Aspen was holding my hand as if I needed comforting. Maybe I did, but I was trying to act unaffected. I was used to the friend zone, even if this time it felt different as I had never fallen in love with a friend before. In case there was any doubt, it made the friend zone a hundred times suckier.

"Oh, Mylanta! This water is cold, boys," Shelby squealed after dipping her toe in. "Back home the water can be as warm as a bath."

I tried not roll my eyes. "Excuse me. I forgot my sunscreen in the Jeep. I'll be right back." I couldn't take it anymore.

"I'll poke a small hole in her tube," Jenna whispered.

"She'd only end up in someone's lap," Aspen responded.

Or worse, she would actually put in motion my plan of getting hypothermia and we all knew whose sleeping bag she would end up in, skin to skin. With that depressing thought, I jogged back to my Jeep. I swore I heard my mom's voice in the light breeze say, "Don't give up, you could totally take her." Physically, I could take the little waif down, but there was no way I could compete with goddess divine.

"Hey," Sawyer called out to me, "where are you going?"

I was irritated with him, so I only mumbled something about getting sunscreen. I wanted to full-out ignore him, but I heard him approaching on the dirt road, so I knew blowing him off wasn't an option. Better to avoid awkward questions like, what's wrong? Oh, I don't know, only that I love you and it kills me to see you with another woman. It also didn't help that he hadn't prepared Shelby for the kind of trip we were taking. Now goddess was sleeping in my tent.

I reached my Jeep and opened the door. The sunscreen was in the door panel. I turned around with it to find Sawyer invading my personal space. That in and of itself was always cause for some heart palpitations, but somewhere along the way he'd ditched his shirt. Holy crap, I needed warning before he did that. I knew it was coming off since we were going in the river, but I needed the cues first, like raising his arms, a little lift of the shirt, etc. He couldn't just come at me all at once half-naked.

I stared at his defined body. He wasn't six-pack ripped, but he was sculpted, as in his nicely carved pecks were begging to be touched. The dark hair his chest boasted called for my head to nestle into it. I couldn't help but wonder why it was evenly tanned. Where was he going without his shirt and why wasn't I invited? I probably didn't want to know.

While I eyed him, his sights were set on the sunscreen. "Do you want some help with that?"

Did I want his hands on my body? That was a big fat yes. "No, thanks." I knew my limits.

He didn't listen and plucked the sunscreen bottle out of my hands. "How will you get your back?"

"I'm more limber than I look."

His eyebrow popped. "Is that so?"

I realized how that comment could be taken. I cleared my throat. "I meant . . . um . . . it's just, I don't need help." I couldn't think around his bare skin.

He stepped closer, not helping my breathless situation. "Turn around, Em." Dang that sounded sexy.

As if I were in a trance, I did what he said.

"Are you having a good time?" he asked while flipping open the lid.

"Yeah." I could hardly speak for the anticipation of his hands on my body. Thankfully, I didn't have back fat. At least not that I knew of; it was kind of hard to see your own back.

"The weather's perfect." His warm hand mixed with cold sunscreen made contact with my shoulders.

I gasped.

"Sorry it's cold. I'll warm it up for you."

I wasn't gasping because of the cold. The rubbing was only going to increase the likelihood of more gasps.

His strong hands went to work. He was doing a thorough job of making sure to rub it in deep.

My breath got caught and was being held hostage by my emotions.

"You're tense." He began to knead my neck. "Relax," he whispered.

I don't know what it was about my body, but it obeyed his every command. I let the breath out I'd been holding. I was putty in his hands.

His hands glided down my back, causing goosebumps. "Are you cold?" Dang, he noticed.

"Um . . ." Lie, Emma, lie. "No." Way to go, self.

He didn't respond, but instead applied more lotion and pressure. I, unfortunately, let myself enjoy the feel of it for longer than I should have and pretended he was enjoying it too. His touch had me mesmerized. Every stroke and each fingertip were felt on a molecular level. I don't know how long we stayed like that. Longer than I should have allowed. My brain finally kicked in and said, *Yo, Emma, there's a size two waiting for him by the river.*

I stepped away from him. "Thank you."

"Do you need me to get anywhere else?"

I had a list. "I'm good." I turned and faced him. "We should probably get back to everyone."

He handed me the sunscreen. "If we must."

Unfortunately, the answer was yes.

Our jaunt down the river started out well and good. This leg of the river was docile, with a few large boulders to deal with. Though the water was cool, the sun warmed us, well, at least most of us. Miss I-Have-No-Fat-On-My-Body kept squealing. She wasn't complaining, it was more like she knew how to draw attention to herself. Kellan and Ashton flanked her to try and prevent cold water from splashing on her. They each tried to impress her and make her laugh. I admit her laugh was pleasant. She had this delicate way of doing everything. No snorting or loud guffaws.

I was happy to see that Ashton was paying attention to her; maybe that meant nothing was going on between him and Macey. I had plans to talk to him about it while we were up here away from my sisters, who refused to camp. Their idea of camping was more like Shelby's. They also had the excuse that their boutique did killer business on the weekends. I had to admit I was surprised they were doing so well. Maybe it was awful for me to say, but between the two of them they couldn't pull a 4.0 GPA at the community college they attended. But they did know fashion and they had Dad's money to back them up.

Ashton kept using a fake Southern drawl and calling her Miss Shelby while quoting her favorite movie, *Gone With the Wind*. I don't know how many times he said "Frankly, my dear, I don't give a damn." Kellan beat him out with a better quote in my opinion. "You should be kissed by someone who knows how." Regardless who was saying what, Shelby ate it right up. She was calling all the men darlin', except for my trusty best friend Brad, who stayed back with Aspen and myself. Shelby also had all those smooth feminine moves down too; she would reach out to take Ashton's and Kellan's hands as if she needed help floating down the river. She'd waved Sawyer up toward her too, but he'd chosen to hang in the middle by himself looking back and forth as if he didn't know who to be with. Or maybe he was annoyed his best friend and brother were vying for Shelby's attention.

I admit I was hoping Ashton or Kellan would sweep Scarlett O'Hara off her feet in Rhett Butler fashion. But if she was smart, she'd stick with Sawyer. Kellan was a womanizer and Ashton was great as far as I could tell, but no one was as good as his brother. With that thought, I did my best to enjoy the journey, per se, without the object of my desire. I leaned back in my tube to soak up the rays until Brad started singing one of our favorite songs from high school, "Yeah" by Usher. Aspen and I joined in. Brad started doing a hip-hop dance routine that included some booty smacking in his tube, making Aspen and I laugh uncontrollably. There was nothing like a gangly, tall white boy trying to pretend he had rhythm to make you snort loudly. No delicate melodic laughs here.

It was all well and good until I wasn't paying attention the way I should have. That, and it truly seemed like life really got a kick out of me being caught in embarrassing situations. I was beginning to suspect it was all part of the Loveless curse.

The chaos came at me all at once. The river's current picked up and I didn't react quick enough, which meant I ended up in the path of an overgrown tree whose branches decided to teach my face a lesson. Stinging pain hit me before I'd realized what had happened. First, I thought I was stung by a yellow jacket—that's how severe the pain was—but the blood dripping down my face and feeling like someone rubbed a pine scented air freshener into an open wound clued me in to what had really happened.

"Fudge biscuits!" I yelled. Don't ask me where my mom came up with that ridiculous substitute for swearing or why as a grown woman I was still saying it. I knew why, I still didn't want to disappoint my mother, no matter whether she was around or not. The next string was from my mom too. "Mothersmucker! Shuzzbutt! Son of a bucket!" The left side of my face felt as if it had been through a meat processor. With one hand, I reached up and touched my raw, bleeding skin, worried about the damage; with my other hand, I was trying to direct my tube to the riverbank.

Sawyer jumped into action and was out of his tube, which he heaved to the bank. Holy crap, he was strong. After that show of manly strength, he marched up the river against the current to help me. Before I knew it, he was dragging my tube and me toward the bank.

"Em, hold on." He sounded so worried that it made me worry. Was I going to need stitches? Plastic surgery? That might not be bad—I could get my insurance to give me some nice contoured cheeks all in the name of fixing my mangled face. Maybe I should try and gouge my butt and stomach. I'm pretty sure they might need to suck some fat out before I could be properly sewn up.

Sawyer had me out of my tube and situated on a rock near the bank before anyone else could get out of the water downstream. Apparently, he was the person you wanted in an emergency. Or in my case, any time.

His cold wet fingers touched my cheek near my eye. "You're lucky it missed your eye, but we need to get these wounds cleaned up to prevent infection and so I can tell if you're going to need stitches." He knelt in front of me. "Are you okay?"

Besides the stinging pain and the ache I felt to throw myself against his wet body, I was super fantastic. I mean this trip was turning out exactly liked I'd hoped. An injury and a man-stealing goddess. I guessed now was the time to fake hypothermia or shock. If only he had a sleeping bag on him, I might have. Instead I nodded. "It's just some scratches, I'll be fine."

He tucked some of my hair back. "Em, it's a little more than scratches."

"Great. I'll get a cool new nickname like Scar Face."

"I think that's been taken." He smiled.

"Dang it." I was trying not to concentrate on the blood dripping down my face and neck. "How about Lady Disfigurement?"

The back of his cold, wet hand glided down my uninjured cheek. "Emma Loveless, you never cease to amaze me."

Talk about amazing. I needed him to run his hand down my cheek a few dozen more times. It was the best pain reliever in the world.

"It is pretty amazing all the trouble I seem to find myself in."

He gave me a breath stopping smile. "You're definitely trouble."

Chapter Eleven

THE TITLE OF Lady Disfigurement was still up in the air, but for now I was half mummy face. Dr. King determined the cuts didn't call for stitches, but he was worried about infection, especially since we were camping. He had fretted about whether we should get back to civilization, but it was one night, and I was no quitter. And I *loved* sitting around the camp fire next to Shelby, who had stolen Sawyer's camp chair, because guess who hadn't brought one?

Shelby took my hand. "Honey, now don't you worry, I have some magic cream at home that is going to make it look like you never ran into that nasty old tree branch. You'll be as pretty as you ever were."

Was that a compliment or a slight? I had to say I think she was sincere. Why did she have to be nice? I wanted to hate her, especially since Sawyer was sitting on a rock on the other side of her. It was probably for the best he wasn't near me, but there was nothing I liked better than when he was near me, unless he was flushing out my wounds with some antiseptic crap he carried around in his doctor kit; that burned like it was molten lava. Even then, though, I wanted to kiss his face off. It had been so close. I loved it when he was all doctory. I'd made sure to make it to my annual eye exams now that he was my optometrist. He'd told me a few months ago that I had beautiful corneas.

I tried not to think about it and instead I smiled at Shelby, who was wearing one of my sweatshirts and swimming in it, I might add. All the girl brought were shorts and tank tops. "Thank you. Maybe the scars will add some character."

She laughed and patted my hand. "Emma, you are a delight."

A delight? I hadn't heard that one before from a peer. "So are you," I breathed out.

Unfortunately, it was true. Ask Kellan, who was drooling across the way for her. He kept asking Sawyer if he wanted his camp chair. Kellan was happy to take the rock. Ashton probably would have offered too, but he had mysteriously disappeared after we'd returned from our excursion. He said he had to get to the nearest town that had reception for an important business call. That was odd. Who had a business call on Saturday? And what business? Was he leaving the Ranch already? I wouldn't blame him. It's not like it was a career that had a lot of upward mobility, and the pay wasn't stellar. Dad was fair and always gave bonuses, but judging by the expensive SUV Ashton drove, he was used to a more lucrative career. He'd done something in construction when he lived in Vegas. He never said exactly what. I hoped he made it back before the sun completely set. These roads at night were hard to navigate.

For a moment, I took in the fire at twilight. The way it crackled and danced. In it I saw my mom. This was her favorite thing to do when we camped. I eyed the dutch oven with her famous pineapple upside down cake that we were going to have for dessert. It was about ready to be enjoyed. I could smell the sweetness. It smelled like Mom. I looked around at the faces that reflected the glow of the firelight: Jenna's, Brad's, Aspen's. Sawyer's I saved for last. His beautiful face was already smiling at mine. Four beautiful people inside and out who had helped me through the most difficult year of my life.

While I was staring at Sawyer, Jenna said, "You know what this reminds me of?"

We all turned our attention to the cute preggers lady.

Jenna gave me a mischievous grin. "Remember when we were about thirteen and we begged your mom to let us spend the night outside because we wanted to set off the firecrackers we had been gifted without anyone knowing?"

By *gifted* she meant we stole them from her older brother.

I shook my head at her. "We were real geniuses."

"Well, maybe if someone hadn't left the bag near the fire pit." Jenna smirked.

"Hey, my s'mores needed saving."

Jenna rolled her eyes.

"What happened?" Sawyer asked.

"Well, let's just say Emma could have been a great pyrotechnician."

I turned to Sawyer. "We lit up the sky like the Fourth of July. My mom and dad came running out after the initial boom to find our backyard lit up in an array of colors. While my dad dragged Jenna and me to safety, my mom stood and smiled, taking it all in. I thought she would have been furious, but she kept saying how beautiful it all was." I choked up.

"She was the best," some emotion crept into Jenna's voice too.

"And could she bake," Brad remembered fondly. "That chocolate peanut butter fudge she made every Christmas was the bomb. She always let me lick the spatula." That meant a lot to Brad, who only grew up with his father.

"I remember when I got my wedding dress back," Aspen tried not to gag, "and the alterations were all wrong. Your mom stayed up all night painstakingly taking stitches out all while telling me not to listen to the naysayers telling me I was wasting my life getting married so young and having a baby. Babies were a blessing, she said, no matter how they came. She never judged me for getting pregnant with Chloe or when Leland ran out on us." Aspen cried. "Every week for a year she brought me a box of diapers with cash hidden in it."

I never knew that. My tears flowed. I had to catch them before they soaked the dressing on the injured side of my face.

"Not once did she ever forget mine or Chloe's birthday."

"Her birthday presents were the best," now Jenna was choking up.

Brad was nodding.

"They really were," I said. "I don't know how she did it, but it was like she knew exactly what would make you supremely happy. And it was never anything you asked for. When I turned nine, she gave me a telescope. Never in a million years would I have ever thought about asking for one. But night after night after my mom put the twins to bed, she would take me out on the deck and she would show me the moon and tell me stories about when she was growing up and where she was when Apollo 11 landed on the moon. We even got to see some of Jupiter's moons through that old thing."

"Your mom was the coolest." Jenna stared into the fire, now ugly crying.

"Yeah, she was," Brad agreed.

"She was my most memorable patient." Sawyer didn't want to be left out.

I gave him a meaningful look. If it wasn't for my mother, I wouldn't be here right now. I wouldn't have had the worst and best year of my life with the man who owned the amber eyes that looked so dang sexy in the fire.

Sawyer gave me a closed lipped smile. "I know I didn't know her well, but I do know how much she loved her daughters. I don't know if she would want me to say this, but I think you were her favorite."

"Oh, hands down," I laughed through my tears. I knew that wasn't true. My mom always said she loved us equally but differently. I do believe, though, that she and I had more in common, so it made our relationship easier. Don't get me wrong, my mom could dress up just as fine as my sisters, and boy could she wow, but she was most comfortable in jeans and a T-shirt like me. She didn't mind getting dirty, in fact, she encouraged it.

I noticed Shelby got awfully quiet and curled into herself, staring into the distance as if her thoughts were a million miles away. I almost asked her what was wrong, because despite the fact that my mom wouldn't have liked that she was impeding her plans for me, Mom never overlooked the opportunity to help someone, even if she didn't like them.

Before I could, Brad jumped up. "I say we have some cake and toast Shannon Carrington, mom to us all and mother of one of the best people I've ever known." Brad gave me his most charming smile.

I waved him off. "You're a goof, but I love you."

Brad pointed at me. "For that, you get the second biggest slice of cake." Brad was one person who could eat more cake than me, though I was always ticked that he seemed to lose weight from the effort while I was guaranteed to have another dimple on my butt tomorrow. Oh, well. No one was seeing my naked butt anytime soon, so I might as well enjoy myself. I knew Mom would want me to, and she'd think my dimples were cute no matter where they were.

⁓

After the lovely night of tributes to my mother, it was time to hit the hay. This was where things got awkward. Since Shelby didn't have a sleeping bag and no one had brought an extra one, Aspen and I put what we had together for the three of us to sleep together. We laid my bag unzipped on the bottom and used Aspen's bag for the top, as well as two blankets, one of mine, and one Sawyer had chipped in for the cause. He was the cause, so it was only right.

We had to put Shelby in the middle because she had no body fat and basically no pajamas, unless you counted the fire red negligée she'd brought. Did she think she was going to parade around in that in front of Sawyer? Feelings of hate were starting to bubble up again even though she was super grateful I let her wear my sweatshirt to bed. I, on the other hand, was wearing thermal underwear with pandas all over them. I wasn't planning on showing those off to Sawyer. Aspen was more cutely dressed in hot pink flannel pajamas.

I was more than ready to go to sleep by the time we settled into our makeshift bed in the flashlight-illuminated tent and got way too cozy for comfort, but Shelby had other ideas.

I had just closed my eyes when I heard the sniffling. She even did that cutely.

"Shelby? Are you okay?" I whispered.

"I'm so sorry." Shelby turned toward me. "It's just, it sounds like you had such a nice momma. I wish I could have known her."

Aspen sat up a bit and even in the dark I could tell she was giving me a look like *what should we do?*

I wasn't sure what to say. Sure, Mom would have been nice to her, but she also would have done her best to make sure Shelby kept her paws off Sawyer. "What about your family? They're from Roswell, right?" It was the best I could come up with.

She sniffled and nodded her head. She had to take a minute to think and compose herself. "Well, to be honest, my family, we . . . well, we don't always see eye-to-eye."

"Is that why you moved here?"

"Not exactly, but it has something to do with it." She seemed hesitant to say anything.

It made me all the more curious, especially considering where she lived and her current job. I didn't want to act nosy though, so I closed my eyes, thinking that was the end of it. Nope.

"You see, I was engaged."

Oh.

Aspen and I both popped up and propped ourselves up on our elbows, intrigued by this revelation. I'd wondered about that tan line on her wedding finger.

Shelby pulled the covers around her tighter as if she needed the comfort. "A few years ago, at a concert my parents wouldn't have wanted me to be at, I met Ryder." Her voice hitched with the pronunciation of his name. Immense loss sounded in the change of her tone when she said his name.

We would get to that in a moment; what I wanted to know first was why did her parents care what kind of concerts she was attending? "Shelby, how old are you?"

"Twenty-eight."

So a few years younger than us, but come on.

"My birthday is on Valentine's Day, the day I got engaged," she cried.

Of course she was born on Valentine's Day. It wouldn't have surprised me if Aphrodite, the goddess of love and beauty herself, hadn't hand carved this woman in her image and sent her down from the heavens.

"What happened?" I tried to sound more sympathetic than curious.

She sat up and took the sleeping bag and blankets off Aspen and me. She pulled her knees up to her chest, along with the covers. This forced Aspen and me to do the same if we wanted to stay warm. Nights at this elevation were chilly no matter the time of year.

Shelby gathered her thoughts while resting her head on her knees. Even in the dark I could see the tears trickle down her beautiful face. And those thick, long eyelashes of hers? I'd found out earlier in the day they were all real.

Shelby let out a meaningful sigh. "Ryder wasn't my parents' ideal boyfriend or husband for me. He was a little rough around the edges and he didn't have the right . . . credentials," she hesitated to say.

"Credentials?" Aspen asked.

Shelby bit her lip as if she knew what she was about to say was a bit snobbish. "His education, financial situation, and family ties were less than desirable to my parents."

"But you didn't care?" I had to ask. Though Sawyer had an impressive resume, I couldn't let him be with someone who would think less of him because he wasn't properly bred.

Shelby shook her head with a sad smile. "Not at all. Ryder," she swallowed, "was, or at least I thought he was, the smartest, funniest man, and when he wanted to be he was all gentleman, but he was a tad unconventional."

Both Aspen's and my eyes said, *what?*

Shelby fidgeted a bit. "Although he never had any formal higher education, he was real smart. He worked for a software company. He was like a Bill Gates." Her voice shined with pride.

"Did he own the company?"

"Oh, no. That might have made it better for my parents, but Ryder was happy without those kinds of pressures. He believed life was too short to spend it living at work. Well, until the end, except I don't think he was really working like he said he was."

Now we were getting to the crux of it.

"Ugh," Aspen spat. "I know where this is going. Men are vile pigs."

Shelby nodded. "They can be." She pulled her knees tighter to her. "My momma and daddy hired a private investigator and there were pictures of him with this woman while he was on a business trip." She full-on started to bawl.

People really hired private investigators? I thought that was just in the movies.

Aspen was good enough to wrap her arm around Shelby. "It's better that you found out before you married the cheater and had a baby with him." Resentment and regret wove through Aspen's words. She never regretted having Chloe, but she wished for a different father to help raise her daughter. Leland was, for the most part, an absentee father. He hadn't lived around here for a long time and he only paid child support when it suited him. Aspen's parents had stepped in and helped raise Chloe. She was with them this weekend.

Shelby nodded. "I suppose so. I just don't know how I could have been so fooled. For three years I gave him my life and defied my parents, all so we could be together," she choked out.

"I've been there," Aspen growled.

"He's why you moved here?" I asked. This way I would know who to properly hate when Shelby rode off into the sunset with my man.

Shelby turned my way and wiped her eyes. "Yes," she didn't sound so sure.

I tilted my head, asking for more clarification.

Shelby lifted her head. "You see, my momma's family are the Hobbs."

I sat up straight. "As in Hobbs Eye Centers?" As in one of the largest eye store chains in the country?

Shelby gave a tentative smile and a slight nod. "That would be correct."

"Whoa," Aspen whistled.

"Does Sawyer know that?"

Shelby shook her head. "I didn't think it would be good to spread that around. I don't want people to look at me any different. My parents thought it would be best if I got as far away as I could for a while, and this is about as far west as our stores go, so they worked it all out."

Wow. They must have really hated this guy—and me, inadvertently.

"It's not really what I would like to be doing. I have a master's degree in nursing. I was a midwife for a hospital in Roswell. It wasn't exactly what my parents wanted me to do. They always hoped I'd go into the family business. I'm here trying that out." No wonder she lived in such a nice place. So, I guess she wasn't growing marijuana on the side like I first figured.

"How do you like it so far?" I asked.

She took in a breath and let out some shudders. "Everyone has been real nice at the center."

I bet they had.

"And it's interesting, but I miss working with mommas and their babies." She wrapped her arms around herself. "I love babies. I wanted to have a house full of them. I thought Ryder wanted that too." Her tears came again. This explained why she had been so excited for Jenna and Brad's baby even though she didn't know them.

This time I put my arms around her. I wanted those same things too.

Shelby turned into me and cried on my shoulder. "Y'all have been so nice to me. I was afraid to move to a new state all by myself, but you all have made me feel so welcome. You even let me borrow your clothes and sleeping bags. Y'all are just so sweet."

I looked at Aspen over Shelby's head; we both were wide-eyed. I wasn't exactly sure we had been nice to her, or even welcoming. I mean, earlier in the day I wanted to rip her arms off and push her into the river.

Shelby continued to snuggle right into me, taking comfort. Once she quit crying, she took a cleansing breath. "You know, I think Colorado could really be a new beginning for me. I think I'd even like to give Sawyer a chance."

My arms fell away from her while my heart stopped beating.

"What do you think of him, Emma, being his stepsister and all? Is he a wicked stepbrother?" she teased. "Or is he a man who is true to his word and character?"

I turned away from her with tears in my own eyes now. Sawyer

My Not So Wicked Stepbrother

was of the not-so-wicked variety, and I had never known a man truer or kinder than him, but that was none of Shelby's business.

Chapter Twelve

"Emma, Emma, wake up."

I better have been dreaming, or more like having a nightmare. All I could hear was some cute, man-stealing voice frantically calling my name, and on top of that I was being poked.

"Please wake up."

One of my eyes popped open. It was still dark, but I could feel Shelby's minty breath in my face. How did she manage to avoid morning breath? She really was a freak of nature.

"What time is it?" I croaked with probably stale breath. Us non-goddesses lacked the minty breath gene.

"I'm so sorry. It's around 4:30. I've been dying for like an hour and I need your help."

I sat up groggy and rubbed my eyes, careful not to touch my wounds. "Are you sick?"

Shelby sat up too, shivering and shaking her head. "I know this is going to sound silly, but . . . I've never peed outside. I don't know how."

"You haven't peed the entire time we've been up here?"

She shook her head. "No, and I'm dying. I can't hold it anymore."

What did she want me to do about it?

"Can you please show me how?"

I was going to kill Sawyer. At the very least, he was not riding home with me and neither was the blonde who was ready to explode.

"Please," she begged.

"Sure," I sighed. "Let me get my shoes on."

She kissed my cheek. "You're the best, thank you."

Before I knew it, we were traipsing in the outdoors with only my flashlight for light before the butt crack of dawn, trying to find a spot Shelby felt comfortable peeing in. I kept telling her no one was awake, so it didn't matter as long as it was level, but the girl said, "My bladder will get shy if it's not in private." I rolled my eyes, not even caring if she saw.

Shelby was gripping my arm as we hiked to a level and private spot among the willow bushes. With every rustle in the wild grass and trees, the girl jumped and squeezed my arm.

"Don't worry, any animals are more afraid of us than we are of them."

"I'm going to have to disagree." She shook.

I pointed with my flashlight to a "private" spot for the princess. "This should work."

She let go of my arm. "Okay," she said through gritted teeth, "what do I do?"

I couldn't believe I was having to give her outdoor peeing lessons. "See how the ground is mostly level. Keep your feet pointed downhill so you don't pee on yourself."

"Pee on myself?"

I shrugged. "It happens if you're not careful."

"Well, how do I be extra careful?"

I needed some Dr. Pepper before I had these kinds of conversations. "It's not that difficult." I tried not to be snippy. I couldn't imagine holding my pee for as long as she had. If she didn't get a UTI, I was going to be surprised. "Just pull your shorts and underwear down to right at your knees, spread your feet at least shoulder width apart, and squat all the way down. Make sure your thighs touch your calves." That may be difficult for her since her thighs were more like bean poles. "Then you can do the rest. I'll turn around."

"Don't do that. I need the light."

I wasn't going to watch this woman pee. "I'll hold the flashlight over my shoulder."

"Oh. Okay. But what do I wipe myself with?"

"If you're only peeing it's best just to air dry. Any toilet paper you use you would have to pack out."

"Are you serious?"

As a freaking heart attack. "You should always leave a campsite as clean or cleaner than you found it."

She nodded, unsure with that assessment. "Well, okay. Here goes nothing."

I turned around but kept shining my flashlight on her.

"Oh Mylanta," she shouted, "it's cold on my wooha and bum."

I had to hold back my laugh.

"I hope I'm doing this right. Do you want to check before I start?"

"I'm good. I'm sure you're doing fine."

"Okay." She sounded like she might cry.

Soon I heard a trickle of urine.

"Oh. My. Gosh. Yes! Yes! Yes!"

Holy crap, she sounded as if she were having a much different experience than relieving herself. She was going to wake everyone up. I gave in to the fits of laughter I had been keeping in. Maybe I should hold my urine for several hours if it felt that good.

I must have stood there for a good ten minutes while she first relieved herself and then air dried. I was impressed she could squat for so long, but that explained her incredible figure.

"Emma," she said after I could no longer hear any tinkling or a downright stream. "Thank you."

"You're welcome."

"I mean thank you for everything. I have this feeling that you and I are going to be best friends."

She might want to get her head checked, because with God as my witness, Goddess Potty and I were never going to be the best of anything unless she married Sawyer. In that case, I might consider her my best enemy.

∽

There was no going back to sleep for me after my way too early wake-up call. I decided to take a bit of a hike up the mountain to the ledge where Dad and I'd had some great heart-to-hearts growing up about everything from what school I should attend to why it wasn't fair that I wasn't as pretty as my sisters. He would wrap his arm around me and say, "Honey, there are all sorts of pretty in this world and you are among the prettiest." He was such a liar. I loved him for it.

The ledge wasn't only good for talks; it was the perfect place to watch the sunrise and think about life. I'd told Shelby where I was going before she fell back asleep just in case something happened to me. Once the sun was up, I would have a clear view of the campsite and I could be seen by any in our group. I didn't expect anyone to get up for at least a couple more hours unless preggers needed to pee too. Jenna said being pregnant meant peeing became your new hobby. At least she would do it quietly.

It didn't take me long to take the dirt path up the mountain a bit. Even in the dark it was easy to traverse. I took special care to watch out for branches. I didn't need the other side of my face to look like I'd been on a date with Freddy Krueger. Sadly, he too would have friend-zoned me I was sure. It was a cold but clear morning, worthy of the jacket and the thermal underwear I was wearing. I looked ridiculous, but what the heck. I could see my breath as I walked with my hands in my jacket pockets. There were still a few stars twinkling in the just-before-dawn sky; the moon was doing its best to hang on too. A few birds were already up and chirping away. In fact, it kind of sounded like the way Josephine whined at my dad. Those poor male birds.

By the time I got situated on the stone-cold, moss-covered ledge, I didn't have to wait long for the sun to start creeping up behind the mountain range in front of me. In the golden and orange hues, I saw my mother. She was a light in the dark. Everything she touched was all the better for it. She helped people feel warmth and to grow. Tears started to stream down my cheeks and bandages just thinking about all the good she had done not only for me, but my friends and family, even strangers.

"Why did you have to go?" I whispered. I swore I heard her say, *I'm still here.* I held my heart, where she would live as long as it still beat.

I pulled up my knees and wrapped myself up. I needed the hug. That's when I noticed some movement down below. Sawyer emerged from his tent looking like a sexy lumberjack in a flannel shirt and tight jeans. Even from this distance I was swooning. Oddly, his sights landed on me as soon as he had zipped his tent and stretched. He waved up at me.

I waved back, even though I was annoyed with him and ready to lay into him about the torture I had endured earlier this morning. I was surprised no one had been awoken by the goddess and her titillating pee session.

He wasted no time making his way up to me.

I ran my fingers through my rat's nest hair and wished I had a breath mint. Oh well, it wasn't like he hadn't seen me first thing in the morning before. We'd fallen asleep together a couple of times on my couch watching movies, but I was never wearing hiking boots and thermal underwear with pandas on them. It was quite the fashion statement. Not that it mattered, right? He'd probably be sneaking off with Shelby soon to have a private rendezvous in the forest. Jenna and Brad already had yesterday. Something about nature was such a turn-on to guys. She'd come back with pine needles and twigs in her hair. I plucked them out like the good friend I was while Brad strutted around like a peacock.

It didn't take long before I heard the telltale signs of someone approaching, the snaps of fallen twigs and the crunch of gravel.

I took a deep breath and tried to steel my heart. I hoped one of these times it would work. No luck, my heart still pitter, pitter, pitter, pattered when Sawyer came around the bend. His dark curls looked even more sexy mussed, and his layer of scruff was the perfect addition to his tight jawline. But I remembered the blonde in my tent stealing my covers and my clothes.

I scowled at him. "I don't like you right now."

He laughed and plopped down right next to me smelling sexy like campfire, musk, and perspiration. "How's your face this morning? Let me check under the bandage." He reached up to do just that.

I batted his hand away. "I'm fine. I'm annoyed with you."

He smirked. "I heard the show this morning."

"You owe me."

"Name it and it's yours."

Sawyer King. If only it was that simple, I would shout his name and claim him all mine. Instead, I rubbed my hands together and blew on them because it was freaking cold out. "I'll think about it and get back to you."

Sawyer took my hands and rubbed them between his own. Oh crap, did that feel good. Don't hyperventilate, Emma.

"Did you forget your gloves?"

All I could do was stare at him. I knew I should be responding but all my mind could focus on was the buzz he was giving me. I was beginning to feel plenty warm all over. "Um . . . surprisingly," I could hardly breathe, "I didn't. Your girlfriend needed them, so I let her borrow them."

His brow crinkled. "Shelby's not my girlfriend."

I rolled my eyes. "Fine, the girl you're dating. Semantics."

"Em." He stopped rubbing my hands but kept ahold of them. "I'm not dating Shelby, nor do I have any plans to."

"Whatever you say, but just so you know, she's a Hobbs."

Sawyer's eyes popped. "As in—"

"Yes, as in the corporate giant you work for, and she's on the rebound, by the way." Hardcore, as far as I could tell.

He shrugged. "That's too bad, but like I said, I'm not interested. She's not really my type."

If that was the case, I had no hope. Who the heck was he looking for? Miss Universe? "You know, as your friend, I should tell you that you really need to lower your standards."

He chuckled. "I have no intention of lowering them."

I took my hands back and shoved them in my jacket pockets, depressed. I stared out into the still landscape, soaking in nature.

"How are you feeling? It's been a year today."

A tear trickled down my cheek. "I'm okay. Thank you for setting all this up, even if I had to teach your girlfriend, I mean *friend,* how to pee."

He didn't laugh. He only tucked some hair behind my ear. "I'm thankful for your mom, Em."

I turned toward him and caught a blast of his sparkling amber eyes. "You are?"

"She brought us together."

I nodded. "Yeah, she did. Even if it was embarrassing."

He flashed me a toothy smile. "That first conversation was something else. I'll never forget it." He poked my chin. "I see you've decided to grow that chin hair out after all."

I batted his hand away, wishing I had some tweezers and privacy. "Hey, you promised to never mention that." And I'd promised to show him how to walk on water, but that was supposed to be on our first date, which never happened. He'd never mentioned it since.

"Did I?" He nudged me.

"Yes, along with some other things."

"I know, Em." His tone turned surprisingly sober. He gazed into my eyes for several seconds without speaking, making it feel as warm as the noonday sun. "I've been wanting to talk to you about some . . . things."

"What things?" I whispered.

He took a deep breath. "Things didn't exactly . . . what I mean to say is . . . I've been waiting."

"Waiting? Waiting for what?"

"Time and—"

"Sawyer! Brother, where are you?" Ashton's booming voice echoed down below.

Sawyer tensed and tried to ignore his brother. "Em . . ." He let out a big breath.

"Sawyer!" Ashton yelled even louder.

"Dammit, I'm always getting interrupted." Sawyer rubbed his neck.

"Are you okay?" He rarely swore.

"Yeah. We'll talk later."

I nodded, confused.

Without another word, he got up and marched off down the trail. He made good time back to camp. I watched from my perch as he talked to Ashton right in his face. He was kicking the dirt around him.

My Not So Wicked Stepbrother

Before I knew it, Ashton had taken off in his SUV. What was all that about? And what was Sawyer going to say to me?

I had this strange feeling of déjà vu, like once again my name had stolen something from me.

Chapter Thirteen

ONE SHOULD NEVER feel sick when they are going home, but that's exactly how I felt when I approached the door of my old home. I couldn't even call it my parents' anymore. Long gone was the cutesy wreath Mom had made with the big C on it and the tacky pink bow to complete the ensemble. Did I ever miss it. Now the only thing left standing were the large double pine doors that Josephine had decided to paint red. It looked as if someone had drenched them in pig's blood. Who knew, maybe she used the extra blood afterward for her rituals with her coven. Okay. Okay. I couldn't think like that. I'd promised Sawyer I would try and get to know his mother better while I helped her plan the Farewell to Summer dance. Even though I was still miffed about her stealing my theme, the Lady of Carrington Ranch.

Sawyer. I had to keep repeating his name in my head. I was doing this for him. Though he had been acting strange and a bit irritable since we'd gone camping. He said he wanted to talk to me alone, but this week had been crazy busy, so there had been no time for it. At work I had KPI reports due, not to mention safety training, which was a huge deal considering I worked around molten steel and fire. Then I'd been called into work one day after my shift was over due to a furnace on the strand going out.

On Sawyer's end, he was the doctor on call this month which

meant he'd had some late evenings too. Not to mention I had to be here tonight with the wicked stepmommy. I offered to beg this off so we could talk, but Sawyer begged me to do it. It was only fair since I'd convinced him to have dinner with his dad and Bridget tomorrow night. Maybe we could talk after that. I was more than curious about what was so important to him that he didn't want to do it over the phone and he wanted us to be completely alone with lots of available time. If tomorrow night didn't work, it would have to wait until the next week when I returned from my AIST conference in Alabama. I was flying out Saturday as soon as my soccer game was over.

The American Iron and Steel Technology Conference and Exposition was kind of nerdy, but I loved it. Even cooler this year was that it was taking place at the Space and Rocket Center in Huntsville. I hadn't been there since my parents sent me out to Space Camp when I was twelve. Pretending to do space missions was the best week of my young life. Besides it being cool, I needed the professional development hours.

I took a deep breath and went to open the blood red door, but then I remembered that Josephine had asked that I knock. She felt it was the polite thing to do. I debated on whether to, one, walk right in or, two, walk right back to my Jeep. *Sawyer.* Fine. I knocked on the stupid door and waited and waited. The longer I waited the more annoyed I became. I became particularly irked when I'd noticed the white rocking chairs that used to sit on the wraparound porch were gone. They'd been replaced with some awful black futuristic-shaped polypropylene chairs. How did you even sit on those? This was a ranch, not an art museum. Did my father approve of these? I couldn't picture him sitting in one. I knew my butt was never hitting one. If it did, I think it might slide right back off.

Finally, Dad answered the door. His brown eyes looked tired when he tried to muster a smile for me. I hadn't talked to him since we'd had our disagreement, which seemed to happen more often than not when we talked now. I never imagined that being the case. Growing up, I never understood when my friends couldn't talk to their parents, especially their dads. My dad talked to me about anything, even periods. He'd told me it was just a biological function and there was nothing to be embarrassed about. It was nothing for him to shop for feminine hygiene products, and with four women in the house it was a regular occurrence.

I looked down at my sandaled feet and then back up at him. "Hi, Dad."

His smile grew a fraction. "Hey, honey." He pulled me to him for a hug.

His arms felt like home, making it not matter that the surroundings no longer felt as such. I sank into his chest and breathed in his wood scent.

He stroked my hair. "Honey—"

"Emma, you finally made it," Josephine shrieked.

Finally? I was on time.

I refused to leave my dad's arms. I buried my head deeper into his chest as if I could bore a hole in there and hide from his new wife.

Like an excavator, she ripped Dad away from me. "Dane, honey." She gave me what I would call a gloating smile. "We have lots of women things to discuss. Why don't you run along?"

Why was she always treating my dad like a child? And since when had the dance become a woman thing? Mom always loved Dad's input. Dad knew the best stringed lights to use and where to place them, as well as great food suggestions, and he always made sure to get in which songs he wanted Grady's band to play. They were usually slow country songs. Dad loved to take Mom for a spin and do the two-step with her. That was when he wasn't holding her close for all the slow songs.

Dad gave me a defeated look before grabbing his cowboy hat from the rack near the door and shoving it on his head. "I'll be out with Ray and the boys," he grumbled. He was talking about the wranglers, Ray being the head of them. He didn't even say goodbye to me.

I thought about going after him until I heard the dulcet tones of my sisters fighting with each other. Something about *quit trying to be nice to me, I'm still mad at you.* That was from Macey, who was normally the sweeter of the two. I wondered what Marlowe had done this time.

Josephine gave me a narrow-eyed glare before spinning on her heels and heading back toward the dining room. Who wore heels at home? Or her short dress ensemble for that matter? I almost mentioned she should really get those varicose veins on the back of her legs checked out, but I remembered who I was here for and kept my mouth shut.

My sisters were in the dining room giving each other stink eyes in between rifling through all the shiny things on the table. It looked like a Las Vegas showgirl's show exploded on it with all the sparkles, but I had to say I was glad it was covering up the stupid black lacquer table Stepmommy Dearest bought to replace the old oak table where so much love and good food had been shared. At least I had been able to make sure Frankie's family got that table.

"Hey girls, what are you doing?" I sing-songed.

"Helping plan the dance," Marlowe responded, annoyed.

Was all this sparkly crap for the dance? The dance that took place in the barn?

"I'm surprised you're sticking around since you can't even help me at our boutique," Macey fired back at her.

Marlowe threw down some sparkly silver fabric she had been holding. "How many times do I have to apologize to you? I'm sorry I didn't make it back on time Sunday."

"You had all of Saturday off!" Macey threw a string of fake diamonds at her.

Marlowe caught them with ease. "You can have this Saturday off, brat!"

It was hard to remember sometimes that they were twenty-five. I felt Mom channeling me. "Ladies, come on. Let's be nice. I'm sure Marlowe has a good reason for not showing up on Sunday." For the record I didn't really think that, but Mom would have said it.

Marlowe stood up stick straight. "I do, as a matter of fact, but it's not anyone's business."

Ah. Now I knew why it was days later and Macey was still upset. Marlowe was keeping a secret from her. Those two shared everything.

Josephine began tsking. "We have work to do."

Macey and Marlowe both huffed but said nothing more on the matter.

I drew closer to the table to see what I was dealing with before I started offering my ideas.

Before I could do anything, though, Josephine shoved a black invitation with sparkling silver letters in my hand. "These are the invites."

She'd already had them made? I looked down at it and read, *The Lady of Carrington Presents a Black-Tie Affair.* Black tie? "Are we holding the dance in the barn?"

Josephine curled her lips. "Yes," she sighed. "I tried talking Dane out of it, but it was the one thing he wouldn't budge on. This would be so much better at the country club in Pine Falls."

"Except it's not at the Ranch, which is kind of the point of the Farewell to Summer dance."

"That name is so trite."

I flexed my fingers and pressed my lips together before I let her have it. My mother had come up with that name. *Sawyer, Sawyer, Sawyer,* I repeated in my head, trying to calm down.

Josephine must have known I wanted to unleash my fury on her. Her dark eyes dared me to. Even Macey and Marlowe were waiting by their expectant eyes.

I disappointed them all by biting my tongue. "Okay, so have you talked to Grady and his band about this new theme and the dress code?" The invite stated formal attire required, which had me seething, but I was doing my best to keep my cool.

Josephine let out an evil laugh. "You're so funny, Emma. I'm hiring a big swing band out of Denver."

"What? Grady's band has always played."

Josephine snatched the invite out of my hand. "Things are changing around here, if you haven't noticed."

Believe me I had, and I hated it with all that I was. I swallowed hard, trying to keep my emotions in check. I looked to my sisters for some help. They each in turn refused to look at me.

"I, for one, think this is a great idea. I have the perfect dress in mind," Marlowe chimed in.

"It's fun trying something new." Macey braved looking at me and gave me a sympathetic smile.

Josephine gave me a victorious smile. "You know, I think we have it handled here. If I need anything, I'll let you know. Feel free to run along."

I looked at Marlowe and Macey to give them one more chance to say something on my behalf, or at least Mom's. Heck, they could have even asked me to stay, but they kept their heads down. I stared at them anyway. "A person who doesn't remember their roots is always in danger of falling. Just remember who will always be there to pick you up when you do."

"That's touching, Emma," Josephine mocked. "Have a good night."

I turned around and marched myself right out of there. I only stopped to scowl at the stupid piece of paint-smattered canvas that Josephine made and called it art hanging above the fireplace where our last family picture had hung. For all I knew, Dad had let her burn that picture. A deep ache in my chest had me catching my breath. I pushed myself out the door in search of Frankie, someone who still had some sanity on this ranch. Instead, I ran right into Ashton, who was coming into the house. Apparently, he didn't have to knock.

"Sorry." I slammed the door behind me.

"Hey there, are you okay?" He sounded so much like his brother, but when I looked up at him, his eyes didn't hold the comfort that Sawyer's did.

I was about to give him a general fine response and move on, but then I remembered I hadn't had a chance to talk to him over the weekend about Macey. He was gone more than he was around. I hope he got that job he said he had been interviewing for. I thought maybe I should ask him about that first. "Have you heard back from the company you interviewed with over the weekend?"

He rubbed the back of his neck like his brother did on occasion. "It was more of a head hunter situation. I'm trying to keep my options open."

"Oh, well, I hope they can help you. Not that we won't miss your Elvis impressions at the weddings here."

He laughed. "I'm trying to find something that will allow me to do both."

"Great."

He reached around me to get the door.

"Wait. I wanted to talk to you about something."

He gave me his full attention. "Shoot."

I bit my lip. "This might be kind of awkward."

He gave me a devilish smile. "I love awkward."

"All right then. It's just, I noticed at the family barbecue a couple of weeks ago that you and Macey left together and—"

He placed his hands on my shoulders. "Let me stop you right there. First of all, she's my *stepsister*," he smirked, "not to mention she's a kid."

I'm glad he recognized that. I nodded.

"She came back to the bunkhouse with me because I had an old vinyl of Frank Sinatra she wanted to borrow."

I didn't even know Macey knew who that was. Maybe she was using it for some inspiration for this godforsaken dance I was thinking about not attending. "Oh, okay."

He patted my shoulders. "Don't worry, *sis*, I would never do anything to hurt this family or make it *awkward*." He gave me a wink.

Yeah, I suppose dating your stepsibling would be the definition of awkward. Too bad that was one awkward situation I would never find myself in.

Chapter Fourteen

I SAT OUTSIDE of Sawyer's dad's house in my car waiting for Sawyer to show up. I was so embarrassed. Who had forgotten that she said she would bring a pasta salad? That would be me. So now I was late *and* bringing store-bought pasta salad. Sawyer was late too, which, on top of being embarrassed, had me worried. He was never late, and he wasn't answering my texts or calls, which had never happened before either. I was hoping he'd run long with a patient and that's all it was. I knew he wasn't thrilled about coming back to his old home, but surely he wouldn't just not show up or let me come by myself. Besides being worried that he was lying dead somewhere on the highway, I thought maybe his mom had gotten ahold of him and tried to convince him how awful I was. I wouldn't put it past her. Because of her, my sisters were turning their backs on me.

I'd cried forever last night at Mom's grave after talking to Frankie, who was on the brink of quitting. Josephine had decided to hire a catering company out of Edenvale to take care of the food for the black-tie affair in the barn instead of Frankie. She'd obviously never had one of those raspberry lemon filled cupcakes of Frankie's. It was a shame. Maybe if she ate some sugar, she'd be nicer. Doubt it. Frankie mentioned that Josephine had been prancing around the Ranch calling herself the Lady of Carrington—not just of the Ranch, all of Carrington.

I stared out the window of my car and it hit me how the house Sawyer grew up in was quite simple and in a very middle-of-the-middle-class neighborhood. The house was a one-story brick rambler. It was cute with yellow shutters and a well-kept yard with peonies and pansies. It looked cheerful, the exact opposite of Josephine. It looked more like my mom. Looking at the house made me wonder how Josephine came off all high and mighty. She'd acted as if where she lived now was a downgrade. As far as I knew, she was living in an apartment before she met my dad. I had to say I found it odd that she hadn't ended up with this house.

I picked up my phone to call Sawyer again. I was sure I had seen Bridget peek out the window. Before I could press his pretty face on speed dial, my phone rang. It wasn't Sawyer, but the eye center number. I immediately answered.

"Hello."

"Hey, sugar, it's Shelby."

Oh, good, my favorite peeing partner. I'd had to take her like four times our last day camping. For some reason she felt more comfortable if I was there.

"Hey, Shelby." I tried to keep any derision out of my voice. After all, Sawyer said she wasn't his type and he had seemed to rebuff her advances on Sunday by declining a walk with her into the woods. The same woods where Jenna and Brad had become one with nature. So maybe the goddess really hadn't caught his eye. I know that didn't help my chances, but it would be much easier to be friends with someone who wasn't going to get my happily ever after.

"Sawyer gave me your number. He's real sorry but we have had a day here and it's still going on. We're dealing with an infection, a foreign object or two, and some double vision. Sawyer wanted me to tell you that he will meet you as soon as he can for dinner, but it's going to be awhile."

"I hope his patients are okay."

"Don't you worry, sugar, we will get them fixed up good. Sawyer is one of the best."

Did she say we? Okay, so maybe we weren't going to be friends.

"I better go. Sawyer needs me to assist."

I bet he did. I threw my phone in my bag. Now what did I do? Go tell his dad and Bridget we needed to cancel? Go in by myself? Move to Fiji? That was a serious consideration after last night. I read that in Fiji they like their women curvy. It's like Hawaii. Why hadn't I considered moving to these places before? I may even be considered too skinny there. It would be like a dream. I could eat pineapple and roasted pig all day long with no judgement.

I decided I better at least make an appearance since I had seen both Warren and Bridget peek out through the curtains. I grabbed my lame pasta salad. I was seriously bummed about it. I made the best pasta salad with roasted tomatoes and mozzarella cheese. What was available at the deli had limp noodles and smooshed olives. What a way to make an impression. I depended on Sawyer to remind me of these things. I was surprised he hadn't.

Oh. I stopped on the sidewalk. I felt a sharp jab in my heart. Maybe that's what Sawyer wanted to talk to me about. He was tired of us palling around. That's probably what last weekend was about. Our final hurrah. He was probably thinking that he had carried me through this past year, but now it was time for him to spend some time looking for a girlfriend or wife. He had been awfully distant this week. Maybe he had been trying to pawn me off on his mom. I shuddered at the thought.

On that depressing note, I headed for the door. A small smile appeared when I noticed a huge red, white, and blue wreath with a sparkly silver bow on the door. I could hear mom say, "These are my kind of people." I had a feeling they were my kind of people too, even if it made me feel disloyal to one of my best friends.

I didn't even have to knock. Bridget and Warren opened the door with big, welcoming smiles.

"We're so happy you could make it," Bridget waved me in.

"I'm sorry Sawyer isn't here yet. There were some emergencies at the eye center. He'll be here as soon as he can."

Relief flooded Warren's face. Poor guy.

I held up the plastic container. "And I'm sorry I forgot to make pasta salad and you have to deal with store bought. You should know

I am chronically forgetful unless it involves dessert. I always seem to remember to make those."

They both laughed at me.

"My kind of woman." Bridget took the container from me. "This is great. Thank you."

"Well, come on back," Warren warmly invited me. "I was just getting ready to throw the steaks on the grill. I wanted them to be fresh. We can grab some beers or soda and chat on the porch."

"Do you have Dr. Pepper?"

"Yes, ma'am," Warren responded.

I already loved these people. "Lead the way, then."

We walked through the cozy home that was minimally decorated, unless you counted the many pictures of his sons on the wall. I had to stop and stare at a few in the family room before we headed through the patio doors. I touched one of a toothless baby Sawyer. He was freaking adorable. He had chubby thighs like me back then too. He had such curly hair as a toddler. I recognized the teenage boy in his football uniform. My heart skipped a few beats.

"He was such a handsome boy," Bridget commented while handing me a Dr. Pepper.

"Uh-huh."

"Still is." She gave me a sly smile.

"For some, I suppose." I grinned.

Warren chuckled while opening the sliding glass door.

While I followed them out, thoughts in the back of my mind kept nagging at me, like why did Warren have all these pictures of his sons and his ex-wife didn't? I had never seen one from Josephine. My thoughts were interrupted by the paradise that awaited me in the backyard. It was landscaped to the hilt, with retaining walls, flower beds, several fruit trees, and a lush lawn that begged to be run across barefoot. A hot tub filled the corner of the large deck with a built-in grill. I could easily picture Sawyer out here playing catch with his dad. A thought that made me both happy and sad.

"It's beautiful back here."

Warren looked out over his yard and sighed with a sad smile. "A lot of good memories happened here." He pointed to the grove of fruit trees. "Every year, Sawyer and I would plant a new tree, and he helped me build this deck."

That was sweet. "What about Ashton?"

Warren shrugged. "Ashton has always been most interested in what Ashton wants."

Huh. "But you still have a relationship with him, right?"

Warren gave Bridget a look that said he wasn't sure what he should say. He took a moment to say anything while he threw some steaks on the grill. Once the steaks were on, he joined us at the patio table. He took Bridget's hand. It wasn't hard to see that such love existed between them.

Warren smiled at me to put me at ease. "I love both my sons with all my heart, but Ashton . . ." he cleared his throat, "is more like his . . . *mother*," he hesitated to say. "Relationships are all about what's in it for them. Ashton mostly calls me when he needs my help. And Sawyer never calls me now, so there's that."

The information about Ashton surprised me. He was a fun-loving guy, but now more than ever I was glad Ashton said he wasn't interested in Macey. Was this why he was divorced? Things to ponder on later. "I'm sorry," I responded to Warren.

He squeezed Bridget's hand. "It's my own fault. I should have handled things differently."

"Me too," Bridget whispered.

"Is my son happy?" Warren begged to know.

I nodded. "I think so. He loves his job. He's saving money to start his own practice so he kind of lives in a dive right now and he drives a beat-up old truck—"

"Old blue?"

"Yeah."

Warren smiled. "That was my dad's old truck. I gave it to Sawyer when he graduated from high school."

"It's seen better days, but Sawyer seems to be fond of it."

A hopeful smiled engulfed Warren's face. He reached across and patted my hand. "I'm glad he has good friends."

I inadvertently winced at the title.

Warren and Bridget laughed.

Warren gave me a pointed look. "You don't like the word."

I tucked some hair behind my ear. "I like it just fine."

Warren stood up to check on the steaks. "You can't kid a kidder."

There was no kidding. I knew where Sawyer and I stood.

Sawyer didn't show up in time for dinner, so we ate without him. Man, could Warren make a good steak. And Bridget was my new culinary hero. Forget Duncan Hines, Betty Crocker, and did I dare say it—Frankie? Bridget made this triple layer chocolate cake that made me want to kiss her. Even better, she was willing to give me the recipe. I loved her. I also loved how welcome they made me feel, how interested they were in my job and me as a person. They even offered to come to one of my girls' soccer games if it was all right with Sawyer. My own dad hadn't even come to one this season. When mom was alive, they never missed one.

After I helped clean up and Sawyer still hadn't shown up, Warren went out to clean his grill. Bridget informed me he was meticulous about it after each use. It also allowed me to have some time alone with Bridget. Maybe Warren sensed I wanted some. There were things I wanted to ask her that I didn't feel comfortable asking Warren. But they were things I needed to know about the woman who was married to my dad, and even about Ashton since he worked for Dad.

Bridget and I sat on the family room couch, which was not mohair. It was a comfortable leather couch like I had. Both of our Dr. Peppers fizzed in their ice-filled glasses on the coffee table. Warren had a pebble ice maker. These people were like my soul. Bridget rested her arm on the back of the couch with her head in her hand. I noticed those dirty fingernails again. They were from helping Warren weed his vegetable and flower gardens.

"You can ask me anything." She read my mind.

"I don't want to seem nosy."

"There is nothing wrong with wanting to be informed."

"Well, in that case," I smiled, "I want to know the why of it all."

"I'm not sure any of us can answer that, but I can tell you some contributing factors. Mind you, there are two sides to every story."

I nodded. That was good of her to say, especially because I

desperately wanted Josephine to be the bad guy in any story she had to tell. But she had to have some redeeming qualities for Sawyer to love her so much. I couldn't see any of them, but they had to be there. Deep down. Maybe?

"When I first moved in next door to take care of my father, I didn't even realize Warren was married. I frequently saw Warren with Sawyer in the backyard or doing yard work in the front. It wasn't until Sawyer started cutting our lawn and he mentioned his mom that I knew there was a mother here. By that time, Ashton was out of high school. He flitted in and out, and between colleges and jobs, sometimes he lived at home, but mostly not. The first time I saw Josephine was late one night when my father and I had returned from an emergency room visit. She looked like she was sneaking into her own home."

My eyebrows raised. "Was that a common occurrence?"

She pressed her lips together and nodded.

"Do you know what she was doing?"

She paused and thought. "Warren had suspicions."

I so badly wanted to ask what those were, but I refrained. She obviously didn't want to say, and I could guess.

She let out a heavy breath. "I can tell you that Josephine was never satisfied with the life she lived here. Warren never made enough money, he wasn't as ambitious as she thought he should be. She got them in a lot of debt opening credit cards and maxing them out under Warren's name. He was close to declaring bankruptcy after the divorce, but thanks to Colorado's economic boom, his business benefited and he managed to eke by. He almost has it all paid off now, including all the student loans he took out to help Sawyer through school."

My head tilted. "Does Sawyer know that?"

She smiled and shook her head. "No. Warren never wanted him to know he didn't have the money saved. He did what he had to do for him. He was so proud of Sawyer; he wanted to make sure all his dreams came true."

I was so confused and a bit alarmed about all this info. "So, did Sawyer know that his parents were having problems? And how was Sawyer's relationship with his mom back then? They seem close now."

"I believe Warren did his best to hide any conflict from Sawyer. He wanted his boys to grow up in a stable environment. As far as Sawyer's and Josephine's relationship, I believe Josephine fawned over him. He was a superstar growing up, and she took great pride in that."

"That makes sense. She still acts like that, but she wishes he showed off his success."

"That doesn't surprise me."

"Thank you, Bridget. I promise to keep what you said confidential."

"I'm not worried about it." She gave me a wicked grin. "I know how you feel about Sawyer."

I went to deny it, but something about her made me stop. I let out a huge breath. "Is it that obvious?"

"You're having dinner with his estranged father without him. I would say that's pretty obvious."

"I guess so." I tucked my feet under me. "It doesn't matter though; he doesn't feel the same way and we have some very odd connections that would make it awkward."

She reached out and rested her warm hand on my knee. "I don't think there would be anything awkward about it."

I shrugged. "Regardless—"

"You're fooling yourself if you don't think he has feelings for you."

I shook my head, not able to believe it. "You know, my mom set us up right before she died. We had the best phone calls ever." My eyes began to tear up. "He even asked me out, but then my mom died and when he came to the funeral and we met face-to-face, he never asked me out again."

She squeezed my knee, looking stumped. "Did you ever ask him why?"

"Now that would be really awkward, but I don't have to ask, I know why. Look at me. I'm not exactly cover girl material. I'm the friend. The girl you down a pizza and pitcher of beer with while yelling loudly at the TV when your favorite team is acting like a bunch of idiots. I've been that way my entire life. Unless you count the polygamist who was more than willing to take me on as his fourth wife."

"What?"

"It's a long story."

"Emma, can I tell you something?"

"Sure."

"Take it from a woman who was never a size four, heck, not even a size six or eight—don't let the size you wear devalue you. I did that for far too long. You know what that led to?"

I shook my head.

"A lot of bad relationships because I thought someone else would make me feel good about myself."

"I do like myself." So I worried about my weight from time to time. Who didn't?

"I know you do; I can see it in your eyes. In the way you carry yourself. I hope that never changes. And I hope you don't sell Sawyer short. You're a beautiful woman inside and out."

"Beautiful may be pushing it."

"I think you should take a better look in the mirror and in Sawyer's eyes."

Believe me, I was well versed in those pretty babies and not once had they ever said, *I want you, Emma.*

Chapter Fifteen

I STARED UP at the Saturn V rocket suspended above my head, trying to pay attention to the presenter droning on about scrap metal supplements and alternative iron making. Usually this stuff totally geeked me out and I had no problem paying attention, but I had a lot on my mind. Starting first with—was Josephine an adulteress? That was a funny word with a very ugly connotation. Would she cheat on my dad? Did she even love him? I knew she loved his bank account.

Then there was Sawyer. He never showed up for dinner at his dad's house. He said by the time he was done working he was beat, so he and Shelby grabbed a bite to eat before he went home. How come he had enough energy to eat with Shelby? I guessed it had worked out. It let me get to know Bridget and Warren better and get some of my questions answered. I didn't like what they had to say, but I figured I wouldn't. I did like them, though—a lot. I kind of sort of mentioned that to Sawyer on the phone when I called him from the airport to let him know I arrived safely in Huntsville Saturday night. He got quiet, like, the deafening kind. I probably should have waited to have that conversation in person, but he'd brought it up. He said, "I never got to ask you how dinner went on Friday."

I mean, I didn't tell him I wanted to kiss Bridget because of her chocolate cake. Or even that when they both hugged me goodbye it felt like when he hugged me. All I said was, "I had a great time. They want us to come over sometime next week when I get back."

Sawyer suddenly had to get off the phone. He and Kellan were watching the Rockies or something. That was three days ago, and we hadn't talked since. It was a good thing I hadn't mentioned I was meeting Bridget at the cute new ice cream shop in Edenvale when I returned.

On top of my Sawyer dilemma, I was struggling with whether or not I should talk to my dad. Would he even listen to me? Or would he chalk it up to me not understanding what marriage was all about? Maybe I didn't have firsthand knowledge, but I sure knew what a good marriage looked like, and his and Josephine's didn't qualify. I was racked with thoughts of what if things didn't work out between them, which I'm not going to lie, I would be A-okay with that, but would he be upset after the fact that I didn't tell him what I knew?

This was all giving me a headache. I was glad when the presenter gave his ending spiel about the company he worked for and all the amazing research they could provide, you know, for the right price.

I stood and took a deep breath and let it out.

"That sigh sounds like it has some meaning," the man next to me said. Of course it was a man. Eighty-five percent of the attendees here were men.

"Scrap metal supplements deserve deep thought."

The stranger chuckled and stood. "I'm Dustin." He held out his hand that looked like it had seen some hard work. Veins popped out under his calloused skin. My own hands had looked that way from time to time. It was a byproduct of my profession.

I took Dustin's hand and shook it. "I'm Emma."

He let go of my hand. "It's nice to meet you, Emma. Where are you from?"

"Colorado. How about you?"

"Born and raised here."

"So, do you work at a local steel plant, or do you just like to crash these kinds of events?"

His grin lit up his pretty blue eyes. I wasn't sure why I noticed that, but then I noticed he was a handsome guy. He wasn't much taller than me, but he was well built with a pleasant face. For a second, I almost felt guilty for thinking he was attractive, like I was cheating on Sawyer. Sawyer had consumed so much of my thoughts the last year, I realized I hadn't really noticed any other men. Don't get me wrong, this Dustin was no Sawyer, but Sawyer was my friend, end of story. Dustin would probably end up that way too. They all did.

"I work at Ducor."

"Oh. I signed up to do a tour of your plant tomorrow."

He leaned in, allowing me to get a whiff of his spicy cologne. I'm not going to lie, it was kind of nice. "Then I will see you tomorrow, Emma from Colorado."

Was he using a flirty voice there?

"See you then."

"I look forward to it." He walked off to join a few other guys, but not before he looked back at me and flashed me a smile.

I looked behind me to see who his pearly whites were directed at. There was no one there. I guess that meant it was me. I smiled back and waved. His smile grew bigger before he turned around. That was weird.

What was weirder was Dustin wasn't the only man who had given me attention since my arrival at the conference. Maybe I should do my hair more often outside of work and wear something besides old T-shirts. It was really time consuming, though, to do all the girly things like blow drying, curling, makeup, shaving your legs. Though I had to do that last one religiously unless I wanted to look like Bigfoot's younger half-sister.

I decided to get takeout for dinner from the Brazilian restaurant near my hotel. I would have loved to take advantage of the running trails near my hotel, but holy mother was it freaking hot and humid in Alabama. How people even breathed here I didn't know. It was like inhaling soup.

I settled onto my bed with a variety of meat, fresh fruit, and a soccer match on the TV. This was the life. Then my life called, I mean Sawyer. Same thing, right? Wrong.

"Hey, what's up?" I decided to act chipper despite our less than cordial conversation a few days ago. I didn't think we had gone this long without talking since, well, you know, when the worst thing that had ever happened to me happened, paving the way for all the other crappy things that had followed.

"How are you, Em? I miss you."

I loved when he said things like that because I used to pretend he meant it in a romantic way, but I had to face reality, like for reals this time. "I'm good. How are you?" You see how I left off how much I seriously missed his face? Baby steps.

"You don't miss me?"

Dang him.

"Should I?" I teased, trying my best to hold on to my iron will. Make that my paper-thin will, but I was getting credit for trying.

"I know we left things a little weird on Saturday."

"Did we?"

"Come on, Em. I know I was short with you and I haven't called, but I have a really good excuse."

"You know, I haven't noticed." I grinned evilly to myself.

"Knife to the heart. I am sorry, for not . . ."

"I know you have a hard time with your dad and Bridget. I get that."

"Regardless, I shouldn't let it affect us. But I didn't call to talk about my," he cleared his throat, "father."

"Why did you call?"

"Like I said, I missed you, and I haven't called because I've been under attack, literally."

"From who?" *Please don't say Shelby.*

"It's not a *who*—it's a *what*."

I was more than confused. "What are you talking about?"

"My apartment has been infested with bees."

"Are you serious?"

"Very. There are thousands of them inside the walls. Not only that, but the honeycomb has soaked into the wall causing an ant infestation as well. There are ants everywhere, not to mention I was stung twice while taking a shower."

I tried to control my laugh. "Should I ask where?"

"Sitting has been a pain. I'll leave it at that."

My laugh escaped. "I'm so sorry. What are you going to do?"

"I've been staying with Kellan while apartment management tries to get in a beekeeper. They are trying to find a specialist because the infestation is that bad."

"You need to move."

"You're probably right."

"I'm more than right."

"They've offered to let me move into a different unit, but it's not available until this weekend."

"You need to move out of that complex, period."

"I will when the time is right. For now, I was hoping you might take pity on me and let me crash at your place. Kellan's place smells like pork rinds and cheap perfume."

"That's telling."

"Yeah, well, his couch isn't all that comfortable either, and someone I know has a spare bedroom."

"You want to use me for free room and board now?" I teased.

"Name your price. Please, I'm desperate. Your house smells good and my body is crying for a bed."

The thought of Sawyer sleeping at my house was making me feel all sorts of things. Like one, why wasn't I home already? Two, I would be home on Thursday, which meant we would be living together for two or three days. It would be like a dream come true minus we weren't married and sharing my bed. So basically, it would be like hell because I could look but not touch.

"So," he interrupted my thoughts, "will you save me?"

Who was going to save my heart from him? "Sure. You have a key—help yourself, but no parties or girls."

He chuckled.

I wasn't kidding. He better not bring any women into my house to live out my fantasies with him.

"You drive a tough bargain, but okay. Honestly, thank you. You're a life saver."

"You're welcome. The sheets on the guest bed are clean and there are fresh towels in the linen closet near the upstairs bathroom."

"You're the best, Em. How's your conference going?"

"Good. I attended a really sexy session today about remelt processes and innovations. I know you're jealous."

"Very." He laughed. "I can't wait to hear all about it when you get home. And," he paused, "I still want to talk to you."

"Is everything okay?"

"I'm hoping it will be."

"You're worrying me."

"No need to worry, just promise me you'll keep Friday night open."

"Is after soccer practice okay?" We had a game on Saturday and there was no telling what Gwendolyn, the worst assistant coach in the history of any sports team, had been teaching them while I was gone this week. I'd left her instructions, but I knew she wasn't following them. She was probably stuffing my girls with caviar and Perrier while her boy toy husband rubbed her feet or something.

"That works. I'll see you when you get home."

"Hey, don't touch my real Dr. Pepper if you know what's good for you."

"I do know what's good for me. Good night."

Strange. I stared at my phone after he hung up. I thought he would laugh and remind me he didn't drink his calories.

Why did I feel like things were changing for us? I had a feeling, like most of the change in my life lately, it wasn't the good kind.

Chapter Sixteen

WAS IT WEIRD how giddy I was to visit Ducor's steel plant? It's not like I didn't work at one. I guess I had been missing the sights and sounds of three-thousand-degree molten steel being tapped out of an electric arc furnace all week. There was something about seeing those amazing oranges and reds light up the mill while a stream of liquid steel poured into a giant ladle. It was raw, and in that stream were a hundred different possibilities. It could be turned into car or appliance parts, tools, even toys. I didn't know why it brought me satisfaction to know that I played a part in that. I could make sure all those things were made out of quality steel. Not only that, I held the key to profit margins. I made sure we were running as efficiently as possible and that every roll of steel that came off our line was quality.

"Impressive, right?" Dustin yelled over the sound of the EAF tap.

I hadn't realized he joined the tour. Or maybe I hadn't noticed him. We were all in hard hats, protective goggles, and sexy orange Nomex jackets, so it was hard to tell who was who on the tour.

"It is!" I yelled hoping he could hear me. We were all wearing ear plugs. "But the furnace at my plant is bigger," I joked.

He leaned closer. "Do you work in a melt shop?"

I nodded. "I'm a melt cast metallurgist."

"Really?"

"You're surprised."

"There aren't a lot of women in our field."

"What's your position here?"

"I'm the melt shop manager." He held the same title as Wallace, my boss.

The tour guide had us start moving down the strand so we could follow the journey of the steel as it was cast.

"Do you want to see the caster pulpit?" Dustin yelled.

Ooh. That wasn't part of the tour. Even though I spent an inordinate amount of time in a caster pulpit—or what we called the observation deck where I worked— I was excited and curious to see how they ran things at this plant. Maybe they were doing something better than we were that I could bring back to my plant.

I nodded my reply, so I didn't have to yell.

I realized as the two of us left the group that it might look like we were sneaking off together. Not like there was anywhere in a melt shop to have romantic pursuits. It would be too dangerous. Besides, there was nothing sexy about 140 degrees with 90 percent humidity.

Dustin helped carefully guide me to the observation deck that was perched back behind the strand where the steel was being cast and molded. It was nice to be in the pulpit where I could take out my earplugs. After all these years I wasn't fond of them, even though they were a necessity. My metallurgist heart felt right at home among the large computer monitors. It almost looked like a control tower for an airport. The monitors in the semi dark room constantly fed the engineers and techs information about the equipment below to make sure everything was functioning as it should. The system was advanced enough to detect impurities in the steel.

Funny how even the men on this crew reminded me of the guys back home. They were all a little rough around the edges with varying stages of beer bellies. The older they were, the bigger the bellies seemed to be.

Dustin introduced me to the engineers and techs on this shift. A plant like this—and ours—ran 24-7. "Emma is visiting from Colorado. She's a melt cast metallurgist."

All the men nodded. One asked what company I worked for. Another asked what we produced. The last one asked, "Where did you go to school?"

"Colorado School of Mines," I replied.

Dustin whistled. "Impressive. We've had a few summer interns from there."

"I hope you have had better luck with your interns than we do."

Apparently not, by the way all the men laughed.

"We had some fool up here in the pu-u-u-lpi-i-i-t," one of the techs overexaggerated his Southern accent, "clipping his toenails last year."

I shared my crying in the bathroom over an Instagram post story. It got a lot of laughs.

Dustin put his hand on the small of my back and pushed me forward. "Don't be shy. Feel free to have a look or make suggestions," he offered.

I felt like a kid at Christmas. One of the engineers even offered me his seat. I readily took it. I didn't expect to see anything out of the ordinary, but I did. I was a little nervous to say anything so as not to step on any toes, but I'd want somebody to say something if they'd noticed. "Hey, it looks like some of your thermocouples are running hot. Do you have a breakout warning system?"

Dustin and the engineer who had given me his seat peered up at the monitor.

"You're right," Dustin said.

I gave the engineer back his seat so he could do his thing.

I was able to watch them for a moment as they tried to resolve the issue. As hard as it was, I kept my mouth shut. This was their show.

Dustin smiled at me as if he knew how difficult it was for me to stay quiet. "I think my guys have this handled. Would you like to join me for lunch?" He gave me a disarming smile that reminded me of Sawyer. It made me think of the text Sawyer had sent me this morning.

Sawyer: Thanks for a good night's sleep. Can't wait to see you.

I'd been missing him too.

Dustin's smile faltered when I didn't answer.

I shook my head, trying to get Sawyer out of it. It seemed like an impossible task. "Thank you. I'd like that," I managed to say.

"Great," Dustin breathed out, relieved. "I have something I would like to discuss with you."

My interest was piqued. I popped in my earplugs and followed him back out. I wasn't sure where we would eat. The plant, like most steel plants, was out in the middle of nowhere. On my drive out there this morning I had mostly seen a lot of cornfields, cows, and a couple of gas stations.

He led me out of the melt shop into the blazing hot day. It was like jumping out of the frying pan right into the fire. I was never going to complain about how hot it was back home. Dry heat was a beautiful thing.

Dustin removed his earplugs. "We have a decent breakroom in our cold mill; do you mind if we eat in there?"

"Um . . . sure, but I didn't bring a lunch."

He gave me a furtive smile. "I might have packed an extra lunch today."

I took my protective eyewear off and bit my lip. "Oh, so you planned this?"

"Do you mind?" He didn't deny it.

Did I? The question should be, why should I? Sawyer was my friend, but I was in love with him. But this was a lunch date? Maybe? I was allowed to go on dates, though I didn't have very many. "Are you a polygamist?"

He squinted his pretty blue eyes. "No."

"Do you have a police record of any sort?"

His cheeks pinked up. "Full disclosure—when I was in high school, some buddies and I got arrested for cow tipping."

"Is that really a thing?"

"We learned the hard way that it's not."

I laughed. "You sound like my kind of person."

That earned me a toothy smile from him. "Shall we, then?"

I nodded before taking off my hard hat and running my fingers through my hair. He'd seen me all girly the day before, so hopefully this charming look today wouldn't frighten him.

"If you would like, we can take my truck; it's kind of a walk over to the cold mill. If that makes you uncomfortable, though, I totally understand."

"I know like five forms of martial arts," I teased.

"I've been warned." He dug into his pocket for his keys.

Dustin drove a nice, new truck with all the bells and whistles, leather, GPS, and air conditioning. Sawyer would have been in heaven. I needed to quit thinking about him. "What did you want to discuss?" I needed a distraction.

"You like to get right to business, huh?" He turned out of the melt shop parking lot.

"Sometimes."

"I wanted to make you aware of some opportunities here."

I looked his way and tilted my head. "Job opportunities?"

"Yes. We're looking to open our galvanized steel mill in the fall and we have two shift supervisor positions to fill."

"Really?" Management was the next step in my career path, but at our plant someone was going to have to retire or die before that happened for me. I didn't want Wallace to do either, so it wasn't something on my radar. Except it was. I reminded myself that I had been thinking about moving. I thought of my evil stepmother and how I felt as if I was losing my family because of her. Then there was Sawyer. He was sure to find a girlfriend soon. Shelby, perhaps? I thought so, even if he denied it.

But did I really want to move to Alabama? The humidity was killer, and they had no mountains. All the green foliage here was beautiful, but it wasn't like back home where a desert plateau landscape met the Rocky Mountains. Perhaps I could get used to the green and heat. They did fry everything here, and there was a rumor that curvy girls were queen in the South, but judging by the way Shelby looked, I wasn't sure if that was true.

"I'm not over the hiring process. We wouldn't be working together, which is good, you know . . ." His face burned red.

I was getting a little warm too. "Are you saying you'd like to see me again?"

The red seemed to disappear from his cheeks when he glanced my way. "I see that as a definite possibility."

Oh? Should I tell him about my curse now or save that for later?

Chapter Seventeen

IT TOOK EVERYTHING I had to keep my eyes open while driving home from the airport at five in the morning. Maybe I should have told Sawyer yes when he'd offered to pick me up, but I'd left my car at the airport and I wasn't sure when I would make it home. My trip home had been the stuff travel nightmares were made of. I should have been home yesterday evening, but did you know that Alabama had tornadoes in the summer and thunderstorms that made you think you needed to board Noah's Ark? There was nothing like being at the airport and having to hide in the bathroom among the blare of tornado sirens. When I wasn't cowering in the bathroom, I watched the sheets of rain pummel the windows at the airport gate while thunder shook the ground.

By the time flights had resumed, the crew for our flight wasn't allowed to fly because of some federal regulation concerning time. We had to wait another four hours for a new crew. To top it off, during one of our bathroom excursions I forgot my iPad, and someone decided to help themselves to it. Needless to say, not even Dr. Pepper or the chocolate chip muffin I was eating to help me stay awake was making me feel any better. It was a good thing I didn't have to go into the plant today. All I wanted was my bed.

Groggily, I pulled into my garage. The first thing I noticed was that Sawyer had made himself at home and parked his rusted clunker in there. I supposed since it was his grandfather's old truck it had some sentimental worth, but if someone stole it, they would be doing him a favor.

Too tired to even grab my bag, I stumbled into the dark house and trudged up the stairs. I could have honestly lain on them and fallen soundly asleep—that's how exhausted I was. When I reached the top of the landing, I looked to my right and noticed the closed door to the guest bedroom. There the love of my life slumbered. Good thing I was too tired to be tempted to enter his room instead of mine. And it was a really good thing I was too mentally out of it to think about Dustin asking for my number and me giving it to him.

I was too tired to even turn on my bedroom light. I only went to the bathroom because I'd downed a lot of Dr. Pepper trying to stay awake. While in the bathroom, I tried to avoid the mirror as I knew it would scare even me. After peeing for five minutes straight, I threw on my pajamas that hung on the door. Why sleep in jeans when I didn't have to?

Sweet bed and sleep, here I come.

"Welcome home."

I grabbed my heart and screamed while taking on a kick-butt karate stance.

My bedside light switched on and illuminated my every hope and wish, Sawyer sitting up in my bed without a shirt on. Holy. Crap. Remember how I said I needed warning when his bare skin was involved? And there I was looking like a deranged ninja in my faded gray T-shirt with plaid boxer shorts after traveling for hours. At least I had peed before this surprise. No telling what other kind of embarrassments might have ensued.

I relaxed my stance. "What are you doing in my room?"

He gave me a come-kiss-me grin, which was only more attractive with his mussed hair and stubble. "Your guest bed is a twin and not as comfortable."

"So you thought you would try out my bed? Who are you, Goldilocks?"

He smoothed out the sheets next to him. "You weren't here, and I didn't think you would mind. I had no idea you had a comfort controlled king-size bed. What do you need all this room for?" He gave me a wicked grin.

Believe me, it wasn't for what his dirty mind was thinking. "I like to sleep like a starfish, thank you very much."

He chuckled.

"I'm serious, so hit the twin, buddy."

He pressed his lips together and studied me for a moment. "I have to get up for work soon anyway, so . . ." he patted the space next to him, "come tell me how your trip was."

He wanted me to crawl in bed with him? Was he freaking insane? My eyes popped like a jack-in-the-box.

He pulled back the covers. "Come on, Em. We're adults here."

That's the part that worried me.

"I'm tired." That was a lie now as the adrenaline had kicked in, but I was trying to find any excuse to avoid my dream.

"Too tired for me?"

I closed my eyes, trying to muster up the courage to lie to him. The truth was I was never too tired for him.

"Em," he whispered. "I've missed you."

My eyes peeked open. I let out a heavy breath and walked toward what would be ecstasy and misery.

Sawyer's grin filled his face while he scooted over for me.

Cautiously, I crept into bed. My exhausted body naturally snuggled down into the pillows, doing its best to avoid any direct eye or physical contact with the glorious chest nearby. It didn't help that my pillows and sheets smelled like him, making all my senses turn on. It was like he sprayed his pheromones all over. If ever I wanted to try out Jenna's stupid plan of kissing him, it was now. I could blame it on being up all night. All I knew was I was never washing my sheets.

Sawyer joined me by resting his head on the pillows next to mine. His happy face was staring right at mine only a foot away. It was then I remembered I hadn't brushed my teeth in hours since I'd been stuck in airports and on planes. Maybe he would leave once he caught a whiff. Though I did really enjoy the view.

Sawyer took a moment to peer into my eyes. In his I could see the wheels turning. What was he so deep in thought about?

"Tell me about your trip, Em."

Where did I even begin? Food was always my go-to. "Did you know they fry Oreos in Alabama?"

"Really?"

"It's true. Unfortunately, it wasn't all that great. But they sell real Dr. Pepper everywhere down there even though they call it Coke."

"What?"

"Coke is synonymous with soda there."

"Weird."

"Yeah, but no worries, I caught on really quick."

Sawyer grinned. "How was the conference?"

"Interesting."

"How so?"

"It wasn't the conference, per se, but during the plant tour I told you about, one of the managers there, Dustin, invited me to apply for a supervisor position in their new galvanized steel mill."

Sawyer's brow crinkled. "You're not interested, are you?"

I shrugged. "Maybe. Dustin said the pay would be more than I'm making now and the opportunity for advancement there is better than here."

"Who's this Dustin, again?" Sawyer's jaw tightened up with the pronunciation of his name.

"He's the melt cast manager. He was great. He let me go up into their observation deck to check it out and he makes a fine chicken salad sandwich."

"He cooked for you?" Sawyer growled.

"Well, kind of, I guess. We had lunch together at the plant."

"Let me guess, in his private office."

I narrowed my eyes. "Are you okay? I didn't mean to upset you. Maybe we should talk about this later."

"I'm not upset," he snarled, "but I think you should be careful about this Dustin guy. What do you even know about him? Sounds like he'd like a casting couch style interview."

"Did you get enough sleep last night? You're awfully grumpy."

He took a breath so deep, when he let it out his cheeks inflated. At least it let me know I wasn't the only one with stale breath. Though I didn't mind it. "I'm sorry, Em, I just didn't know you were thinking about moving. You've never said anything."

"Well, I'm not sure I want to, but I think it's good to keep my options open."

"Is Dustin an option for you?"

I flipped on my back and stared at my trey ceiling and the spinning fan. "I don't know. I don't know anything anymore. I'm not even sure where I belong," I choked out.

"Hey there." Sawyer scooted closer. His body heat enveloped me. "Em."

I turned to find his face inches from my own. His warm amber eyes radiated in the dark room. I held my breath, which made me feel even more fuzzy. Where had the oxygen in the room gone? I kept telling myself this meant nothing to him, but then his strong hand combed through my hair.

"Em," he repeated. "I know where you belong."

"You do?" I whispered.

He nodded and moved in closer. I could feel his warm breath on my face. His eyes searched my own while his hand caressed my cheek. "Your cuts are healing nicely." He shook his head as if he had said something stupid.

Okay, maybe I was reading him wrong. I thought we were having a moment. Like *the* moment I'd been waiting for, for a year now. "That cream Shelby recommended has helped. How is Shelby?" I asked out of nervousness and uncertainty about what exactly was happening here.

His finger began to outline my lips. "I don't want to talk about Shelby."

Me either. I was more focused on how every cell in my body was chanting Sawyer's name and every goose bump possible was raised and singing hallelujah. Could this be real? My body said yes and closed our eyes to wait.

Sawyer's hand glided down my cheek, then my arm. His breath had become warmer the closer he got, making the anticipation grow.

Holy crap this was really happening. My breath caught in my chest, waiting.

Sawyer's slow hand continued a downward path until he reached my bare stomach where my shirt had come up. When he landed on my less-than-tight abs, I felt his warm hand freeze before it popped off. I opened my eyes to find the spell was broken. Sawyer's eyes were wide and confused—or was that disappointed that his suspicions about my figure had been confirmed?

I shot up and ran my fingers through my hair. "Wow. That was awkward." I kept my head facing forward, avoiding any eye contact.

Sawyer sat up too. "Wait, that wasn't the way this was supposed to go."

"That was apparent." I threw off the covers to go anywhere but here.

Sawyer grabbed my hand. "Please, don't go."

I was about to ignore him and flee, but my ancient landline started ringing violently on my nightstand, which meant it was the plant and it was probably an emergency. Work was the only reason I had the landline in case cell service was interrupted or I left it in my car like I had today.

My head was buzzing from all the stimulation. I didn't know what to do as the phone kept ringing. Finally, I took my hand back from Sawyer and used it to answer the phone.

"Hello," I growled.

"Emma, this is Hayes." He was a member of the production staff, which meant this wasn't good. "I know you're off today, but we've had four breakouts in the last twenty-four hours and we can't figure out the cause. Please, we need your help."

I could picture the mess now of molten steel overflowing the shell. I let out a heavy breath. "Yeah, of course. Lock out and tag down. Make sure everything is deenergized. I'll be there in about a half hour."

"You're a life saver. Thank you."

I hung up and jumped out of bed.

"Em, please, we need to talk."

I headed for my dresser in the corner. "No, we don't." I was absolutely mortified and planning on a séance later or something to sell my soul to the devil in return for scrubbing this event from my mind for eternity. I pulled open my top drawer with gusto.

Sawyer, in all his half naked glory, joined me at the dresser running his hand through his mussed hair. He pushed the drawer back in.

"Excuse me." I pulled the drawer back out, not caring that it was filled with panties and bras.

Sawyer took my hand and pressed it against his bare chest. I felt his heart pounding.

My eyes drifted up and met his. "I need to go."

"I know, but please promise me you'll still meet me tonight. I have a plan, and this wasn't a part of it."

"What are you talking about?"

"Please, Emma, let me do this the right way. I'll pick you up at eight tonight."

"I don't know. I think maybe..." His hand pressed harder against mine, making me more aware of how warm and tight his skin felt under my fingers. How much my fingers yearned to stay right where they were among the soft hair on his chest. It made me lose my train of thought.

"Please," he pleaded.

I ripped my hand away like I should have done to the stupid Band-Aid I'd been using ever since I met him and fell in love with him. "Fine," I cried.

"You won't be sorry, I promise."

I ran my hand across my mid-section. Somehow, I had a feeling he wasn't going to be able to keep that promise.

Chapter Eighteen

"SOMEBODY BETTER HAVE died," Jenna's scratchy voice filled my Jeep. I had her on speaker as I sped down the highway.

"Sawyer and I almost kissed, or at least I think we did."

"What!!! Dish, girl." She sounded wide awake now.

"Baby, are you okay?" I heard Brad ask.

"Go back to bed," Jenna whispered, before focusing back on me. "Don't spare any details. Go."

My head pounded while I thought about what to say. "I don't know. It was weird. We were in my bed together."

"Whoa, whoa, whoa! You were in bed together? Dang girl, I thought you said you almost kissed. What did you do before that?"

"It's not like that."

"Right."

"Seriously, Jenna, this isn't a happy story." Tears leaked out of my tired eyes.

"Oh, Em. What happened?"

"I don't know. No, that's not true, I do know; and I feel so stupid now. I totally thought he was going to kiss me. I had my eyes closed and everything. And then . . . well, he touched my squishy middle and that was that. No kiss."

"That b-hole. Did he say anything?"

"He said it wasn't the way he wanted this all to happen and he wants to take me out tonight."

"Wait, wait, wait."

"What?"

"Well, maybe you're reading the situation wrong."

"Jen, how can that be?"

"Well, I don't know exactly, but why would he want to take you out? Is this like a date?"

"He didn't call it that. And he'd already asked me earlier in the week if we could get together tonight and talk."

"Ooh, that's interesting."

"I'm living off zero sleep and I've just been humiliated in my bed, of all places—which makes it worse, by the way—so *interesting* is the last word I would use."

"Take a breath. I'm on your side."

"I know. I'm sorry. It's just, I've been waiting for this for forever and then instead of a magical moment, I got a kick to the gut."

"Maybe he's been planning this night so he could kiss you in a special way."

"A special way," I snorted.

"You know what I mean."

"I guess, but believe me, I don't think it would have topped what almost happened."

"That good, huh?"

I shivered thinking about it until that last bit, and then I cringed. "I know this sounds cheesy, but it was surreal, and it felt like we were in this magic bubble where only we existed." Tears began to stream down my face instead of trickle

"Oh, Em. Maybe he's one of those guys who feels like you should date before you kiss."

"You really think that?"

"No. Guys will take whatever they can get, when they can get it."

"Exactly, unless you have a doughboy middle because you love the Doughboy."

"Sawyer doesn't seem like that type. Regardless, I hope it doesn't affect the way you feel about yourself."

I thought for a second. I'd always known who I was and wasn't. I knew my love affair with all things sugar and yummy carb related made me not the prettiest girl on the block. I'd always been okay with it. I liked me. Yes, it hurt sometimes when I wasn't chosen, but it wasn't because I felt less, it was because the other person couldn't see more. They couldn't see that I was *more* than my waist size. If Sawyer was one of those people, it would break my heart but not my spirit.

"Em, you're beautiful. I hope you know that."

"Beautiful is an exaggeration, but I like myself."

"Stop that, please. You are beautiful. You can ask Brad. He said more guys didn't ask you out in high school because you intimidated them. No guy wants to think his girl can play ball better than him."

"I don't think that's Sawyer's problem. He could kick my butt on the field."

"Em, I don't know what happened this morning, but don't give up hope yet."

"I don't know, but now I need to go climb into a caster and figure out why molten steel is oozing out of it."

"See how intimidating you are?"

I laughed through my tears. "I'm just me."

"Just me, you're the best person I know. I love your guts. Call me later."

"Love you too. Get some rest for my godson."

"If only he would stay off my bladder."

I hung up feeling a tad less depressed. This tiny strand of hope stretched across my heart, holding it together thinking there was a chance with Sawyer. In the next second, that string frayed because I couldn't think of one good reason why he didn't kiss me this morning unless he was turned off by my less-than-perfect figure.

Those conflicting emotions carried me into the melt shop. It felt more like the cold mill this morning with all the equipment shut down.

Sawyer played in my tired brain all day while I crawled in and out of the caster trying to figure out what was causing the problem. My brain could hardly concentrate on all the process data I was having to muddle through. The problem was that my life felt like a bigger problem at the moment. Add to that no sleep and a heart that was on the verge of breaking. Sawyer's and my conversation kept running through my head. My hopes rose when I heard him say, *I know where you belong.* Did he think it was with him? But as soon as that wonderful thought took hold, I would remember the sting of rejection. His hand repulsed by my squishy middle.

The misery of not knowing would be over tonight. I would finally know one way or the other, because there was no going back after what happened this morning. There was no way for me to hide my feelings for him any longer. No matter what, he knew I wanted him. It was clear by how I had responded to him in my bed. His actions, though, were puzzling. This was all assuming I made it that far. I was exhausted. Not even all the Dr. Pepper I was downing was helping.

By two that afternoon I was exhausted, filthy, and had managed to rule out a bad encoder and misalignment. It also wasn't the mold powder, which was like a crazy expensive industrial cooking spray. In frustration, I looked at the data once more and somehow my brain began to function.

"Can someone bring me an infrared gun?" I shouted. I should have done this earlier, but the thermocouple data looked good. "We need to run a ghost slab!" I yelled to my tech guys.

While they went to work getting the caster and furnaces back up and running, I went up into the observation deck and took a small but much needed nap curled up in the corner on the floor. For a beautiful hour my brain was void of any thoughts or dreams. That was until Wallace came up and nudged me. "Wake up, kiddo. The higher ups are on me to get the strand back up and running."

With barely opened eyes, I looked up at him. "I don't like this job." That was a lie, but in the second it felt very true.

Wallace chuckled deeply while reaching out to help me up. That was a good call on his part. I needed all the help I could get. With one hoist I was on my feet. One of my guys was standing ready with a cold Dr. Pepper. I took it and downed it all in one long drink. I crushed the can with my hand and belched loud enough to fill the entire deck. And I wondered why Sawyer was turned off by me. "Let's do this."

We marched back down like soldiers off to war with my infrared gun as our weapon of choice. I fired that baby at the thermocouples, and lo and behold, they were a bunch of liars. Ugh. It was the thermocouples all along. "Well, there's our problem. Call the mechanics down here and get those replaced, and you should be ready go," I instructed the tech.

Wallace patted my back. "Go get some rest, kiddo. You did good."

Rest. Yes, it sounded so good. Too bad I had soccer practice and something with Sawyer tonight. Maybe Sawyer could just tell me quickly he was abhorred by me and then I could cry myself to sleep. At least I would be sleeping. Or, maybe, just maybe, he would tell me something different and I could fall asleep in his arms. That sounded like heaven.

I walked into the blaring sunlight and remembered not to complain about the heat or the sun after what I'd experienced in Alabama. That made me think—did I really want to live there? We didn't have tornadoes here. In Denver, sure, but not on this side of the mountains. So we had blizzards, but you got plenty of warning before those, and snow was fun to play in. Tornadoes not so much. Depending on what Sawyer said tonight, I might want to take my chances with the tornadoes.

As soon as I reached my Jeep, my phone rang. I reached into my pocket with my black-streaked hand. I needed a shower something fierce. Frankie's name was on my screen. I hope she wasn't calling me to tell me she was quitting before the end of summer, though at this point I felt like my dad deserved it for thrusting that wicked witch wife of his on all of us. Maybe that was Sawyer's hang-up—he didn't want to make out with his stepsister. If that was his problem, I hated Josephine even more.

"Hey, Frankie. How are you?"

"Emma, you gotta get up here."

"What's wrong? Did something happen to my dad? My sisters?"

She paused, making my heart beat out of my chest.

"Frankie!"

"Everyone is physically fine, but your dad has lost his damn mind. You've got to get up here now before he makes a serious mistake."

"What is going on?"

"One of our guests claims she had some money and jewelry stolen from her cabin."

"What? That's never happened before."

"Exactly. But Ashton conveniently found the jewelry in Morgan's room in the bunkhouse."

"Morgan, as in Ray's son? No way." We'd known that family forever and they were as true as true could be.

"No way is right. I think . . . Emma, I think Ashton is the real culprit."

I dropped my phone on the pavement. It was a miracle it didn't crack. I hastily picked it up. "Frankie, why do you think that?"

"Emma, please just come. I'll explain more when you get here."

I hung up and tapped my phone against my head. Did someone hate me? So much for showering or maybe even making soccer practice, at this rate. And worse, how was this going to affect my already shaky family dynamics? I knew Frankie would never make such an accusation unless she was certain. My gut began to wriggle. Sawyer's thoughts and feelings about this new twist in the plot entered the picture. Should I call him? What would I say? Maybe it was best for me to go and see what I was dealing with first.

Honestly, though, I don't know why Frankie thought I could be of any help. No one in my family cared about my feelings or what I had to say as of late. Dad was pretty much non-existent in my life now. No more phone calls or visits. When I was there, Josephine made sure we never had any quality time together.

I called Aspen on my way up to the Ranch to see if there was any way she could help out at soccer practice tonight. I knew Fridays at the bank were busy, but I was desperate and wanted my girls to be ready for the game tomorrow. I'd heard from Aspen via Chloe that the practice earlier in the week run by Gwendolyn was more like a fashion tutorial and they all went home with a set of fake eyelashes and bright ruby-red lips. No telling what they would get tonight if some sanity didn't show up. Padding for their training bras?

Thankfully, Aspen said she could make it work. I owed her big time. At least it was something I didn't have to worry about.

The mountains and the valley that were usually such a comfort to me no longer brought me the peace I had been longing for ever since my mother had died. The flood of tourists strolling through our postcard worthy Main Street were just another reminder of how things were changing, and I didn't like it. I was happy for my sisters that it meant good business for them, but I missed the days when there were only two stoplights and you never had to stop at them because rarely was anyone coming from the other direction. Now there were five lights and you always had to stop because pedestrians were everywhere. Today it wasn't a bad thing. I wasn't looking forward to going to the Ranch. My stomach was tied in knots over it.

When I drove onto the property it didn't take me long to spot where all the trouble was brewing. There was a good-sized group gathered near the barn. Dad was the most prominent figure among them due to his height and the poise he was naturally blessed with that said he was in charge. His awful wife was glued to him, as her usual. These women that lean. Morgan, the accused, was standing next to his dad, Ray, who was shaking his head while taking a protective stance. Surprisingly, my sisters were there, but unfortunately, I wasn't surprised that they were standing too close to Ashton. That gave me an uneasy feeling, but not as uneasy as when I realized Sawyer was there standing back from the fray. Back behind people I didn't recognize. Why was he there?

As soon as I parked my Jeep, Frankie ran up to me, her long, gray hair whipping behind her. She was a woman on a mission.

She wasn't the only one.

As soon as Josephine caught wind that I was there, she made a mad dash toward me.

"Emma," Frankie said in a rush. "You have to listen to me, I saw Ashton coming out of the cabin of the couple who has been robbed. He seems to be a frequent visitor for a lot of—"

"Did you call Emma out here to tell lies to her too?" Josephine sneered at me with such disdain while her dark eyes judged my appearance.

I got it—I was winning no beauty contests in my filthy jeans and long-sleeved cotton shirt with hair that was caked in grime from crawling around the caster all day. Believe me, it wasn't my dream to be here like this.

Frankie turned on a dime to face Josephine. "Don't you dare call me a liar. What you're doing to Ray's boy isn't right. Come to think of it, what you've done to this family and place isn't right."

Rage filled Josephine's unnaturally taut face. "Dane!" she shrieked.

In a herd, the group near the barn moved the scene to the parking area where I was.

Sawyer's and my eyes met. He looked confused, in his shirt and tie looking as if he had come from work, as to why he was there. That was a good question. Who called him?

Next, I turned my focus on Dad, who looked as exhausted as I was both physically and emotionally. His lined face was haggard, and he walked as if he had to force each step.

An irate Ray and a scared Morgan who was all of nineteen joined Frankie and me as if we were forming teams. Then and there I knew this wasn't going to end well. Mom had always said don't draw dividing lines with those you love.

A couple I didn't know walked up and the woman of the pair gave me the same look Josephine did. Sue me for having a job.

"Who is this?" the snotty princess with an uppity nose asked.

Oddly, several people answered. Dad said, "This is my oldest daughter."

But Ray, Morgan, and Frankie all said in unison, "She's the Lady of Carrington Ranch."

That filled me with such sweet pride to be called by my mother's title, but oh, that did not go over well with Stepmommy Dearest. Her nostrils flared while she gave each of them withering glances.

I looked at Sawyer, who was now looking down at the gravel, shaking his head.

I stepped forward to speak to the couple. "I'm Emma, Dane's daughter." I used deductive reasoning to conclude this was the couple who had been robbed. "Can you tell me what happened?"

The snotty princess clucked her tongue. "Are you even in charge here?"

"No, she's not," Josephine answered.

The princess's man looked like he was embarrassed by his wife or girlfriend's reaction. He put his arm around her. "Honey, she's just trying to help."

Princess pointed at Morgan. "We already know who did it, so fire the creep before I call the police."

"Wait a minute, please. Maybe this was all a misunderstanding." I tried to reason with her.

Ashton stepped forward proudly, looking like a cowboy. "I found her diamond earrings in Morgan's bunk."

"I didn't take them," Morgan swore with a crack in his voice. "I don't know how they got there." The poor kid was scared stiff.

"Did you see Morgan near your cabin?" I asked the man, hoping his partner didn't go off. It didn't work.

"Of course we didn't see him; that's how crimes are committed, you idiot."

"Hey," Sawyer chimed in. "We don't need to call anyone names."

Sawyer's defense of me didn't sit well with his mother. "Emma, we have this handled here. You should have never been called."

That did it. Frankie had hit her limit. "Someone with some sense needs to be here." Frankie faced me. "Emma, I swear to you on your mother's grave that," she turned and pointed, "I saw Ashton sneaking out of their cabin yesterday evening. And it wasn't the first time."

"She's lying." Ashton's face turned red, but he kept his cool.

Oddly though, I caught a glimpse of the princess and her cheeks had turned a few shades of pink. "That couldn't be," snotty girl said, "I was there all evening."

I bet she was. "Were you by yourself?" I asked.

Princess's eyes popped. "Why does that matter?"

"Yes, Emma, why does that matter?" Josephine seethed. "You wouldn't be accusing my son of something would you?"

"I'm just trying to get the facts."

"Emma," Marlowe whined, "Ashton is totally innocent. He turned *in* the earrings."

The princess's partner squeezed her tighter. "I don't think I like what you're implying about my fiancée."

Dad finally stepped in. "Listen folks, I will take care of any cash you say was stolen, as well as refund your entire stay."

"Oh, you better," princess snotty snarled, "but I'll still be leaving a scathing review on Trip Advisor telling people they better not pack any valuables if they stay here. I may still call the police." She turned and marched off with her man trailing behind her with his tail between his legs. If he was smart, he would run far away.

The fact that she hadn't called the police in the first place spoke volumes to me. I think if we called them now, their investigation would show a much different picture than the one trying to be repainted.

There were two camps left, though I really only cared about one person's reaction at the moment. Sawyer was looking at me with disbelief as if begging me to do the right thing. The problem was I think we had much different opinions on who was right and who was dead wrong.

"Emma, I can't believe you are blaming Ashton for this." Macey frowned.

Josephine took that as her cue. "Oh, she doesn't really believe Frankie, now do you? She would never take the word of an employee over her family, right?" A triumphant smile blazed on her face as she looked between me and Sawyer. It became painfully clear who had invited Sawyer and why he was here.

Frankie took my hand and squeezed it.

I looked at Dad who closed his eyes and shook his head. No surprise there. Where was the man who had always been my champion?

Tears filled my eyes for the loss I had incurred and the one that I knew was about to happen. I stared straight at Sawyer. "I believe Frankie. I know Morgan would never do such a thing."

"Are you saying I did this, sis?" Ashton used the term of endearment with such a snake-like hiss. It was enough to make me shiver in the warm evening sun.

Sawyer's brows raised waiting for my response. His incredulous look was killing me. I was losing another champion.

I turned from Sawyer and faced Ashton. It was as if I was looking at him for the first time. Where I used to see a warm, kind face, I now recognized it was an act. He looked like Josephine now more than ever. Conniving and vicious. She had put on the same act to catch my father. Now the façade was long gone. Ashton's was too.

"Ashton, I'm not your sister and you better stay away from mine."

"How dare you talk like that to my son." Josephine whipped her head toward Sawyer. "Do you see what I'm talking about now? I've done everything I can." She started to cry. "She wouldn't even help me plan the dance, when all I've tried to do is be a friend to her."

I spat out a laugh. She was such a liar. "If you were trying to be my friend, please stop."

She gave me a scathing look before facing my father. "Do you see this?" She really poured on the tears before she stomped off sobbing. Ashton chased after her, but not before glaring at me.

My sisters both looked at me as if I had lost my mind. "That was really mean, Emma," Macey threw at me. "Mind your own business from now on," Marlowe added in.

Sawyer stood frozen, staring at me coldly, but I couldn't deal with him yet.

Frankie gave my hand one more good squeeze. "Honey, I'm done here. I can't work like this." She faced my father. "Mr. Carrington, I always thought you were a good man, but I'm not sure anymore." She shook her head. "Shannon wouldn't have wanted this for you or your girls." She wrapped me in her arms. "Take care. I'm only a call away if you need anything."

"Frankie," I cried.

"I know." She walked away.

Dad let her.

Ray took off his cowboy hat and ran his hand over his balding head. "I gotta say, Dane, Frankie's right. Things haven't been the same since Shannon died. I think it's time for us to part ways."

Dad's brown eyes widened. "Listen, Ray, we can work this out."

"I don't think so. When you didn't stand up for my boy or your girl here," he patted my back, "it told me all I needed to know about where your head is."

Ray and Morgan headed for the bunkhouse. Dad looked between me and them as if he wasn't sure what he should do, that was, until he looked at Sawyer. It was then he made his choice.

I was left alone with the man I loved.

Chapter Nineteen

SAWYER STOOD EERILY still near one of the signs that had a map of the property on it for guests.

I wiped my eyes, which was a mistake with how much grime was left on my hands even though I had washed them. I could picture the streaks on my tear stained face. "Sawyer, please say something."

He began to stretch his neck from side to side. "What do you want me to say, Emma? I knew you didn't like my mom, but I can't believe you hate her so much that you would accuse my brother of stealing and cheating. What have they ever done to you?"

I stepped over the stones that marked off the gravel parking lot with a laundry list of what his family had done to me, but I was holding it back in hopes of salvaging at least my friendship with someone who had meant more to me than words could express. Not even my thoughts could do our friendship justice; you would have to listen to the beat of my heart to understand the breadth of it.

"Sawyer, I don't think you're seeing the full picture."

"I just watched you accuse my brother and humiliate my mother," he spat through gritted teeth.

"Don't you know me well enough to know I wouldn't falsely accuse someone?"

He blinked an inordinate amount of times. "You truly believe he's guilty? What proof do you have?"

I took a deep breath, not knowing how to finesse my response. "Your dad and Bridget said some things—"

Sawyer's eyes bulged while his face turned an ugly red. "You want to talk about cheaters and liars, there's a pair. How could you believe them?"

I stood up tall, though I was wearier than I had ever felt. "You want to know why I believe them?" I shouted. "Because your father reminds me of you, and you are one of the best people I know."

Sawyer's eyes flickered for a moment with some pause. His face lost a shade of red.

It gave me courage to proceed. "Your dad and Bridget, unlike your mother, have treated me with nothing but kindness. You don't even know everything your father has done for you."

"What are you talking about?"

"You need to ask him. And while you're at it, why don't you ask him why they got divorced. The real reason."

His hands clenched. "Dammit, Emma, why can't you just be happy that your dad has found love and happiness again with my mom?"

There was a loud ringing in my ears. Did he really just say that? "You know, for an eye doctor, you're sure blind. If you think that's what our parents have together then you don't know what happiness is."

The blood drained from his face while he stood stunned as if I had slapped him. Once he shook off the metaphorical slap, he rushed toward me and took me firmly by the arms. His eyes bore into mine, making me catch my breath. "I know exactly what happiness is." He leaned in as if he was going to kiss me and, like this morning, I felt his breath so close I could taste it. Live off it. In an instant, though, it was gone. He stole the air from me. He dropped my arms and pushed himself away from me. "I'm just never meant to have it." He turned and headed toward the barn, kicking rocks and swearing as he went.

I wanted to shout, *well, join the club, buddy!* Instead, that tiny strand of hope holding my heart together burst, allowing my heart to shatter. The Loveless curse had struck again. I had to get out of there.

This was no longer my home. As quick as I could, I ran to my Jeep and opened the door, but it wasn't quick enough.

"Emma, did you really think Sawyer would be yours?" Josephine slinked toward me in her ridiculous coral jumpsuit. Where had she been hiding this entire time?

I ignored her and jumped in my Jeep.

She wasn't done with me. "I hope you've finally learned who the Lady of Carrington is now. You're not even a Carrington. Have you ever wondered why your father kept that name from you?"

I grabbed my gut and faced the vile witch. "He didn't keep it from me."

"Didn't he?"

I shook my head, though I was now unsure. How could I be sure of anything? I had just lost almost everyone I loved.

"Oh, you are delusional, aren't you? Have a good night. I know I will." She waved and slithered away toward the barn.

I threw my Jeep in reverse and gunned it, kicking up rocks. I debated on whether I should do a little four-wheeling and run over the snake slinking through the wild grass headed for her son. She wasn't worth jail time, I decided. I tore out of there like I was running from the law. If only. It would have been better than leaving behind those I loved who obviously didn't feel the same way. Racking sobs came while I raced home. It was the same pain I felt when I was told my mother had died. An empty ache consumed me.

When I got home, the torture continued. Reminders of Sawyer were everywhere, from the used towels in my bathroom to the stupid note he left on my pillow.

I can't wait until tonight.

I crumpled the note and threw it across the room. Then I ripped off all my bedding. His clean scent filled my senses. I was washing him away literally and figuratively. The Band-Aid had come off. It hurt worse than I could have ever imagined. But how would I have known? I'd never been in love before. I was going on record as saying it wasn't all it was cracked up to be.

I shoved all my bedding in the washer and put it on hot with lots of detergent. If there was even a hint of his scent on them, I was burning them. I might anyway for the satisfaction.

Next on my reign of terror was my guest bedroom. Anger was better than pain. But, boy, did the pain ever want to overtake me. I was refusing it. I'd known too much of it this past year. Now the person who had helped ease it the most inflicted the worst kind on me. If he'd just rejected me, that would have been one thing, but he hadn't believed in me. He didn't trust me. And he was related to the vilest person I knew.

With my tough-guy attitude, I threw open my guest bedroom door. It was a huge mistake. The first thing that caught my eye was the picture he had placed on the nightstand as if he lived there. It was the same picture of us that I kept on my desk. The one of us in the hot air balloon. I had given him a copy of the photo but didn't know he had it framed. I went from tough to goo in seconds. I crumpled, landing on the lumpy twin-size bed that smelled too much like him. Exhaustion overcame me. I curled up in what I had left of him and cried myself to sleep.

I woke up sore and with a crick in my neck. Maybe I should replace that bed.

In the dawn's early light that filtered through the window blinds to the small room, I was able to come to my senses. I wasn't going to wallow for what I never had. I had enough to mourn with my dad, sisters, and forever my mother. Sickening thoughts of my dad never wanting me to have his name filled me. Was that true? Lately it felt as if it could be. Maybe that's why he'd been so distant since Mom had died. Was it all an act for my mother? More sobbing ensued.

With my last shudder, I stretched and berated myself for not showering last night. I smelled foul. Before I could shower, I had one more thing left to do. I shoved all of Sawyer's belongings in his duffle bag, not stopping to think or reminisce. I didn't even look at the photo of us before I placed it on top and zipped up his bag. I tossed his bag on my porch and texted him.

Me: Your crap is on my porch. You can leave my house key under the flowerpot.

I sounded much braver than I felt.

While I showered, I talked to Jenna on speaker. She wouldn't be put off anymore. She thought the reason I hadn't texted her back last night was because I was with Sawyer. I cleared that up real quick by recounting the awful events from the night before. I ended with me tossing his stuff on the porch.

"So, you broke up," she shouted so I could hear her while showering.

"What?" I shut off the water. "Didn't you hear me?"

"I heard everything. Sounds like a bad breakup to me."

"You have to be dating to break up," I reminded her while grabbing my towel. It felt so good to be clean.

"Please, you two were dating. It was a shame you never got the full physical benefits of it, but you were unconsciously coupling."

"What does that even mean?"

"It means you were totally a couple, but you didn't know you were a couple."

"Not even close. I obviously repulse him."

"I don't believe that."

"You should have seen the way he looked at me last night."

"You mean when you thought he might kiss you?"

"The hate in his eyes was unmistakable." I buried my head in my towel, trying not to cry.

"Honey, that's what happens when you fight with the person you love."

"That makes no sense at all."

"Think about the loss you feel right now. Think about how you felt throwing his things out of your house. Has it stopped you from loving him?"

"I wish," I whimpered. "But he doesn't love me."

"Hate is born from love. I've never hated anyone more than Brad."

"Does Brad know that?"

"I tell him as often as I can, especially when his baby is sitting on my bladder all night while he's fast asleep snoring."

I stepped out of the shower with my towel wrapped around me. "I don't think Sawyer snores," my voice cracked.

"Aww, Em. Do you want me to start slapping some people? Because I will. I'll start with his mom, then your dad and sisters, and last but not least, that fetcher for breaking your heart."

"Don't waste your time. I'm done with them all."

"You're such a liar."

"Probably, but I have to try, right? They all couldn't care less about me."

"They've all lost their minds, obviously, but I have a feeling when they find them, they're going to be sorry, and you better make them all grovel. Like, your dad should buy you and all your friends new cars, especially the ones who are having a baby."

I wiped the steam off my mirror and laughed. "Don't count on that. Besides, Josephine," I could barely say her name, "has some kind of hold on my dad and she's not going to let go without a fight. And I'm tired."

"You need to quit fighting, Em. They should be fighting for you."

My eyes began to water. "I don't see that happening."

"You know I'm always in your corner. Come to the club when your game is over, and we'll break out the karaoke machine. Nothing makes you feel better than singing the Spice Girls' greatest hits. The vat of slime and clothing are totally optional."

"I love you."

"Right back at ya. It's going to be all right, Em."

"I know. I still have Doughboy and Duncan Hines. This may call for Betty, though."

"Go straight to the chick; men are fickle pigs."

"Good thinking, sister. See you later."

I was breaking out the box of Brownie Supreme by my girl, Betty Crocker. I could taste the chocolate frosting now. She and Dr. Pepper would see me through. Those two should really think about hooking up. They would have delicious babies. Meanwhile, I was going to start planning my celibate life in Fiji.

When I left my house for the game, his crap was still on my porch. I hoped he would come and get it today while I wasn't around. Or maybe it would get stolen; I didn't really care. That was a lie, but I was going to try my best to make it true.

The soccer field helped calm my soul. There was something about a sunny day, freshly cut grass, and soccer balls that brought me comfort. Maybe because I only had good memories of playing. It was something I was skilled at and I always had great coaches and friends, supportive parents. Or at least my mom was. Was Dad truly putting on an act? He was an award-winning actor if that was the case. He sure had me fooled. Sawyer had too.

I shook my head. I had to stop thinking about all of them. Jenna was right, I needed to stop fighting for people who didn't think I was worth the effort. Anyone who was happier with Josephine than me deserved her. That even went for her younger son whom I was no longer calling by name or thinking about. From now on he would be the S-word. It seemed fitting.

When my girls started to arrive, my spirits only rose with each hug and high five. I was still loved, not by as many as I thought or hoped, but it was enough.

I was enough.

Chapter Twenty

BETWEEN BETTY, THE Spice Girls, and my *real* best friends, I survived the weekend. Actually, I thrived. My girls won their game, which meant we were headed for the playoffs. So, they might have been a little—or a lot—disappointed that the S-word hadn't shown up. And that he would be breaking his promise to them that if they won the league championship, he would personally pay for the entire team to go to the amusement park in Edenvale.

But it was the first time I'd ever heard any sense come out of Gwendolyn, who, by the way, wore a bikini top to the game on Saturday, but I digress. When the girls were mourning what was probably for some of them their first crush, Gwendolyn blew on her freshly painted nails she'd done while I was doing warm-ups with the girls and said, "My little darlings, there are two things you can count on in life, shoe sales, and that men will disappoint you."

Amen. Gwendolyn and I had different shoe tastes, but when my favorite brand of running shoes went on sale, I was a happy girl.

I wasn't happy, though, that as of Monday evening when I got home from work, a certain duffle bag was still on my front porch and my housekey hadn't been returned. I hoped he had to return to his bee and ant infested place to get some other clothes. While he was there, I hoped he got stung a few more times. The least he could do for me was to remove any reminders of him from my life. That stupid duffle bag was a symbol of the pain I was doing my best to hide from. But his handsome face kept popping up in my head and heart.

I had to tell Dustin today when he called to talk that I was consciously uncoupling with someone who I didn't know I was subconsciously coupled with. He didn't know what that meant, but he hoped I got it straightened out soon because he was hoping I was still considering applying for that position out there because he wanted to take me out, if and when I flew out for an interview. He wasn't even afraid that I was cursed. He obviously didn't know better.

I was torn about applying for that position in Alabama. Between tornadoes and humidity, I wasn't sure Alabama was the place for me. I mentioned to Dustin that I was thinking about moving to Fiji. After he got done laughing, he promised me that Alabama had some of the most beautiful beaches I would ever visit. He offered to be my tour guide. The poor man was a glutton for punishment. He had no idea we would only become friends or worse. Look at Sawy . . . I meant S-word and me now. And my friends were begging me not to go, especially Jenna, who wanted me here to share in the joy of her baby. I wanted that too. And I guess now I didn't have to worry about awkward family gatherings because I no longer had a family, real, step, or otherwise. I rubbed my heart.

How had it come to this? My poor mother was probably in heaven blaming herself. Who we really needed to blame was Dr. Alvarez, my mom's optometrist who had retired. Had my mom not needed a new eye doctor, none of this would have ever happened. I wouldn't have just had the best and worst year of my life. It still would have been the worst, because Mom still would have climbed that ladder, but Josephine wouldn't have come to the funeral if the best part hadn't shown up. I'd still have my family, and I would have had one less person to mourn.

Perhaps I was to blame. I should have given more credence to the curse. I should have known better than to have tried.

I scowled at the duffle bag one more time before I entered my garage. If it wasn't gone in a few days, I was tossing it in the garbage.

It was a good thing I was already meeting Bridget for ice cream; I needed some, stat. Though I had to admit I was a tad hesitant to go now. It's not that I didn't like her—I really did—but I wondered if I should cut all ties with anyone associated with you know who. And I wasn't too sure how Warren would feel about me accusing his son of stealing and cheating. Deep in the pit of my stomach I knew it was him. I was sick thinking Ashton might do it to more guests, or worse, my sisters. I figured it didn't hurt to have more friends, so I agreed to meet her at a cute shop named Ice Cream Social and decided I wouldn't talk about either son or what had happened last Friday. I mean, it's not like you know who was talking to them, and I had a feeling Ashton wouldn't want to say a word about it either.

I knew Bridget and I would be lifelong friends when she ordered a brownie sundae and told them to go heavy on the hot fudge. We were soul sisters. I ordered a Dr. Pepper float, heavy on the DP and ice cream. At first it was going great with pleasantries of *how are you?* and *how was your business trip?* Easy answers. Okay, so I lied when I told her I was fantastic. I did my best to keep her talking about her job as a court reporter. You didn't meet one of those every day, I guess unless you were a lawyer or judge, but as I was neither, I found it fascinating. She'd been the assigned court reporter for some pretty scary cases.

After my tenth question, she finally reached her hand across the table and rested it on mine. "Do you want to tell me why Sawyer called his dad demanding to meet with him?"

I stared down at my half-eaten float and shrugged. "I don't know. I guess he wants to talk."

A small laugh escaped her. "We figured that much out. The question is why he's blaming his dad for taking you away from him."

My head popped up. "I don't know what you mean," my voice cracked.

She patted my hand. "What's going on, honey?"

"Have Sa . . . I mean, have father and son met yet?"

She narrowed her eyes. "Oh, this is bad. You won't even say his name."

"I know it's juvenile. I'm just trying to forget about him."

"How's that going for you?"

I gave her a crooked smile. "Not so well."

"I've been there. Those King men, they get under your skin and take your heart hostage."

I nodded. That's exactly how I felt.

"Did you guys break up?"

"Why does everyone keep saying that? We were never a couple."

"Uh-huh." She grinned. "You two weren't fooling anyone except maybe yourselves."

I took a big bite of my ice cream soaked in Dr. Pepper. Food at its finest. Bridget waited for me to revel and then swallow.

"Have they talked?" I asked.

She shook her head. "Not yet. I think Warren is a little afraid. He wanted to get some background information first."

"So, you're his spy."

"I'm his partner and your friend."

"I could use a few more of those after last weekend." The tears I had been so good about not shedding filled my eyes. I regurgitated the entire ugly affair, but made sure she knew I didn't divulge the conversation we'd had before I went to Alabama. "I didn't tell Sawyer,"—there I said his name—"what you told me. I only recommended he talk to his dad and get the full picture. And I'm sorry if you and Warren hate me now for thinking Ashton is a cheating thief." I leaned back in my seat and let out a deep breath.

Bridget dropped her hot fudge covered spoon in her mostly eaten dessert bowl. "You had quite the weekend, didn't you? I'm so sorry about your family and Sawyer. Don't worry about Warren and me; we aren't going anywhere." She sighed. "Unfortunately, what you've said about Ashton isn't all that surprising."

My brows jumped to my hairline. "It's not?"

She hemmed and hawed a bit. "Warren has been worried that Ashton wasn't exactly truthful about why he got divorced and had to leave Vegas in such a hurry. He asked to borrow a pretty good sum of money when he got here."

"Did Warren give it to him?"

Bridget shook her head. "He gave him a few hundred dollars and a place to stay until he started working for your dad."

"Does Warren know what kind of trouble he was in?"

"Not exactly, but Warren overheard a few conversations that made him think he owed a lot of money to a lot of people."

"Is Warren in contact with Ashton's ex-wife?"

"We never met her. They weren't married that long. It was one of those quickie Vegas weddings. We offered to come visit them or to have them visit us, but Ashton always had some excuse as to why that wouldn't work."

This was fantastic freaking news. Ashton had portrayed his marriage and divorce much differently to me. He'd acted so heartbroken. He'd even cried and said they'd known each other forever, so it came as a shock to him when she left him with nothing.

I was at a complete loss for words. There was nothing I could do. My family had made their choice, and it wasn't me. "I don't even know what to say."

Neither of us had to say anything because, lo and behold, a blonde goddess entered unexpectedly. That pretty much summed up my life anymore, a series of unexpected events. At first, she didn't see me, which I was grateful for and hoping to keep it that way. I watched Shelby walk with purpose in her heels and tiny wrap dress across the tiled floor to the counter. Both teenage boys manning the ice cream scoops began fighting over who would serve her.

Shelby charmed them, "Now boys, I'll take two scoops of your nonfat peach frozen yogurt, so you can both help me."

I couldn't be friends with someone who came into an ice cream shop and ordered nonfat frozen yogurt. Why was that even a thing? What joy would you get out of eating that? Apparently, Shelby must have gotten some pleasure out of it because as soon as they handed her the paper bowl with two very generous scoops, she took a large bite, closed her eyes, and sighed as if she'd had a bad day. When she opened them they lasered right in on me. I probably shouldn't have been staring at her from our small table near the entrance.

"Oh, my goodness." Shelby began prancing toward me. "Emma, sugar, this is an answer to my prayers," she spoke loudly. "I've been wondering if I should call you and here you are." She landed in front

My Not So Wicked Stepbrother

of us and looked between Bridget and me. "Oh, I'm so sorry, I'm interrupting you."

I couldn't help but be nice to her. There was something about her, and dang if she wasn't polite. "That's okay. This is my friend Bridget." No need to mention how she was affiliated with my former friend.

Shelby gave Bridget a warm smile. "It's a pleasure to meet you. Any friend of my friend Emma is a friend of mine. This woman saved me from the fullest bladder I've ever had."

Bridget gave me a curious smile. Mine in return said I would tell her later.

"Do you mind if I join y'all?" She didn't wait for our response—she set down her frozen yogurt on our table and grabbed one of the white wooden chairs from a nearby table. She sat down and let out a deep breath. "Mylanta, has it been a day. I've been feeling awful all day."

"Are you sick?" I asked.

She reached out and took my hand. "Darlin', I am heartsick. I owe you an apology."

"What for?"

She took another bite of what I assumed was basically orange colored ice. No way that nonfat crap had any flavor. The way she savored it, though, made me wonder. She swallowed and breathed out. "I'm a horrible, awful friend." She looked between Bridget and me. "This might be a delicate, private situation."

I was more than perplexed. "I'm sure whatever it is you have to say, you can say it in front of Bridget."

Shelby's shoulders relaxed. "Okay, then here it goes." She reached out and took both my hands. "Emma, why didn't you tell me that you and Sawyer were a thing?"

For not wanting to talk about the man, that was all I was doing. I pulled my hands away from her delicate, perfectly polished ones. "That's because we weren't."

Bridget rolled her eyes.

"Now, Emma, I know that to be an untruth, and here I was going on and on about him and fawning all over him. My goodness, you must hate me."

Oh, I had tried to hate her, but how do you hate pure, sweet perfection? "I don't hate you. Like I said, there was nothing between us."

Bridget coughed out, "Liar."

Shelby gave her a dazzling smile. "I knew it."

"How do you know that, Shelby?"

"Well, on Saturday I asked Sawyer to dinner and I was thrilled he said yes because he'd turned me down before." She bit her lip. "This was before I figured it all out."

I was suddenly feeling ill. I knew I shouldn't care that he had dinner with her, but I did.

"There we were in that nice chateau up on the mountain. Lovely, by the way, and the food was fantastic. I could tell he wasn't himself from the beginning, so I did my best to cheer him up by . . ." her face tinged pink, "you know, never mind."

My mind was swirling with unsavory possibilities. She was lucky I didn't kick her stick legs under the table.

"My point," Shelby continued, "is all that sweet man talked about was you, Miss Emma."

I tucked some hair behind my ear. "What did he say?" Not like I really cared, but I thought I should at least ask to be polite.

She pursed her pretty pink lips together. "First, he was kind of angry, which surprised me. He was lamenting something fierce about you just not understanding, though he wouldn't say what about. Then as the night went on, every little thing reminded him of you. Like when he looked over the menu and said, 'If Emma were here, she'd want to me to order the shrimp scampi so that she could order the ribeye and we could share.'" Shelby flashed me a smile. "He did order that shrimp scampi and only ate half of it."

"He did?" That sounded good right now. I wonder if he had the other half boxed up to go. What a dumb thought. I shouldn't care.

"Yes, ma'am. That should have told me all I needed to know," she added, embarrassed, "but I kept thinking you were stepbrother and stepsister. Then today it all clicked when he was downright ugly with some of our staff today and not as caring and personable as he normally is with his patients. It started reminding me of when I found out that my fiancé had been cheating on me. I'm ashamed to say how unpleasant I was to be around." She placed her hand across her chest.

I couldn't picture her being anything but sparkling and kind.

"I started thinking back about all the times I'd seen you together and I remembered the first time I saw you two together at the café and I thought you were a sweet couple before I knew about how you were related. Sawyer doted on you. I realize now he did that a lot. He always wanted to be near you, make sure you were taken care of. My Ryder used to do the same for me." She began to tear up.

My eyes started leaking too. He really had doted on me. Had I been reading him wrong this entire time?

Shelby took my hand. "I'm so sorry, Emma. You must think I'm a hussy."

"I don't think that at all." Okay, so maybe I had, but I didn't now. "Sawyer and I were never really together, and we never will be. You have nothing to be sorry for."

"Oh, but I do. I was going on and on about him that night in the tent. And there you were being so nice to me and listening to my personal pain and teaching me how to pee in the woods."

Bridget snorted a bit. I was liking her more and more. Any woman who could snort was a winner.

Shelby took a breath and held up her hand as if she was taking an oath. "I promise from here on out, I will only have a professional relationship with Sawyer and I will do everything in my power to see that you two are rightfully back together like you belong."

"No. No. That won't be necessary."

"It is absolutely necessary. That's what best friends are for."

When had we become best friends?

"Shelby, really, there's nothing you can do."

"Oh, honey, you have no idea what I can do."

"Whatever it is, I'm in." Bridget gave me a wicked grin.

I shook my head. "Ladies, if neither of you have noticed, my last name is Loveless. It's my curse, and nothing anybody does will ever change that." Not even my mom could.

Shelby gave me a coy smile. "You know what my memaw used to say about curses?"

I shook my head.

"She said they are nothing but self-fulfilled prophecies—they only work if you believe them."

Well, I was a believer.

Chapter Twenty-One

I WOULD HAVE thought talking to Shelby was the most interesting conversation I was going to have all week, but I was wrong. Again.

My phone rang the next day while I was in my dingy office working on some analytical data. I was surprised to see Macey's name on the screen. I ignored it at first, thinking she must have butt dialed me with that bony thing she passed off as a rear end. Besides, I had nothing to say to her. She called me three more times. It finally annoyed me enough that I answered.

"Why are you calling me?"

Sniffles filled my ear. "Emma," Macey's pathetic voice squeaked.

Someone died. I knew it. Why else would she call? Was it awful that I had a list of who I was hoping it would be? Then panic set in. Please don't let it be Marlowe or Dad. Sure, I didn't like them right now, but I loved them even if they didn't love me.

"What's wrong, Macey?"

"We need your help."

"We?"

"Marlowe and me."

"Why are you calling me for help? Why don't you ask Josephine or Ashton?"

Macey's sniffling increased. "They can't help us."

"Why?"

"Because no one knows where Ashton is, and Josephine and Dad aren't speaking to each other."

Oh, really? Huh. "I still don't understand why you are calling me. Didn't you tell me to mind my own business?"

"I didn't say that. Marlowe did."

"What did I say?" Marlowe yelled in the background.

"You told Emma to mind her own business."

"I told you she wouldn't help us," Marlowe responded.

"Please, Emma. We need you."

"You both have a lot of nerve asking me for help right now. What is it you need help with anyway?" I thought I should ask before I outright told them no.

"I know we haven't been very nice to you. I'm sorry."

"Because you want my help?"

"No, Emma, everything is a mess right now. Almost all the wranglers have quit, and Dad can't find anyone to replace Frankie. No one in town wants to work at the Ranch. Several guests have left."

I wasn't surprised, but it broke my heart. "What can I do about that?"

"That's not what we need help with. We've made a big mistake at the store."

"What kind of a mistake?"

"The thousands of dollars kind."

"What did you do?"

"We don't know," she cried. "We were balancing the cash drawer and reconciling the receipts and we are off by over $6,000."

Holy crap. I didn't know they made that kind of money. "How much do you make in a day?"

"Normally around $2500 in the summer."

"Then how can you be off by that much?"

She paused. And paused some more.

"Macey?"

"We haven't balanced the drawer in a while or—"

"How long is a while?"

"Like, two months."

This was why when Mom was alive, she wouldn't let Dad give them the money to open their own store. "Macey, you can't run a business like that."

"We thought our point of sale software would keep track of everything, so it didn't matter."

I wanted to bang my head against the desk.

"You're smart. You know how to do all this stuff. Will you please help us? If Dad finds out right now, he'll probably make us close the store."

"It sounds like you would deserve it."

"I know," she sniffled.

Marlowe got on the phone. "Emma," she took a deep breath and let it out slowly, "we know we've been brats to you. If you don't help us, we'll understand."

I'd never heard Marlowe grovel before. She wasn't all that good at it, to be honest, but for her I guess it was something. I debated on whether I should help the brats or not. I wanted to tell them no, but then I heard Mom's voice in my head saying, "Sometimes you have to be the one to start mending the fence even if you didn't break it. Never be afraid of being the bigger person." Mom's final assault on me was to remind me what was written on her headstone, *Where there is great love there are miracles.*

"Fine," I breathed out. "I can be there in about an hour." I wasn't expecting any miracles, but I knew Mom was. She always did.

"You're the best," Macey shouted.

"Thank you," Marlowe whispered.

On the drive to Carrington Cove, all I could think about was what the girls had said about the Ranch. What had happened to Dad? How could he let Mom's dream die such a cruel death? What kind of spell had Josephine cast on him? It had to be in the bedroom, and that thought grossed me out. Scrubbing that from my memory and moving on. Where had Ashton disappeared to? Was Sawyer seeing all this? Did he really think this was happiness? I would never know. I hadn't heard from him and I wasn't planning on it. He hadn't even picked up his stupid bag on my porch.

Now here I was bailing my sisters out.

I parallel parked in front of M&M on Main. A chalkboard closed sign hung on the door even though it was only four in the afternoon. They must really be in a state to close their store early, especially with so many tourists flocking the streets. I had to admit their storefront was darling with a striped black and white awning and a simple glass and black door with their insignia on it. An array of all white clothes on black mannequins was displayed in the windows in an artsy sort of way. Their storefront was a lot like them. A beautiful exterior, but the substance inside was lacking. I knew Mom worried that Macey and Marlowe let the Carrington name and looks go to their heads. She wanted them to work for this store. Work for something.

I took a deep breath of the mountain air before I knocked on their door.

Macey rushed to open it and pull me in. "Thank you, Emma." She wrapped her skinny arms around me. She was so much taller than me that my face landed in her boobs.

I tried to lighten the moment. "There's a lot of padding in your bra."

She pulled away. "We didn't luck out and get Mom's boobs like you did."

I looked down at my ample, but not too ample girls. Huh. I'd never thought about it. I guess I did have a pretty nice set.

Marlowe came out of the back holding a fistful of receipts. "We're still off."

"Let's see what we can find."

Both of the girls gave me sheepish grins.

Their back office area was a mess with receipts and cash spread out in piles across both of their desks. I had to roll my eyes.

"Where have you been keeping all this cash? Don't you make daily bank deposits?"

"We have a safe," Macey offered.

I rubbed my head. This was going to be a long night.

As I started sorting through their mess, I found one of their biggest problems was they were each taking cash for personal use and leaving notes saying how much they took. I warned them to stop doing that. They were begging to be audited by the IRS. They had no idea what that meant.

I was there so long we ordered Chinese food. While I ate and scoured through each and every receipt and report from the last two months trying to find the difference, I decided I might as well be bold and try and get some answers about what was going on at home. They did live at the Ranch, after all, and had a front row seat to what was going on.

"Why is everyone quitting?"

A look of guilt passed between my sisters. At first they shrugged. I gave them a pointed look. "Come on."

Macey dropped her chopsticks. "No one likes Josephine. And Ashton . . ."

Marlowe nudged her and shook her head.

"Ashton what?"

Marlowe curled her lips. "It's just stupid rumors. Ashton's a good guy."

"Are you sure about that?"

"Yes," Marlowe was quick to answer.

"Then where is he?"

"Well, you would want to leave too if people were saying . . . well, saying the stuff you accused him of."

I set my food to the side and picked up a balance statement sheet. "Yeah, well, I know what it's like to want to leave home and not come back."

It was silent for several minutes. I didn't bother to even look at my sisters. I was here to help them sort their mess out and then I was out of there.

Macey finally broke the silence. "Do you really think Ashton robbed that couple and . . . you know?"

"It's called sex," Marlowe said bluntly.

I looked up from the report, still unable to find their discrepancy. "I do."

"You have no proof," Marlowe challenged me.

I decided to focus on Macey. "Why are you asking?"

Her face burned red and she started to shake. "It's just . . . it's just . . . we met here a few times." And before I knew it, she ran toward me and curled up on my lap like a child and started bawling.

I wrapped my arms around her. "Macey, what happened?"

Marlowe was now shaking too, but in a furious sort of manner. "What were you two doing here?"

"Stuff," Macey eked against my chest.

My stomach churned. "Macey, please tell me you weren't."

"He said he loved me," she wailed.

Marlowe jumped up. "That lying, cheating . . ." She grabbed her phone.

"Marlowe, put your phone down," I demanded. "Were you seeing him too?"

"What?" Macey sat up and rubbed her eyes.

Marlowe lowered her phone, but she wouldn't answer.

"Marlowe, were you seeing him, and did you bring him here too?"

She threw her phone on the desk. "We met all over."

That made Macey curl right back up into me and lose it.

"You didn't answer the question," I had to yell over Macey's wailing.

"Yes!" she barked.

"Did he know about the kind of cash you kept here?"

"Maybe." Macey snuggled more into my chest.

I had a feeling as to why they were off by so much. "We are going to go through every receipt and report and then you are going to call the police and then Dad."

"The police?" Macey cried.

"If my suspicions are right, you've been robbed." And of more than just money. This entire situation made me feel dirty and like I needed a shower.

"Emma, I'm so sorry," Macey cried. "I thought he loved me. He was my first. He told me I was special and that's why I couldn't tell anyone."

Let that be a lesson. If a man is keeping you secret, you aren't his only one.

I wanted to kill him.

Marlowe wasn't devastated like Macey; she was enraged. She started listing out loud how she was going to make him pay. She started by pulling out their security camera tapes. At least they were smart enough to have those.

While Marlowe searched those for evidence, I went through their paper trail. To my dismay, they both started comparing notes about their rendezvous with Ashton. Marlowe confessed that the weekend she disappeared she had met the sleazeball in Aspen. It was the same weekend of our camping trip. That pig was sneaking off, not for a job interview, but to hook up with my sister. The thought made my skin crawl.

By the time I left that night, we couldn't account for $4,500. I found the other $1,500 and change in the form of credit card transactions that they hadn't accounted for. I made them write out a deposit slip for cash they hadn't deposited and promise me that they would take it to the bank's night depository.

Marlowe was still searching their tapes for evidence. Apparently, there were plenty of instances where they had both brought him here after closing, so there was a lot to look through. I left them to it. I couldn't stand the thought of having to watch the conniving man take advantage of my sisters.

Before I left, Marlowe took a break and put her arms around me. She hadn't done that in forever. "I miss Mom," her voice cracked.

I did too. Now more than ever.

Chapter Twenty-Two

I MISSED MOM so much that I decided to sneak onto the Ranch and visit her. Josephine may have stolen a lot of things from me, but she wasn't taking this. I took the back road and turned off my lights when I got close to Shannon's Meadow. There was no need for artificial light. I knew the way, and the moon was aiding and abetting me tonight.

When I got out of my Jeep parked just past Mom's cabin, I noticed how deafeningly quiet it was. Grady's band wasn't playing in the background. The sounds of happy guests were only echoes of the past now. It was as if the Ranch had died. I felt my mother mourning it and begging me to fix it. What could I do? "Love," I heard her whisper in the breeze.

"I'm Loveless," I whispered back.

I swore I heard her laugh. "That's what you think."

I shook my head at her, or at me, because either she was delusional or I was for believing I could hear her. I tiptoed through the tall grass and wildflowers toward the gate leading to my mother. That gate opened and closed, startling me. I grabbed my phone and turned on the flashlight to see what or who made the noise. A tall who of a person stared back at me, just as surprised to see me as I was to see him. I'd thought he'd all but forgotten my mother. I glowered at him before turning and running back to my Jeep.

"Emma, stop," Dad called.

I refused to listen to him, so he proved to me that he could still outrun me. It was those long Carrington legs. For a middle-aged man in cowboy boots, he could sure move. He was to me in no time, wrapping his arms around me.

"Emma," he whispered.

"Let go of me." I tried wriggling out of his arms.

"No." He held on tighter.

"Please let go," I cried against his chest.

"No, Emma Bear."

He hadn't called me that in forever. I burst into tears against his chest. "Why? Just why?" That's all I wanted to know. Why had he brought that awful woman into our lives? Why had he forgotten about our mother? And did he ever really think of himself as my father?

His strong arms held on for dear life while he rested his chin on my head. "You remind me so much of your mother it hurts sometimes."

"Is that why you hate me?"

He leaned away and looked down at me with regret-filled eyes. "I could never hate you."

"Why didn't you ever give me your last name?" That question had been eating at me for the last several days.

He closed his eyes and let out a heavy breath. "I wanted to." He let go of me only to take my hand. "Let's go sit on the porch and talk."

We turned toward Mom's cabin with the pink door, but something was wrong. Even in the dark I could tell the door was the wrong color. I let go of Dad's hand and raced to the now blood-red door. The smell of new paint hit me like a slap in the face. I went for the thermometer to grab the spare key only to find it was missing. I turned and unleashed my fury on my father, who stood on the steps looking at the door with wide eyes.

"How dare you let her touch this cabin! Was it not enough that she's ruined everything else, you had to give her this too?" I started to march off the porch until I saw the tears leaking out of my father's eyes.

"Dammit, I told her not to come near this place." In defeat, he sat down on the top step with his face in hands. "I've made a mess out of things."

Amen to that. I sat down next to him. "Why her?" I went back to my original question, or the one I really should have asked to begin with.

Dad lifted his head and slowly turned my way. Tired, red eyes stared at me. "I miss your mom."

"So you replaced her with a psycho?" I was past trying to play nice.

"I could never replace your mother. She was one of a kind."

"Yes, she was." I wiped away my tears. "So why? Why Josephine?"

He stared into the starry Colorado night. "For a while, she helped me forget."

"You wanted to forget Mom?"

"I wanted to forget the pain of losing her."

I leaned my head on his shoulder. "Yeah, well, you could have picked someone better for the job."

He turned and kissed my head. "I know."

"She said you withheld your name from me. Is that true?"

His entire body went rigid. "Damn her." He put his arm around me and pulled me closer. "I never adopted you because I felt guilty. Anders was the best man I'd ever known. The kind of friend who would give you his last dollar and rush into a burning building to save your life. He loved you and your mom so much. I fell in love with both of you, too. I'm ashamed to say it was before he died. I never acted on those feelings until he was gone. Your mother never knew. The least I felt like I could do was let you have Anders's name since I got everything else. Honey, I'd give you anything you ask for, including my name if that's what you want, but believe me, you got the better man's name."

I nestled into him like I used to. "Dad, what are you going to do?"

"I've got to fix this mess, don't I?"

"Yes, you do." He had no idea how much of a mess it was. I was going to let my sisters fill him in on the pieces he was missing.

"I'm sorry, honey. Your mom was having some words with me tonight. She's not all that happy with me."

"I don't suppose she would be."

"I was blind, but not anymore."

"I'm glad to hear that. I've missed you."

He pulled me closer. "Kid, I've missed you. You are the daughter of my heart. If making it legal will make you feel better, let's do it, but . . ."

"But what?"

He chuckled. "I have a feeling there's another man who would like to change your last name."

I popped up. "Who are you talking about?"

"Emma," he brushed back my hair, "are you blind like your old man?"

"What do you mean?"

"Sawyer. I like that kid."

I grabbed my heart and swallowed. "Dad," I shook my head, "he doesn't, I mean we're not—"

Dad took my hands. "I've seen the way you two look and act around each other. I'm sorry if my *relationship* with his mother has done anything to impede your own relationship."

"Well, it hasn't helped much. He's not very happy with me right now."

Dad shook his head. "Nah. I think, like me, he knows the truth deep down. We've both been fools. We've both hurt you."

I nodded with tears in my eyes.

"I am sorry, Emma Bear, the Lady of Carrington Ranch."

"I think I'm going to start signing my Christmas cards like that."

Dad laughed. "Your mom would love that."

Then I was for sure doing it.

"You know what else she would love?"

"What?"

"To see you with Sawyer. She thought he was the one."

"I did too," I choked out.

"So, what are you going to do about it?"

I shrugged. "I don't know if there's anything I can do. I'm not even sure he feels the same way."

"Your old man may be wrong about a lot of things lately, but take my word for it and your mother's—he loves you."

"How does mom know?"

He rested his hand on my cheek. "You don't think she's watching over you?"

My tears trickled down his hand.

He kissed my forehead. "I love you."

"I love you, too."

See, I told you, where there is love there are miracles, Mom whispered in the breeze.

Chapter Twenty-Three

ALL DAY WEDNESDAY I felt like singing "Ding-Dong! The Witch Is Dead." Well, she wasn't exactly dead, but Dad said last night while we talked on the porch that he was filing for a legal separation, which was just as good, in my mind. Was it awful that I would love to be there when he told Josephine, to capture the look on her collagenized face? It was going to be even better after Dad told her that he and the girls went to the sheriff's office to file a report. Per the girls, Dad was on the warpath.

It was about time.

The only damper to it all was, I knew this would hurt Sawyer. He thought our parents were happy and that his brother was a good guy. I guess, in turn, it hurt me too, because I knew my chances with him now were zilch, nada, nothing. Even if I did have the heavenliest of angels watching over me. I'm telling you, my last name meant business. Maybe I should take Dad up on his offer to become a Carrington, but after what he said last night about Anders, I didn't know if I could. It was all I had of Anders, even if it really had been a crap parting gift on his part. It was the gift that kept on giving. But Anders was a good man, even if he had left me Loveless.

With Josephine on her way out, I decided I better get on my Lady of Carrington Ranch duties and get the anniversary gift baskets out for

July. I couldn't have Mom blaming herself for anyone's breakup. I pulled out her chocolate truffle recipe. Her thumbprint smudge could still be seen on it. It was weird how much I treasured seeing it each time I pulled it out.

While I was finely chopping the chocolate and singing loudly to the Backstreet Boys, my doorbell rang. I popped a piece of chocolate in my mouth and headed for the door. I peeked through the blinds on the door to see who was interrupting my groove. Oh crap. I swallowed the chocolate the wrong way and started to splutter. What was he doing here? He was probably getting his stuff, so why did he ring the doorbell?

Sawyer pounded on the door. "I know you're in there, Em. I can hear you. By the way, put your arms up."

Dang him. I put my arms up and stopped coughing enough to say, "Take your stuff and leave my key."

"Emma, please let me in."

"Go away, Sawyer."

"You forgot something in there that belongs with me," he yelled.

Of course I did. "Well, it must not be that important if you've lived without it for several days. If I find it, I'll mail it to you," I shouted back.

"Em," his voice turned low, "she's the most important thing to me and I don't want to live without her anymore."

I leaned my forehead against the door and breathed in and out several times.

"It's you, by the way, if you didn't catch on to that," he said when I didn't respond.

"How can you say that? You can't even stand the thought of kissing me."

"Are you crazy? All I've wanted to do for the last year is kiss you."

"Friday morning in my bed, when you touched my stomach, it grossed you out so much you didn't kiss me."

"I don't know what you're talking about. That morning in your bed, all I thought was how warm and soft you were and how I wanted to touch every part of you. I knew if I kissed you, I wouldn't want to stop, and I didn't want you to think that's the only reason I wanted you because it's not even close to the truth."

Whoa. Whoa. I felt like I was going to internally combust. Was he saying what I thought he was saying? "You want to have sex with me?"

"When the time is right, I want to make love to you, Em, all day, every day."

"We would take snack breaks and naps, right? I mean, that could get exhausting and you know how much I love food. And we both have jobs."

"Em," he chuckled, "will you please open the door?"

I rubbed the door taking in deep breaths and letting them out. "Sawyer, you didn't believe me," I choked out.

He paused. "I'm sorry. I've been waiting so long to tell you how I feel about you, but between you grieving your mother and our parents doing their thing, it seemed like I was never going to get my chance. I kept waiting for you to come to terms with our family situation because I was afraid you wouldn't give us a shot until you did. So, when everything blew up last weekend, I thought I would never get my chance. I'm sorry. I didn't want to believe those things about my family. But I've always believed in you, Em."

I clasped my hands together and prayed this was all true. "How do you feel about me?"

"Open the door and find out."

The internal struggle was real. More than anything, I wanted to whip that door open, but I had been here before—just when I thought things would work out, the curse of my last name struck. I was afraid if I opened the door I'd have an aneurysm, or maybe a plane would fall out of the sky and land on my house. Or worse, Sawyer would hold out his hand and be like, psych, we're only friends. But he did say someday he wanted to make love to me.

"Open the door!" That was my mother, not Sawyer.

I looked up and smiled. *You're so pushy.*

I took a deep breath and unlocked the door. Before I could open it all the way, Sawyer pushed his way in and picked me up. His lips crushed mine before I knew what was happening. I caught on real quick as I savored the feel of his warm lips. I wrapped my arms around his neck and my legs around his body, drawing myself as close to him as I could. His tongue parted my lips while he backed me up against my wall, knocking a picture down. Amid the crashing glass he groaned hungrily as his tongue delved deeper and his hands ran through my hair. He tasted every bit as good as I thought he would—sweet and savory, my favorite combination.

"Em," he breathed out my name, exciting me. He began trailing kisses down my neck. His warm, sensuous lips made me gasp. He kissed the hollow of my neck before making his way back up where he kissed the corner of my mouth. He paused to peer into my eyes while brushing away some of the happy tears gliding down my cheek. "You're so beautiful. I love you."

I could hardly believe my ears. "Well, that escalated quickly."

He chuckled before kissing my nose. "I was hoping for a different response."

"Oh. Did I forget to mention that I love you? So much." I could hardly say it without choking up.

"I'm glad to hear you say that, because you've never told me how to walk on water."

"I thought you forgot."

He rested his warm hand on my cheek and I leaned into it. "Never. I was only waiting for the right moment to ask you out again."

"Is this the right moment?"

His thumb glided across my cheek. "Will you please go on a date with me?"

I couldn't keep from smiling. "When?"

"Now." He brushed back my hair.

I nodded. "What do you have in mind?"

"Food will definitely be involved."

"You speak my love language." I kissed him, realizing I could and how amazing that was. "So food. What else?"

"Definitely more of this." He leaned in and pressed his lips against mine. His tongue danced across my lips, making me shiver. "I'm sorry

I didn't ask you if you wanted to touch my papillae before I shoved my tongue in your mouth."

I laughed at him. "I told you, that would have been a mood killer."

He narrowed his eyes. "Would it have really?"

I touched his cheeks and ran my hands through his hair, all because I could. "Coming from you, no."

He was staring at me as if he was amazed by all this too. "Let's go to dinner. I want to look across the table at you and know you're finally mine and that we'll share more than our food."

"I think that is the most attractive thing anyone has ever said to me. You know, besides the whole I love you thing." I grinned.

He gently set me down. "Are you ready to go?"

"Just a second. I need to grab something and call in a favor."

"I'll be waiting." He flashed me his beautiful smile.

I dashed upstairs, excited about everything. I had been anxiously waiting to show him how to walk on water. I wanted it to be a surprise, so I grabbed a bandanna to act as a blindfold for when the time came tonight. While I was shoving it in my bag, I swore I heard my mom say, *I told you so.* I was happy to let her take full credit.

After my quick phone call to an old family friend to make sure the place I needed tonight would be available, I rushed back down to be with my man. That's right, he was all mine. Walking out my door together felt entirely different than it ever had, though we had done it dozens of times before. It probably had something to do with the way he held my hand and ran his thumb across it, or maybe when he kissed me deeply before opening the door to his crappy old truck. Or maybe it was the way I sat in the middle like we were from Shelby's neck of the woods and we couldn't keep our hands off each other.

Or perhaps it was the way he stared at me contentedly from across the table at dinner where we shared smothered burritos and pollo loco, as if this was the way it was always meant to be.

Sawyer grinned at me. "You know, Shelby is a huge fan of yours."

"Is that so?"

"Not so much of me anymore. She threatened to have me fired unless I came to my senses and took the best girl ever off the market, as she put it. She said if firing my butt didn't work, she would bring out the big guns. Whatever that means."

I laughed. "You know, I think the Southern Belle isn't all that bad."

Sawyer chuckled before reaching across the table and taking my hands. "You have another fan too. I talked to my dad last night."

Funny. I talked to my dad last night too, but I didn't mention it since it involved leaving his mother. That was a weird bridge we would have to cross when the time came. That one and the one where my dad was trying to get his brother's butt thrown in jail. Oh, yeah, and the disgusting one of his brother sleeping with both of my sisters. For now, though, I was going to stay off all those bridges and savor this first date with my Sawyer.

"How did that go?" I gave his hand a squeeze for support.

He stretched his neck from side to side. "I'm not going to lie, it was tough."

"I'm sorry."

"No, I'm sorry. My dad said I was a fool for taking so long to let you know how I feel about you. He was right. He said some other things, too, that I didn't want to hear."

"About your mom?" I bit my lip.

Sawyer nodded.

"You don't have to tell me."

"I want to tell you everything."

"Then I'm here to listen."

He lifted my hand to his lips. "I love you. I can't say that enough."

"I'm not going to stop you." I couldn't quit smiling.

He held my hand tight as if he needed the strength. "After talking to my dad, I've been thinking a lot about how anger can skew your memories of the past. How it creates tunnel vision. Now I'm angry at both my parents and myself for not believing what was before my eyes when I was growing up."

"I don't think you should be too hard on yourself. Every kid wants to believe their family is happy and it's difficult when you know it's not. I know I can't completely relate to you, but I do understand how that feels. I find it helps to have someone to help you work through it.

Someone who loves you and wants more than anything for you to be happy."

"Em, I'm never happier than when I'm with you."

"The feeling is mutual. You've helped me more than you know this past year, even if I was in love with you and thinking the entire time that you only wanted to be my friend, but I totally forgive you for that." I grinned.

He leaned over the table and kissed me. The back of his hand ran down my cheek. "Had I known that's how you felt I wouldn't have wasted a second." He sat back down. "You know what? Let's not waste any more time talking about our parents right now because I'm not going to let their decisions affect mine anymore. I don't care who they marry or don't marry; they aren't going to keep me from you."

"Well, then I think we should get out of here." I pulled the bandanna out of my bag. "You're going to need to wear this."

His mouth dropped. It took him a second to compose himself. "I always knew dating you was going to be a lot of fun."

I tossed him the blindfold. "We're not going to have that kind of fun . . . yet."

"Em, I meant what I said earlier. You and me, this is a forever kind of thing for me, and I want to do it right."

Every butterfly in the world took off in my stomach. The one he didn't find repulsive at all. It felt like a dream, but I knew I was awake because as good as my dreams of him had been over the last year, this was better than I could have ever imagined. "I better keep my promise to you then."

I drove us in his truck all the way out to Carrington Cove. I would have loved to do this in Shannon's Meadow, but we would have had to wait until winter for that to happen and I was done waiting. My life with Sawyer began now.

I helped my blindfolded man out of his truck.

"Where are we?" he asked.

"You'll see. Hold on tight to me."

"Your wish is my command." He pulled me closer.

We entered the establishment of one of my favorite places

growing up. The owner, Marvin, was there waiting for us at the door to unlock it since they had been closed for a few hours.

"Emma." Marvin grinned at me with his old, stained teeth. "Who do you have with you?"

"This is . . . my boyfriend, Sawyer." Holy crap, I loved saying that.

Sawyer held out his hand even though he had no idea that Marvin was nowhere near him. "Nice to meet you."

Marvin shook his head at us and laughed. "I'm not even going to ask what you're going to do, but the place is all yours. I'll be in my office not listening to or watching a thing; just let me know when you leave."

I had a feeling there were going to be some kinky rumors about us going around Carrington Cove very soon, the least of those being that we were stepsiblings. Though hopefully not for long.

"Thanks, Marvin," I called out to his retreating figure.

"It's kind of cold. Where have you taken me?"

"Don't worry, I plan to warm you up very soon."

Sawyer groaned. "If I haven't mentioned it before, I really love you."

"Good, because I really love you. Now take my hand and be prepared to learn my ways."

"Now that you've officially introduced me as your boyfriend, will you change your Facebook relationship status?"

"There's totally room on there for you with all my other loves. I'll even put you above Poppin' Fresh."

"What about Betty?"

"We'll see how good you are tonight and then I'll decide."

"Consider it a done deal then."

Dang, he was sexy. I shivered, and not because it was chilly.

"It's getting colder." Sawyer pulled me closer.

"Be careful." I led him around the benches to one of the entrances. "Are you ready for this?"

"Yes, but I'm still not sure how anyone can walk on water."

"You have good balance, so it will be easy, I promise."

"Okay," he sounded skeptical.

"Are you ready?" I reached up to take off his blindfold. When it dropped, he looked around at the small ice-skating rink and started to laugh.

I pulled him onto the ice with me. "Look at you walking on *frozen* water."

He wrapped me up in his arms. "Very clever, Em."

I snuggled into his chest and breathed in his clean scent. "I've been waiting for this moment."

He stroked my hair and kissed the top of my head. "Me too, Em. Me too."

Epilogue

"Hey, let's go easy on the teasing, there." I batted Marlowe's hand away from my hair. My sisters insisted on playing Barbie Doll with me before the Farewell to Summer dance. It felt more like a new beginning to me, or maybe a reset. This dance wasn't going to be any black-tie affair. It was going to be the way my mother would have wanted it.

Marlowe didn't listen to me and continued her assault on my hair. "It looks so much better with a little volume."

I rolled my eyes in her vanity mirror. I looked around at all the cosmetics and hair products she kept on it. If this is what it took to be beautiful, forget it.

Macey, meanwhile, was filing my nails and complaining about how little care I put into them.

"You both realize I work in a steel mill, right?"

They looked at me like, *so?*

"Stop your complaining. You can dress up for Sawyer for one night." Marlowe pulled out a large can of hairspray.

"He doesn't care about that kind of thing." It was one of the reasons I loved him.

"Tonight's special." Macey smiled at me.

Yes, it was. We were celebrating the twenty-fifth anniversary of this dance and doing a tribute to our mother.

"Fine, just go easy on that hairspray."

Marlowe ignored me and fogged my head. I had to admit, once it cleared, my curled hair did look good. I even felt a little glamorous.

"How's everything going at the store?" I asked.

Both of their tall frames deflated. Macey even sighed. "Dad says he's going to find a buyer for the store, but he'll try and find someone who will keep us on as employees."

"That's good."

"I guess," Marlowe growled.

"Let's not talk about the store." Macey jumped up and grabbed the dress I would be wearing tonight. The girls had found it in mom's old things that the wicked witch had hidden in the attic. The wicked witch who no longer lived here. She wasn't all that happy about it and swore to take Dad for everything he had. Thankfully, Dad had been at least smart enough to have her sign a prenup. I wasn't sure what was more awkward for Sawyer and me—that our parents were married or that they were getting divorced. I was more than happy about the latter, though I tried not to convey it around Sawyer.

We also didn't talk much about his sleazeball brother, who had a warrant out for his arrest not only here but in Vegas too. Poor Sawyer was sick over it. His brother was more of a swindler than we previously thought. His ex-wife's family was on the lookout for him too. The construction company he'd work for was owned by his ex-wife's family and they too had some missing money, but it was a lot more than four thousand dollars. Ashton was never mentioned around my sisters. I think they were both still struggling with the idea that they had been so fooled, and it kind of grossed them out that they'd had relations with the same guy. I knew I was still ill over it, which was why I was choosing to push it out of my head for the night. This night was all about what was good in my life.

Macey held up a lacey mauve dress with spaghetti straps. Mom had worn it to the very first Farewell to Summer dance. It was my honor to wear it, as long as the Spanx was going to hold up. I had no idea how Mom had looked so good after giving birth to twins earlier that year.

"Pink really isn't my color."

"Actually, it is." Marlowe smoothed one of my curls until she was pleased with it.

"Let's get you in Mom's dress," Macey's voice cracked.

I looked at my sisters through the mirror. They were already dressed to perfection with their hair up and makeup done. Macey was in a long, flowing maxi dress, and Marlowe was wearing a strapless dress. Both casual but classy. "I think us together makes her very happy."

Both the girls smiled before hoisting me up. "She's going to be happier once you get dressed." Marlowe always knew how to ruin a sweet moment.

"Fine. Why are you both in such a hurry?"

They looked between themselves and did their twin talking with no words thing.

Marlowe didn't answer but unceremoniously started disrobing me.

"Sawyer will be here soon." Macey took Mom's dress off the hanger.

That was always good news for me, but we had some time, or so I thought. Dad knocked on the door. "Is she ready?"

"Just about," Macey called.

I yanked up the Spanx over my abdomen. Who needed to breathe? "What's going on?"

"Nothing," Marlowe lied in a high-pitched voice.

I shimmied into Mom's dress, and by some miracle we were able to get it to zip up. I slipped into some semi-comfortable bone colored heels with a bit of a sparkle to them, and stood in front of Marlowe's standing mirror and stared at myself, but I only saw my mother staring back at me. Macey handed me a tissue. "Don't cry yet—you'll ruin your makeup."

"Yet?" I dabbed my eyes.

Marlowe stared at me too. "You know, you're beautiful." She walked off with Macey and let Dad in.

Dad walked in tall and proud in his jeans and a plaid button-up, just the way Mom would have wanted him to. His smile was back and the light in his brown eyes hit me. Dad had returned. He stopped and stared at me. "Honey, you look as beautiful as your mother did the night she wore that dress." A sheen of mist covered his eyes. He held out his hand to me. "I have the privilege of escorting you to the dance."

"Now? It doesn't start for an hour."

He gave me a wink. "You aren't in charge of everything tonight."

I placed my hand in his strong capable one. The one I had needed all my life and had missed so dearly this past year. "What's going on, Dad?"

He pulled me to him and wrapped me up. "Emma Bear, I love you. I want you to remember that you will always be my little girl."

"Are you dying?"

He chuckled in my ear. "Not that I know of."

I leaned away from him. "Why is everyone acting so weird?"

He took my hand. "Come see for yourself."

Without a word, Dad led me out of the house. My home. No more mohair couches, thank you very much. The comfy leather ones had returned, along with all our family pictures and the pink door and the ridiculous wreaths with poufy bows Mom loved. Once we made it to the porch, a string of paper lanterns lit a path filled with pink rose petals all the way to the barn. In the light of dusk, it was a beautiful sight.

"What's all this?"

Dad said not a word, but patted my hand and led me down the beautiful path. The closer we got to the barn, I could hear Grady's band playing an old country song, "You and I." It was a beautiful duet about two people in love who looked forward to building their dreams together. It reminded me of the man I wanted to build my future with. The man who was standing at the end of the lighted path in front of the open barn door in a dark suit and tie wearing a big grin. Dang, did he look good, even if I told him this was no longer a black-tie affair, I'm glad he still went with it. My pulse was racing. The way his eyes looked me up and down made me catch my breath.

Dad kissed my cheek before handing me over to the love of my life and walking into the well-lit barn.

Sawyer took my hand with such love. "I wanted the first dance tonight."

"I didn't know there was any doubt that all the dances belonged to you."

His free hand cupped my face. I leaned into it. "You are so beautiful."

"You know I'm totally Spanxed up here, right?"

He shook his head at me. "Come dance with me."

He led me into the barn where most of our family and friends waited. Jenna, Brad, Aspen, Kellan—and even my new best friend Shelby was there holding her hands to her mouth and crying as if this were the happiest day of her life. Frankie, Ray, and all the employees who had previously quit were employed once again by the Ranch and smiling at us. You don't know how happy I was to see the table full of Frankie's cupcakes. Dad stood near Warren and Bridget in front of the punch table. I had to admit I was surprised to see them there. I had wanted to invite them but left it up to Sawyer to extend the invitation. As much as I had grown to love the two, Sawyer was working on his relationship with them. I was happy to see he had extended the olive branch. My sisters ended up near Shelby, and immediately I could tell the girls were thinking this was someone they could be friends with.

Everyone was looking at Sawyer and me with bated breath as we made it to the middle of the wooden dance floor. It made me feel a tad self-conscious. Grady's band quieted to a low hum and all the lights except for those that lit the dance floor magically turned off. That was Sawyer's cue to drop to one knee. We were in our own world, just him and me. He didn't have to say a word. The makeup my sisters had caked on me was toast. I hoped they used waterproof mascara.

Sawyer took my hand. "Em, I know technically we haven't been dating all that long, but for the last year this is all I've wanted to do. I've known from our first phone call that you were the one for me." He reached into his pocket and pulled out a familiar ring, but there was something unfamiliar about it. He held the beautiful diamond ring deftly between his fingers. "Your dad gave me both of your mother's rings."

I seriously lost it, like there-was-no-hope-for-the-makeup lost it.

I recognized the gold band from my mother's first wedding ring and the round diamond from her second. They were so beautiful together. Like they were meant to be one.

"Emma Elaine Loveless, I love you, will you marry me under the pergola?"

Words escaped me when I realized I would no longer be loveless. My mom whispered I never was and to hurry up and answer the man. I nodded my response furiously.

"Is that a yes?"

"Yes!" I shouted, making everyone laugh.

Sawyer placed the ring on my finger before standing up and kissing me like we were alone. A dipping me down, parting my lips, tingles everywhere, and hands for days kind of a kiss. Holy crap, I wanted to be alone with him. When we came up for air, I realized everyone was clapping and the music had started again. Sawyer pulled me close to him. We began to sway to the beat of the music.

I skimmed his lips with my own. "You realize we're still related."

"I guess that makes me your wicked stepbrother," he groaned low in my ear.

I played with the curls in the back of his hair while I stared into his beautiful amber eyes. "You're not so wicked."

His hand glided down my back, entering the danger zone while he pulled me as close as he could. "Believe me, Em," he whispered in my ear, "I can be wicked. Very wicked."

SNEAK PEEK

My Not So Wicked Ex-Fiancé

OH MYLANTA, MYLANTA. This cannot be happening. I scanned through the article my cousin had sent me on my phone, hardly able to comprehend what I was reading.

Edenvale welcomes Prescott Technology, the up and coming software company started by owner and CEO, Ryder Prescott. In the past five years, Edenvale has become one of Colorado's upcoming technological centers due to its . . .

How could this be? I couldn't breathe. I needed to talk to Emma. I walked out of the boutique's back offices to find only a few customers browsing our new summer line. Macey and Marlowe were taking care of them beautifully. Weekdays were slower than weekends for now, until the summer months began. At least that's what the sales data that Mr. Carrington had provided me when I bought M&M on Main last year said. Now it was M&M'S on Main. Memaw loaned me the money to take on this new adventure. She more than anyone knew how much I wanted out of my family's business and my family out of my business.

"Ladies, I will be right back." I waved as I walked out the door into the beautiful late May day. I loved the Colorado sunshine and less humid days than I was used to in Georgia, but I was happy to see the snow go. This Southern girl had missed her mild winter, but it was worth it not to have to worry about running into my ex-fiancé, Ryder Prescott, cheater among men, love of my life and crusher of my soul.

I scooted my heels down the cobblestone sidewalks of Main Street. Carrington Cove was right out of a Hallmark Channel town—darling. Close together shops and boutiques with brick storefronts, some with cute awnings like my store. Most of them had welcoming display windows. Some of the cafés had outdoor seating when it was warm enough, though the natives around here walked around in shorts in two feet of snow.

The sun's rays felt good on me as I hustled to Carrington Cove's Eye Center, owned by some of the best friends I had ever had, Emma and Dr. Sawyer King. They weren't open for business quite yet, but would be in the next two weeks. Carrington Cove was happy to finally get their own optometry practice. Not as happy as the newlyweds were to be fulfilling one of their dreams.

The eye center was two blocks down from us on Willow Street. They were renovating an old coffee shop nestled between a family practice and an old-fashioned candy shop. I peeked through the frameport glass door with Carrington Cove Eye Center etched into it to find the lovebirds painting—more like kissing and pretending to paint—the reception area wall. I tried not to be jealous of the sweetest couple I had ever known.

I knocked before letting myself in. "I'm sorry to interrupt."

The happy couple covered in paint from head to toe as if they had rolled around in it, which wouldn't have surprised me, gave each other one last peck before turning my way with big grins.

"Hey, Shelby, what's up?" Emma set her paint brush down in the rolling tray.

"I'm having sort of a dilemma and I need someone to talk to."

"Is this female related? Should I leave?" Sawyer asked.

I shook my head. "No. Actually it might be good to have a male perspective." I approached their reception desk covered in plastic, trying not to inhale too many paint fumes.

Both Emma and Sawyer hopped on the plastic covered desk, ready to hear my tale.

"Remember when I told you I was engaged?"

They both nodded.

"Well . . ." I paused, hardly able to say it, "it appears my ex-fiancé has started his own company and is moving to Edenvale."

Emma's mouth dropped. "Does he know you live nearby?"

"I don't think so. I haven't talked to him since, well, since I left town and never said a word to him." Not to mention I had done my best to keep my whereabouts a secret from him, everything from deleting my social media and email accounts to blocking him from my phone. Momma and Daddy had convinced me it would be better this way. And after seeing those pictures of him with that woman on his supposed business trip, I had agreed.

"Maybe it's a coincidence," Sawyer offered.

Emma patted her husband's cheeks, adding more paint to his scruff. "You men are so clueless sometimes."

He took her hands and kissed her as if I wasn't there.

I cleared my throat.

They broke apart with apologetic smiles.

"Sorry." Emma grinned. "Hmm. This is interesting."

"Ryder Prescott . . ." I almost hated to say his name. It used to be the most wonderful bits of alphabet to escape my mouth. Now I felt like wiping my tongue off each time I had to speak it. ". . . moving to Colorado is more than interesting. I'm not even sure he's been west of the Mississippi."

Emma squinted. "Ryder Prescott? That name sounds so familiar."

"You probably remember me talking about him."

She shook her head. "No. It's more recent than that." Emma thought for a second. "Holy crap." She jumped off the desk. "A Ryder Prescott from Georgia booked one of our cabins at the Ranch for the entire summer. It caught my attention yesterday when I was going through our reservation site because of the length of his stay."

I reached for my heart, the one Ryder broke. "Please tell me this is one of your practical jokes." I was living at Carrington Ranch in the main house until I could secure a place in town. It was part of the deal when I bought the store since my parents had cut me off for leaving the family business. Real estate was expensive in Carrington Cove so I was waiting until after the busy summer months to move into my own place. How could I avoid him if we were both there? And why out of all the places in the world had he chosen the Ranch? It was forty-five minutes away from Edenvale where his headquarters would be.

"I'm sorry, Shelby," Emma interrupted my thoughts.

Not as sorry as I was. I fanned my face. "It's fine. It's all fine." I stood tall and proud while lying. My heart raced.

Emma tilted her head. "It's not fine. Maybe I can find some legitimate excuse to cancel the reservation."

I shook my head. "Goodness no, don't do that. You and your daddy have a business to run. I'm sure," I cleared my throat, "Ryder's money is as good as anyone else's." Though I had to wonder how he'd come into all this money. An entire summer at Carrington Ranch would be well into the tens of thousands of dollars.

Emma bit her lip and approached me in paint coated cutoffs and one of Sawyer's old T-shirts. I wished I was more like her, comfortable in anything including her own skin. I loved how she was able to throw her hair up in a ponytail and not wear any makeup. Though she was naturally beautiful whether she thought so or not, her confidence and personality made her more so. I was taught growing up to never leave the house, not even to go grocery shopping, unless you were looking your best. I knew that was a turnoff to some people. But it's not like I had to do a lot of those type of domestic things growing up or for most of my adult life. That's what delivery services and the help were for, Momma would say. As silly as it sounded, I liked strolling through each aisle of the store. It reminded me of . . . well, different times. A time when I wanted nothing more than to be blissfully domestic and even clip coupons if I had to. What an evil thought for a Duchane.

Emma got close but not too close as she was covered in wet paint. "Shelby, we don't need the money and we always have a waiting list."

"I appreciate your offer, but Ryder Prescott means nothing to me. If I saw him today, I would . . ." My breath got caught in my chest. What would I do? Slap him? Ignore him? I knew one thing that would not happen. I would not let his dark chocolate eyes capture mine and melt into my soul. My breath came out in a rush thinking about that first moment, four years ago, when our eyes had locked. "Excuse me." I turned on my heels.

"Shelby," Emma called, "Let's go grab lunch. My treat."

I waved from behind; my whole body was shaking. "Thank you, but I have to go." I opened the door and ran into the bright sun. I soaked in the rays and warmth, letting that feeling settle my heart. I silently berated myself for allowing him to affect me after all this time while I took a seat at the nearby bench under the gaslit lamppost.

Ever my momma's daughter I crossed my legs, smoothed out my pencil skirt, and sat up straight as a pin. I could hear Momma now yelling at me to keep my shoulders back and head held high. For once I didn't listen to her as I sank against the wrought iron. That was a lie, it wasn't the first time. There was a time, a beautiful time, almost like a dream now where I didn't worry about the expectations of my family. When, for once in my life, I could be me, with *him,* curled up in his arms nestled under a blanket of stars out in the hay field on his momma's and daddy's farm. It was not befitting of a lady or a Duchane, Momma would have said. But I thought it fit me perfectly. Oh, how wrong I had been.

At least the man left me with something. He made me see I was more than my name. I forgot that for a while last year when I came running here under the thumb of my family, but once the shock of his betrayal had worn off, I realized I was exactly right back where I had promised myself I would never be, living under the Duchane law. Ryder was right, I needed to be my own person. The question now was what was I going to do? And why was he coming here?

If you enjoyed *My Not So Wicked Stepbrother,* here are some other books by Jennifer Peel that you may enjoy:

All's Fair in Love and Blood
Love the One You're With
Facial Recognition
The Sidelined Wife
How to Get Over Your Ex in Ninety Days
Narcissistic Tendencies
Honeymoon for One- A Christmas at the Falls Romance
Trouble in Loveland
Paige's Turn
My Not So Wicked Ex-Fiancé
My Not So Wicked Boss

For a complete list of all her books, visit her Amazon page.

About the Author

Jennifer Peel is a *USA Today* best-selling author who didn't grow up wanting to be a writer—she was aiming for something more realistic, like being the first female president. When that didn't work out, she started writing just before her fortieth birthday. Now, after publishing several award-winning and best-selling novels, she's addicted to typing and chocolate. When she's not glued to her laptop and a bag of Dove dark chocolates, she loves spending time with her family, making daily Target runs, reading, and pretending she can do Zumba.

***

If you enjoyed this book, please rate and review it.
You can also connect with Jennifer on social media:
Facebook
Instagram
Pinterest

To learn more about Jennifer and her books, visit her website at www.jenniferpeel.com

Made in United States
Orlando, FL
27 January 2022